The Dolphin Chronicle

A novel by

Norm Kohn

PublishAmerica
Baltimore

Books by Norm Kohn

Beginnings
STARS
The Chandana Tree

ISBN: 1-4241-6071-5
PUBLISHED BY PUBLISHAMERICA, LLLP
www.publishamerica.com
Baltimore

Printed in the United States of America

For
Bryan, Grace, Robert, Hunter,
Alan, Pam and Jamie—shipmates.

Acknowledgements

No story is every created in a vacuum. With grateful appreciation to those who made this adventure possible: Hilda Brucker for her support and back-fence literary mentoring; Linda Heaviside and Judy McDowell for manning the fort; Terry Kay who refused to take no for an answer; and my wife Kathy for her editorial nudges and unflagging commitment to the journey.

"What matters it how far we go?" his scaly friend replied. "There is another shore, you know, upon the other side. The further off from England the nearer is to France. Then turn not pale, beloved snail, but come and join the dance."

"Will you, won't you, will you, won't you, will you join the dance? Will you, won't you, will you, won't you, will you join the dance?"

- The Lobster-Quadrille from *Alice in Wonderland*

CHAPTER 1

The afternoon Peter Jamison felt the first cool kiss of death, he formulated the plan.

He stood, still dazed and wet, his hair matted like marsh grass, in the mud and weeds next to South Carolina Highway 42. Most of the crowd had left, and the paramedics were loading up. The state patrolmen had filled out their forms and gone, and Jamison, numbed by their insistent interrogation, was left alone for a moment, scrubbing his glasses with the long end of his tie and licking rain off the end of his nose.

He reached back through a fog of conflicting emotions and tried to focus on the events of the past fifty minutes. He and Sandy had completed their client presentation in Beaufort and started home. The afternoon was dark as squalls laced with lightning blew in off the cold Atlantic, battering the low country with a vengeance. A Hilton Head radio announcer extolled the virtues of island living, as rain pounded the road into a tight ribbon of water that followed the high ground of the grey marsh, and traced a twisting corridor through sullen pine thickets and clumps of live oak.

Jamison squinted over the steering wheel, trying to find his way through the cascading gloom. Gusts of rain rocked the car and drummed on the roof. He reached for the radio and turned it off.

"How long have we known each other, Sandy?" he asked his companion seated next to him in the dim, rain-splattered light. His eyes never left the road.

Sandy loosened his tie, settled back in the leather seat and sipped a Coke. "Thirty-five years next month."

The windshield wipers slapped back and forth, sending spray into the air to be caught instantly in a vortex and sucked over the roof out of sight.

"You probably know me better than anybody except for Tommy."

Sandy polished the rim of the Coke can with his finger. "Even a few things that may have escaped her." The car hit a puddle, and a shower of spray arched out into the marsh. Sandy looked up. "Well enough to know when there's something on your mind."

A wry smile creased Jamison's comfortable face. "We've been together too long."

Sandy grinned. "What's up?"

Jamison paused and gathered his thoughts. "Do you ever have dreams of flying?" he asked.

"You mean in airplanes, or self-propelled?"

"Self-propelled: stepping into space and flapping your arms."

Sandy thought for a moment. "Sure, every now and then."

"How does it feel?"

Sandy smiled. "Great. I specialize in stunts. All kinds of maneuvers: loops, barrel rolls, even—"

Jamison interrupted. "Complete control?"

"Always."

Jamison nodded. "That's the way it was for me, too."

A bolt of lightning illuminated the inside of the car and they both flinched. Jamison tightened his grip on the wheel and continued as if nothing had happened.

"When I'm up there, it's so good that I never want it to end." He hesitated, picking his words. "Have you ever crashed?"

"Crashed?" Sandy considered the question. "No, I don't think so. At least I don't remember it if I did." He looked quizzically at Jamison. "Why do you ask?"

Jamison glanced in the rearview mirror. There had been no traffic for the past twenty minutes. He refocused on the road ahead. "Because six months ago I crashed."

He paused, sorting through memories of sleepless nights and cold sweats. "I dreamed I was standing on the peak of a mountain. I stepped off, leaned into the wind, stretched out my arms, and nothing. No wings, absolutely nothing to hold me up. For the first time in my life, I couldn't fly."

Sandy finished the Coke and put it in the drink holder. "Having trouble keeping it up these days?" He looked amused.

The wind pushed the car right and Jamison adjusted left. "Easy, Sandy," Jamison said quietly. His blue eyes tightened.

Sandy studied his partner for a long moment. "I'm sorry, old friend. Go on," he said carefully.

"Since that night, I've crashed five times. Every time I have the dream, it's a disaster. Sometimes I start out okay, gain a little altitude; then I lose it. I flap and twist, suck in air and try to will myself up, but nothing works. I'm Icarus in a gray flannel suit."

"What are you trying to say?"

Jamison caught his breath. "After all these years of flying, I think I've lost it, Sandy. The magic's gone. I've lost the touch, and it's really messing with my head."

"But they're only dreams, Jamison," Sandy protested.

"No, believe me, there's more to it than that. Part of me is missing. For the first time in my life, I'm having to reach for ideas—thumbing through magazines looking at other people's ads."

"Hell, everybody looks at other people's ads."

"Yeah, Sandy, but lately the music and the poetry are gone. I can't hear them, but worse than that, I can't see them. The art has vanished; all the images and colors, and I can't find them much less create them. It's like midnight in a Hieronymus Bosch painting." He hesitated. "It's as if I've lost my soul."

Sandy stared through the rain-swept windshield. "Shit, I think you're serious."

"I've never been more serious about anything in my life, and the problem is, I don't know—"

He never finished the thought. Like a scarlet goblin, a one-eyed, red pickup truck burst out of an advancing wall of rain running fast and low. Suddenly, the truck slid across the yellow line, halfway into their lane.

"Oh, my God!" Sandy gasped.

Jamison swerved frantically to the right. The red pickup jerked back the opposite way, its unlit headlight missing them by inches, but Jamison was out of control, a ton and a half of Lexus spinning off the wet pavement and then flipping— airborne, upside down into the weeds and slash pine.

It was a violent but strangely serene flight: life's little way of reminding him how fragile he was and how forgiving it can be. At least it was on this dark October afternoon when the angels lifted him, unharmed, and whispered in his ear the tentative melody of a new song that was sweet and fresh and clear— really clear.

Sandy got out with only a bump on his head, from falling against the roof when he released his safety belt. No one else saw the red pickup. It never stopped, vanishing into the murky shadows as quickly as it had come. An hour later, as Jamison collapsed into the well-worn vinyl of Bobby Lee Tucker's red and gold wrecker, he knew what he had to do.

The red sunball fused with the low tree line beyond the western edge of the marsh, transforming the sky into a thousand shades of purple, accented with delicate traces of iridescent pink and mauve. The orchestra of the night began a hesitant overture: a gust of wind in the rigging, a nightbird's call somewhere out in the dark sea of cordgrass, the wissss of a dolphin sounding along the edge of the creek. Peace settled over Broad Creek, South Carolina, which is just off the Cooper River, just off Calibogue Sound, just off the Atlantic Ocean and, on this particular evening, just off the edge of the world.

Jamison checked the anchor line one more time. It was stretched tight by the pull of the tide but seemed to be firmly set. The plastic chaff guard was securely in place. He could relax; it looked as if they were set for the night. As he moved aft toward the companionway, the steamy aroma of pasta drifted forward on the cool salt air to meet him.

Charlie poked his head through the hatch. "You about through up there? Dinner's almost ready."

"Be right down." Jamison took one last look at the banks on either side of the creek. *Plenty of room to swing*, he thought. Then he turned and climbed down the steps into the cabin. The table was set, and Charlie was dishing out the spaghetti. Before they sat down to eat, Jamison opened a bottle of wine he had bought just for the occasion. He carefully filled two orange juice glasses, handed one to his son and raised the other.

"To the adventure," he proposed. The glass caught the sunset through a port, and the wine glowed like an ember.

Charlie raised his glass and touched the glowing rim. "To the adventure."

The wreck had saved Jamison the inconvenience of having a breakdown. Those few seconds, when his life hung by a thread of Japanese sheet metal, were an elegant and brutally efficient alternative to two years on a therapist's couch. For a fleeting second, his windshield was wiped clean, and in a flash of clarity, he saw that he was headed down a dead-end street in a landscape littered with the wreckage of his crashed dreams.

He had no idea when the psychic shredding had begun, but he was amazed at how stealthy the loss had been. It was like a gradual deprivation of visual acuity: an imperceptible change of focus; a slight shift in colors; the slow fuzzing of perception until the brain could no longer reconcile the altered optical input with preconceived, imbedded images. In the resulting confusion, visions that were once clear lost their lucidity and degraded into dim apparitions devoid of spontaneity and inspiration.

Something had gone terribly wrong, and it was painfully obvious to Jamison that he didn't have a lifetime left to sort it out. He wasn't thirty or even forty anymore. In fact, he was sliding down the slippery slope on the back side of fifty, and as he saw it, that didn't give him much of a choice. He could either get out of Dodge, go in search of the missing juice and, if he found it, either reinvent his life or end up a bitter and bewildered old fart stumbling into the dustbin of mid-life angst. The thought of doing nothing and prolonging the misery was unbearable. He had to suck up what courage he had left and make the leap.

Jamison zipped the collar of his jacket tight around his neck, stepped out of the rental car and closed the door. *It's now or never*, he thought. He crossed the gravel parking lot and walked onto a dock that pointed like a weathered finger into a pine-sheltered cove. A chilly breeze ruffled his slate-colored hair and raised cat's paws along the far shore as he stopped beside a sailboat bobbing gently in its slip. He paused, then reached out and ran his hand along the rail. He felt an almost imperceptible shiver, and then a familiar thrill as the hull rose on a small wave and strained against the dock lines holding it in place.

He noted with satisfaction that she was tidy, clean and shipshape; the obvious result of meticulous attention to detail, hours of polishing, and quarts of carefully applied varnish. He studied the sturdy rig and the confident lines of her hull. Then he nodded as if answering his own question. *There's no doubt about it. She's up to the challenge,* he thought. It was on that wet, dark ride in Bobby Lee's wrecker, as he tried to reconstruct the pieces of his life, that Jamison had realized the twenty-eight foot sloop might be his saving grace.

September Song had a diesel engine, a galley, a head, hot and cold water, and enough space sleep three to four people—two to three in comfort. She had been in the family for three years, number four in a series of sailboats going back thirty years. Tommy had suggested the name. The inspiration dated to the autumn of their college years, when they would make their final toast to summer accompanied by "September Song's" pensive melody. In time the tune became their theme song, so the lyric seemed an apt sentiment to grace the stern of this small vessel that held the promise of so much romance and adventure. She was a lake boat, but only because fresh water had been closer to home than salt water. *But she's seaworthy,* Jamison thought, *and that's what matters.* He had satisfied himself on that count before they bought her, but there was still work to be done to prepare her for an extended journey.

He stepped up onto the rail and swung his five-foot-ten-inch frame easily aboard. He was pleased that he hadn't lost his balance, agility, or too much of his waistline to five-thirty vodkas, vermouth, and chicken wings. Jamison removed the companionway drop boards, went down the three steps into the main cabin, and sat down at the dining table. He pulled a pad from his pocket and examined the snug interior. *I'll need to add a cabinet over the settee, a bin in the galley, and upgrade the nav station,* he thought.

He found a pencil in the nav station and started making notes. Thirty minutes later, he tallied up his list of modifications. All doable, he decided. He climbed back into the cockpit and sat down behind the wheel. He noted the compass was pointing one hundred and eighty degrees, due south. He pondered the compass card for a moment. His life needed a complete turnaround: one hundred and eighty degrees from where it was headed. Was it possible that the solution to his predicament lay in the confluence of the magnetic fields, ruby bearings, and embryonic fluid that oriented the rotating oval?

He pondered the compass again. It was a stretch, but it was as good a place to start as any. Jamison made a decision. He and

September Song would head south, but if he was going in search of his Holy Grail, he needed a crew—someone to man the bridge while he jousted with his personal dragons. He thought for a moment, then smiled, unsnapped the case on his belt and took out a cell phone.

The depth and passion of their son's talent had caught Jamison and Tommy totally off guard. Charlie's huge paintings dominated the space around them with bold, slashing, urgent color that demanded, and got, immediate attention. It was the sort of raw power of youth that spoke of greatness to come once it was refined and focused. But lately it had not been going well. He had become so caught up in the paraphernalia of art and the seductive song of his muse that he had lost touch with the physical act of putting paint on canvas. The colors and images were all there dancing in his right brain, but his hands refused to respond to their inspiration, and the harder he worked, the more frustrated he became. It was a pain in the ass. Even deep breathing and the dog-eared volume of Jack Kerouac that he had liberated from his parents' library couldn't get him back on track.

Maybe he needed a break. Maybe he needed to get away from the insular world and familiar routines he had created for himself. Except for a summer in Italy, the small-town university art colony had been his safe house for seven years, three since graduation. Hell, even his love life was a disaster. Painting absorbed so much of his creative energy that there was little left for the intricacies of intimate relationships. Seven years was long enough. It was time to shed the cocoon and get on with his life, so when his father called and laid out the plans for the voyage, Charlie didn't hesitate. His instincts told him that a rare window was opening. Not only would it be a great adventure, but maybe he could catch a breath of fresh air. *Carpe diem.*

With dinner over and the dishes and utensils washed and stowed, Jamison got out the charts for the next day's trip. The purple twilight had faded to black. The anchor light had been turned on, and the cabin was bathed in a warm twelve-volt glow.

Jamison always did his chart work the night before he went offshore. In the quiet of the evening, he had time to plot courses and check and recheck calculations. For him it was a labor of love, and like the best love, it brought with it the anticipation of mystery and adventure.

As he spread out the charts, it occurred to him how ironic it was that to find his way around on the planet, he had to flatten it out and define it with four corners. Jamison knew this hadn't always been true for all cultures. He had read the stories of South Pacific islanders who routinely sailed thousands of miles across open ocean without the aid of a straight edge, guided only by their mystic connection to the stars and the suppleness of their terrestrial senses. There was something incredibly sane in their ability to find their place in the shape of a wave, the scent of the breeze or the call of a seabird.

He couldn't help feeling that during the translation of that primal passion and wisdom into science something irreplaceable had been lost. But perhaps not everything, for he knew that while the pencil lines he drew appeared to be straight, in reality they represented arcs on the surface of the globe. These lines he so carefully scribed with parallel rules and compass were both the efficient delineation of science and the supple curve of romance.

Therein lies hope, he thought, for in their manipulation he momentarily transcended the limits of his linear calculations and heard, from somewhere far before the machinations of time, the healing call of an ancient sea bird and felt the swell of an aboriginal wave.

The lines that he drew tonight would guide them southward along the Georgia coast to Sapelo Island, where they would turn inland and anchor. Jamison took his time. As he plotted and measured the various legs of the course, he read out the information to Charlie, who recorded it in a deck log for them to use in the cockpit while underway. He left nothing to chance. They were both convinced that Murphy's Law had originated at sea.

Once the last notation was entered, the charts, deck log, logbook, parallel rules, dividers and pencils were laid out in the nav station ready for use in the morning. Satisfied that they were prepared, they climbed the companionway steps for a final anchor check before crawling into their bunks.

The stars were out. Stars like this were beyond imagination. The Milky Way poured from horizon to horizon as a background for Venus, the Dippers, the Twins and their cousins of the Zodiac. Jamison and Charlie stood at the rail, caught in the crystal clarity of the moment.

It seemed to Jamison that in that instant even their thoughts would echo forever through the universe. Eternity was as close as the breath on their cheeks, tomorrow was just over the horizon, and the months of preparation seemed light years away in another world.

It was to be a spring departure. *September Song* would be shipped to Hilton Head, South Carolina, and on the first of May, Jamison and Charlie would shove off, headed south. Sometime in June, Tommy would join them in Nassau for a status check.

Charlie quit his job at the chicken processing plant where he had been working as a truck driver to support his painting. He negotiated an early end to the lease on his studio apartment, loaded easels, canvases and everything he owned into the back of his battered pickup, had a final beer with some friends, and headed home.

Meanwhile, at the Atlanta advertising agency of Jamison, Langford & Linder, pandemonium had broken loose. The reception area had become a loading dock, much to the amusement of the creative department and chagrin of the account people. Anything that irritated the account execs was a not-so-well concealed delight to the creatives. Jamison was their guy, and they reveled in the random disorder that struck every afternoon at two o'clock when Sarah, the UPS lady, wheeled in his daily consignment of boxes, crates, and odd-shaped packages from chandlers and nautical supply companies.

When Jamison had talked with his partners, Mac and Sandy, he hadn't given them much choice. The car wreck had become a metaphor for his life, and it was either a leave of absence or he was gone forever. But Mac and Sandy didn't have to think twice about signing on. The business was in good shape, they had the personnel to cover for him, and they had five months to get ready for his absence. But, if the truth were really known, the deciding factor was they had come to recognize something of themselves in his plight. As they shook hands over a round of martinis they both knew that the next casualty might be one of them. Ten days later, Sarah rolled a loaded hand truck up to JL&L's tastefully elegant mahogany and brass doors with Jamison's first equipment order.

The passing days and weeks became a blur to Jamison. He had less and less to do at the agency as his assistant assumed more of his responsibilities. Everyone on the staff continued to be supportive, but he realized, with some satisfaction and no small amount of dismay, that they were going to get along fine without him.

Finally, on the first of April, *September Song* came out of the water for new bottom paint and the final outfitting. The work effort shifted to a boatyard. After months of checking and cross-checking lists, wiring electronics, and fitting teak, they were down to the final details: adding backing plates to the cleats, tightening keel bolts, checking the engine. Tommy and Charlie made a trip to a discount grocery store and bought two months' worth of basic staples. Food, clothing, linens, charts, and books were loaded aboard. There were the usual last-minute delays, but on the evening of April 21, the transport truck backed into the yard and hooked up to *September Song's* trailer. They would pull out at six the next morning.

Later, after the crew left and Charlie had taken the station wagon home to pack it, Jamison and Tommy sat in the tall grass beneath the boat.

"Jamey, I'm not losing you, am I?" she asked.

There was a cool breeze blowing, and Jamison had pulled her close to him. He smiled. "You haven't called me Jamey in a long time."

"I know."

He felt the tightness of her slender body, like a cage protecting a small bird.

"You're not losing me," he said reassuringly. "I'm only going away for a little while."

"That's not what I mean. I feel like we're changing and I don't know who you'll be when you come back. I don't even know who I'll be, and it scares me."

"I didn't know you felt this way, Tom." He spoke gently.

"I haven't known what to say. I think it's a great idea for you and Charlie to do this thing. You both need it, and God knows, maybe I do, too, but lately…" She turned to him, her deep eyes damp. "Damn you, Jamison, I love you so much."

His lips brushed across her eyes, and he tasted the salt of her fear as he pulled her into his arms. The sweetness of her auburn hair engulfed him as Tommy straddled his lap and buried her face in his shoulder. Then he felt her hot tears and her lips moving.

"Make love to me, Jamey," she whispered with an urgency he hadn't heard in years. Her hands groped for his shirt and pulled it up out of his jeans. She lifted her face, and his lips found hers. Then she lay back and pulled him down through the translucent harbor of the gathering twilight into the soft cradle of the spring earth. That night, sheltered by *September Song's* hull, searching for courage in their passion, Tommy and Peter Jamison cast off into the unknown.

CHAPTER 2

There was not a ripple on Calibogue Sound. Not a breath of air stirred, and other than the throaty purr of *September Song's* diesel, there was not a sound. It was 7:30 a.m., and they were on a course of one hundred and eighty degrees, due south, headed for Tybee Roads.

They were up early, eager to be off. After a breakfast of cereal and donuts, Charlie weighed anchor, and they slipped quietly out of Bull Creek.

For Jamison, leaving an anchorage had to be done with care and respect. It was the day's first act of seamanship, the rebonding with the natural order, and after the moment of awakening, the second act of faith. They left no evidence of their presence behind, no ashes of a campfire, no artifacts, and no straight lines drawn in the sand. Fish and crabs were already swimming where their keel had divided the murky waters. It was a reminder that, more often than not, history at sea is recorded only in the heart and mind.

Jamison adjusted the sweat band of his cap and ran through the checklist in his head for what seemed like the hundredth time. He knew he was being compulsive, but it had become his way of dealing with the vague but persistent anxiety brought on by the recent turmoil in his life. Besides, they were heading to sea, and it was a virtue to be a little anal-retentive.

The cap was still loose, so he took it off and pulled the Velcro tighter. *That's better,* he thought, as he slipped it back on. After he finished running the numbers, he was satisfied that everything was in order, except for one persistent glitch.

"You seem preoccupied," Charlie said, looking up from the chart book.

"I was thinking about the GPS. I wish to hell it was working." The Global Positioning System was on loan from a friend. It was mounted in the nav station and gave them satellite navigation capability but, much to their frustration, it refused to work. They had spent hours fooling with it, all to no avail.

Charlie studied his father. "Dad, I'm sure we can get it fixed somewhere down the way." Then as an afterthought, "We really won't really need it until we leave for the Bahamas, anyway."

Jamison knew that to Charlie it was no big deal, just further evidence that technology was an uncertain savior. He had to admit that Charlie was right, but it was something beyond his control, and it irritated him.

"Besides," Charlie pointed out, "we can always do it the old-fashioned way."

Jamison nodded. "It's been awhile. Can you still plot a compass position?"

Charlie laughed. "Has a cat got a tail?"

Jamison smiled in spite of himself. "Has a dog got a bark?"

"Does a chicken quack?"

"Can a snake dance?"

"Can a moose fly?"

It was a nonsense game they had played since Charlie had been a child. Jamison started it one night when Charlie was afraid there were monsters hiding in his bedroom closet, and they ended up laughing so hard that the night-beasts were vanquished and Charlie fell asleep with a smile on his face. As the years passed, the words became more sophisticated, but sooner or later, they always came back to Charlie's favorite: the flying moose. It was the one that had driven the fear away that first night.

Jamison grinned. "Just checking." The moose had risen to the occasion once again; the anxiety was gone, blown away by a playful absurdity. Charlie had returned the favor. Jamison smiled and noted that the cap fit just right.

The late afternoon sun was turning St. Augustine golden as Hinkley Prescott muscled the red Stingray out of the SouthCoast Yacht Services parking lot and headed for downtown. He considered the events of the past few months and marveled at the turn his life had taken.

Goddamn, it's amazing. You go to bed one night trying to find the lost pieces of the puzzle, and the next morning—poof, it's all there spread out before you, he thought. *One minute nothing, the next minute Xanadu.*

Hink could hardly stand it. In a couple of weeks, he would be able to walk into Charleston, buy his father's bank, and then, just for the hell of it, foreclose on the board of director's fucking country club. He knew it was an absurd scenario, but just the possibility of it warmed his heart.

Bobo was the one who had made it all possible. He had come up with the contact. Or maybe it was the contact that had come up with Bobo. Hell, it didn't make any difference who had come up with what. The only thing that mattered was that it worked. The Miami tans with the mother lode hanging around their necks needed a pick up and delivery service, and for once in his life, Hinkley Prescott had been at the right place at the right time.

He and Bobo fancied themselves treasure hunters. They had met on a dive in the Bahamas and had decided to join forces. It was no secret that there were tons of booty spread all up and down the Florida coast just waiting to be scooped up. Hell, the odds were better than the lottery, and diving was a damn sight more fun. It was only a question of who found it and when. Everybody knew that some hunters had been outrageously successful, bringing up half the Spanish treasury. A piece of cake, or so it seemed.

But the going had been slow and frustrating, and they soon discovered that to make a big score in an underwater El Dorado took time, research, personnel, and money: big-ass money. They had been at it for six months, and Hink could see another failure blowing up on the horizon when Bobo called him at SouthCoast and asked him to meet for a drink at Las Chitas Restaurant as soon as he could.

"It's a fucking tourist bar," Hink had complained.

"Goddamn it, I know that; that's why I picked it! Nobody will recognize us there."

"Oh, for Christ's sake, Bobo, this had better be damn good."

"Trust me, pardner."

Hink sighed. "OK, see you at 5:30."

"Is that th' best you can do?"

"Dammit, Bobo, it's 4:30 now. I'm sitting here with a radar in five hundred pieces. If I don't have it back together by 5:00, Jake will have my ass."

"Shit, Jake loves your ass."

"Bobo, 5:30."

There was a long pause. "Okay, Hink, 5:30."

But Hink never heard Bobo's reply. He had already hung up the phone.

The early morning haze was lifting off the water as *September Song's* bow swung toward the east and for the first time began to rise and fall to the heartbeat of the open sea. There were no waves to speak of yet, but the visceral swell spoke of mystery and awesome power sleeping somewhere beneath the surface. Jamison felt as if some ageless memory was stirring deep in his consciousness, tuning his senses for communion with a fearsome but, he hoped, merciful god.

A breeze began to freckle the water's smooth skin as they continued east between large red and green channel buoys. By the time they arrived at the buoy where they would turn south, the breeze had freshened and the freckles had become small waves.

As they rounded the mark, Jamison raised the sails. Although the breeze was light, it was a thrill to be under sail for the first time. *September Song* seemed to sense the moment and lifted upwind, alive at last. The murmur of the diesel was replaced by the whisper of the wind sighing through the rigging, the gurgle of water slipping out from under the stern, and the *puc...puc* of waves slapping against the red dinghy which followed close behind at the end of its line.

Once they were settled down and on course, Jamison walked forward on the deck to enjoy the sun and the view. He leaned against the mast and looked out toward the horizon. No ship or telltale smudge of smoke marked the blue sky; they had the ocean all to themselves. A gust of wind probed the collar of his shirt and sent a shiver chasing down his spine. He suddenly had an inexplicable feeling that he was being watched. He glanced back at Charlie but saw that he was absorbed in the chart. Charlie looked up and smiled, then returned to studying the course.

The feeling of another presence became more intense. Then Jamison's eye caught a movement in the water. Flapping along just below the surface was a spotted skate. Its right eye was following Jamison's every move. He grabbed the rigging for support and leaned out over the water. The unblinking eye never left him as he stared into its soulless gaze. It was an unnerving connection that took his breath away. He felt as if he were being stalked.

Finally, he found his voice. "Charlie, quick, look over the port side!" He had just called Charlie when another of the bat-like creatures swept out from under the boat, then another and another. The water surrounding them was taking on a primeval urgency.

Charlie left the wheel and peered over the rail. "Where are they coming from?" he exclaimed.

Jamison was mesmerized. Their motion and speckled patterns were magnified by the waves. The eyes were hypnotic. Was their course simply coincidental, or were they all bound by some primal helix that still stirred a common soup within their cells? He wasn't sure, but suddenly the spell was broken, and he was torn back into the present by the thunder of two silver-bodied Navy jets flashing low overhead. Wings above and wings below, and the wings of their sails in between; all fused in a symmetry of form and function, but light years apart on Darwin's curve. Jamison felt as if he were sailing out of a momentary twilight zone, caught somewhere between high-tech transcendence and ancient incantations, but he wasn't sure where he fit on the morphological scale.

After lunch, the breeze picked up to fifteen knots. The seas were up to about three feet, and *September Song* was close-hauled, beating into them at five knots. They were on course, running along the thirty-foot curve off Wassaw Island. From five miles out, the shoreline was a smoky blur, broken only by an occasional water tower. The boat became a small, isolated island in the expanse of the sea. Arriving at a buoy was a landfall of sorts: tangible proof of their position and cause for a small celebration. To Jamison's satisfaction, the Wassaw sea buoy appeared right on schedule, tossing in the sun-spanked waves. His confidence was returning.

Peter McKinzie Jamison Jr. was born September 15, 1942, in Pittsburgh, Pennsylvania. His mother, Dorothy, was a painter and his father, Peter Senior, was an architect and actor. The Jamison family moved south to Atlanta when he was six months old. They were the first of the Jamison clan to cross the Mason-Dixon Line. It was not an easy decision, but it was wartime and jobs for architects were scarce. It was a particularly difficult time for his father, for he had been rejected for military service, the only one of three brothers not in uniform. He had been a childhood victim of polio that left him without the use of his left arm, and although he had learned to compensate for his disability, the military establishment considered him unacceptable. So Peter Jamison Senior had accepted the offer of an Atlanta architectural firm that was heavily involved in defense contracting, even though it was in the South, far from the lakes and rolling hills of western New York and Pennsylvania where he had grown up, gone to school, fallen in love, and married Dorothy Franklin.

Young Peter's mother was the first person to call him Jamison. It began as a convenience when he was three years old. Peter Jr. was just too awkward, and his father refused to call him Petie, so when his mother suggested Jamison, it stuck.

In the Atlanta of the forties, the Jamisons were a bit of a novelty. They were in the early vanguard of a migration of Northerners and Californians that would eventually change the face of the city and region forever.

For young Jamison, it was a mixed blessing. He discovered, all too soon, that he was a "damned Yankee." He wasn't exactly certain what that meant, but one thing for sure, it meant that he had to be able to run, and run fast. It also meant that he was different. The stories his father told were of a different culture than the stories he heard from his friends and their parents. On top of that, his parents were artists and lived life with an openness, passion and perspective that was clearly different from the community around him. But Jamison adjusted, and as the years passed, he came to love his adopted city and the many friends he made. He came to think of himself as "from the South" but not "of the South." Jamison knew in his heart that he could never be a "good ole' boy."

One of his most persistent memories from boyhood, was spending hours wandering through the woods and golden fields near his home, then climbing his favorite tree in the evening, drifting off into the stars and wondering if he would ever find out where he truly belonged.

Six hours after turning south, *September Song* entered the Sapelo Channel along with a large fleet of shrimp boats that were trawling the entrance to the sound. They left the wilderness of Blackbeard Island close to port, then winged past High Point on Sapelo Island before swinging south into the Front River and into the Intracoastal Waterway.

The sweet, musky smell of the land reached out and absorbed the salty edge of the sea breeze as Charlie dropped the mainsail and they coasted along under the jib, basking in the late afternoon sun. They continued south down Teakettle Creek and into Doboy Sound. Under power, they crossed the sound, and turned into the North River. It was wide, deep and quiet, a welcome change from the bite of the wind and the roller coaster ride of the breaking seas. They found a place in mid-stream that felt right, and Charlie dropped the anchor.

A flight of egrets broke formation over a nearby island and settled onto a live oak, turning it white as early snow. Jamison reached down and pulled the engine stop. The chugging of the diesel was replaced by the muted sounds of the marsh and the rustling of a fish swarm by the shore.

After they cleaned up the cockpit, Jamison went below, peeled off his jacket and sailing gloves and threw them on his bunk. Then he rummaged through the galley and dug out a bottle of wine, a tin of pâté and some cheese and crackers, and they kicked back in the warm blush of the evening.

"How do you feel?" Jamison asked as he poured a glass of wine.

"Damn good. It's been a great day." Charlie pushed his sneakers off and stretched, then he sliced some cheese and spread pâté on a cracker. "How about you?"

"Couldn't be better." Jamison took a sip of wine. It tasted especially sweet.

The feeling of returning safely from the sea was something they never talked about. It was restricted territory, acknowledged but never entered. Jamison could see it hunting in his son's eyes, and he knew that Charlie could hear it probing the defenses of his laugh. They had ventured beyond the bays and harbors of their natural habitat, and the god that tends to those things had suffered their impertinence one more time. There had been no meteorological blockbusters that had escaped the weather forecasters. The boat and its equipment had functioned properly, and they had been up to the challenge and made all the right decisions. On another day, it might not be so. Anything or everything could go haywire, and they might have to depend on their wits to survive. But today had been a great day, and it was, as Charlie so eloquently put it, a damn good feeling.

CHAPTER 3

The Dolphin Chronicle of Peter Jamison #1

One of the first things an artist learns is that there are no straight lines in nature. Nature is fluid, made up of arcs and curves. Edges bend and twist. Masses shape themselves and flow into molds created by unseen rhythms, weaving subtle and majestic forms that delight and mystify. What seems to be predictable one moment is unpredictable the next. There are no calendars in nature, only seasons and cycles, and even they cannot be measured with absolute precision. Of all the creatures on the planet, it is only man who tries to set things straight.

The discovery of the principle of the straight line was a watershed in human history. Man for the first time had a conceptual tool for rearranging the natural order to suit his whims. With the ability to conjure linear patterns and structure he had the power to design, build, reason, even create and measure "time." Armed with a grid and a straight edge, Man had the means to find his way around in the wilderness. He was free to follow the biblical injunction to "go and subdue the earth." It was the beginning of the end in the Garden of Eden.

"What do you say we stick to the Waterway today and do some sightseeing for a change?" Jamison asked, as he turned the page on the chart book and slipped it into its protective cover.

Charlie was putting away the breakfast dishes. He nodded. "Sounds good to me. We shouldn't have any trouble making St. Simons." They had already decided that St. Simons Island would be their first marina stop.

It looked like an easy day—warm sun and no breeze now, ten knots later on. Charlie eased *September Song* out of the North River a hundred yards or so down from one of the few island houses they had seen since leaving Hilton Head's condos behind. Its sun-bleached and wind-scarred frame was snugged back in a sheltering grove of live oak, pine, wax myrtle and palmetto. The front porch was only a few feet above high tide. There was a dock of sorts, a few planks and pilings large enough to tie up a skiff or a small motorboat. Although the house had a lived-in look, there was no one in sight. It appeared that the sand crabs and blackbirds had the place to themselves.

The channel was narrow as they nudged their way down the Little Mud River past Wolf Island. At times they were no more than twenty feet from shore, almost close enough to count the blades of cordgrass that wove the tight fabric of the marsh.

The drone of the engine and warmth of the sun began to work their spell. Enfolded by the dreamy shade of the Bimini top Jamison felt like he was aboard the African Queen. The view ahead could just as easily have been the Zambezi as south Georgia. Charlie yawned, adjusted his baseball cap, and settled back comfortably behind the wheel. Jamison stretched out on a cockpit seat. He loosened his belt and propped his feet up on the cockpit coaming. His body absorbed the opiate heat like a sponge. He closed his eyes and began to drift.

In the years to come, Jamison would look back on the next few moments and remember them as his Alpha, the point from which he would forever measure time. He would later return on another boat to try to find the exact place, the precise spot where she had first appeared, but he would never be successful. It was like chasing a will-o'-the-wisp.

She materialized out of nowhere.

"Jamison, you've got to let go."

"What do you mean, let go?"

My God, she's beautiful. He was captivated.

"Just exactly what I said, let go."

"Let go of what?"

She smiled and studied him.

"Do you like my hair?"

"You changed the subject."

"Umhummm. Do you like my hair?"

"Yes. I like your hair."

"Tell me what you like about my hair."

"It's beautiful. The curls, I like the way the curls fall across your shoulders."

"What about the color?"

This is crazy, he thought. He knew that solo sailors on long voyages sometimes hallucinate, and if she was typical of that experience then he could understand some of the attraction of prolonged solitude. But this was the Intracoastal Waterway, not the Indian Ocean. He wanted to pinch himself to see if he was awake, but he was afraid she might disappear.

"It shines like silver. When the light is behind it, I can see little rainbows in the strands."

Who the hell is she? he wondered.

"How does it feel?"

Jamison ran his hands through her hair, letting the curls fall through his fingers.

"Like woven honey—soft, flaxen. I can taste it with my fingers."

Her eyes sparkled.

"That's nice, there may still be hope for you—"

"Dad, we've got a tug!" The spell was suddenly broken. "I can see the superstructure beyond the marsh."

The vision was fading. Her eyes were the last to vanish.

Jamison tried to pull himself together and concentrate on the scene ahead. Charlie was right. A tugboat *was* rounding the next bend, pushing two very large black barges directly at them! They appeared to fill the whole channel. From the look of the bow wave he estimated the tug to be making six knots.

He fumbled for the chart. A quick check indicated that the channel was barely wide and deep enough for them to pass without colliding or running aground. As the tug settled on course, the captain sounded two blasts on his whistle.

"He wants to pass on our port side." Charlie was standing to get a clearer view.

"It'll be close, but we don't have much choice. That thing could make driftwood out of us." Jamison looked at the right bank where a band of mud separated the grass from the water. "We're past high tide but I think we can make it."

September Song's draft was five and a half feet, so with an eye on the depth sounder's rapidly changing numbers, Charlie cut back on the throttle and eased as far to the right as he could, trying to trace the eight-foot bottom contour with the keel. The tug, pushing its train of barges before it like a massive battering ram, churned past while Charlie attempted to keep off the bank and out of its prop wash.

The depth alarm began ringing incessantly as the bottom of the channel came up to six feet, but he was finally able to catch his breath and swing back into midstream and deep water before they hit anything.

"Any tighter and we'd be walking," he muttered.

"You got that right," Jamison said. "Did you see the birds standing on the water just in front of us?"

"Birds, where?" Charlie turned and looked behind them. He could see the light color of a sand bar beginning to break through the dark water they had just passed. A half-dozen seagulls were lined up on the emerging shoal, like a small band of guardian angels marking the boundary between safety and the edge of the road.

The shadows had turned from gold to pink when Hink squeezed through the stucco and wrought iron entrance of Las Chitas. *Shee-it, Bobo was right,* he thought. If two locals wanted to meet incognito this was the place. Except for the employees, there couldn't possibly be anyone in here from south of Newark or north of Havana.

The restaurant was divided into three sections: an upstairs deck that wrapped around two sides of the building, an indoor dining room, and a patio and bar. The patio and bar were open air with tables randomly spaced inside the stucco and tile enclosure.

It took him a minute to spot Bobo at a table toward the back, partially obscured by a large potted plant. *Jesus, with that beach-blasted hair and that shirt he looks just like one of the fucking plants. If he was in a pot somebody would try to water him,* Hink thought. He couldn't make up his mind if Bobo thought he was camouflaged, or if it was his idea of what tourists were supposed to wear. He found the whole scene amusing.

"How d'you like the shirt?" Bobo asked, as Hink slid into a chair across from him.

"How many geraniums did you have to kill to get it?"

"Figured I'd blend right in."

A waitress appeared with two drinks and set them on floral coasters.

Hink grinned. "Camouflage."

"What d'you mean by that?" Bobo asked suspiciously.

"Just what you said, you blend right in, absolutely invisible."

Hink took a sip of his drink. *Bourbon and Coke, that's one thing Bobo always gets right,* he thought.

"I thought it was a nice touch." Bobo seemed reassured.

"Down to business, Bobo: why are we hiding out among the aliens?"

Bobo took a long pull on his margarita, then leaned across the table. "You're not gonna believe this, Hink."

"Try me." Hink settled back in his chair. He thought Bobo was going to climb right over the table.

"I was down at the docks this mornin' loadin' the tanks aboard *Gold Rush* when two heavy lookin' dudes walked up and asked for us."

"Heavy lookin' dudes?"

"Miami Beach—suntanned, white pants, flamingo shirts, sunglasses, the kind you see yourself in, and so much gold; shit, damn near blinded me."

"Right out of South Beach."

"You got it. Anyway, I told 'em you weren't aboard, but I was and what could I do for 'em?"

"They knew our names?"

"Yep. The tall one with blond hair, he did all the talkin', said he had a business opportunity he would like to discuss with us. So I invited them aboard." He paused for dramatic emphasis and took another sip of the tequila.

"How did they know our names?" Hink squinted over the top of his glass.

"Goddammit, Hink, how should I know? Maybe they asked at the dockmaster's office; maybe they looked us up in the phone book; maybe they've got a voodoo chicken. What difference does it make?"

Hink could hardly stand it. "Bobo, what the fuck is a voodoo chicken?"

"Jesus Christ, Hink, you know what I mean. Maybe the guy has magic or somethin'." Bobo's voice had gone up two octaves. A middle-aged woman in a fuchsia shirt and spandex shorts was staring at them from the next table.

Hink leaned forward. "Keep your voice down; you're blowing our cover."

Bobo was beside himself. "Dammit, Hink, do you wanna hear what happened or not?" he hissed.

"Sure, Bobo." Hink swirled his drink. "Go on."

Bobo regrouped. "Well, we went below and the blonde dude and I sat on the settee. The other one stood by the door and lit up a cigar—one of those skinny ones with the little wooden tips."

"Come on, Bobo." Hink was becoming impatient.

"Okay, okay." He pushed his drink out of the way and bent over the table. "The long and the short of it is they want us to pick up packages that someone is gonna drop off near the sites of sunken ships," he said in a tight whisper.

"Pick up packages?" Hink leaned forward.

"Yeah, off the bottom."

"Off the bottom?"

"It's a work of art. Everybody knows that we're always divin' around those places lookin' for stuff, so it's perfectly natural for us to be out there. And every now and then we do bring somethin' up, so everythin' *looks* real natural. The beauty of it is we do it in broad daylight, Hink, broad fuckin' daylight." Bobo leaned back and finished off the tequila.

Hink put his drink on the table. "What's in the packages, Bobo?"

"I didn't ask. Barbie Dolls for all I know."

"Are we going to do this for free?"

"Twenty thousand dollars a trip."

Hink stared at Bobo. "Holy shee-it!"

Bobo had him. It was clear that the chicken was ancient history.

Bobo Grinned. "What'd I tell you, pardner? You can count on ol' Bobo."

Hink regained his composure. "How does it work?"

Bobo was in command. "We give 'em a list of four or five wrecks that would make good drops; then they let us know a week in advance which site they're gonna use. After they make the splash they'll call and give us the exact GPS coordinates where the goods went down. All we have to do is let it be known that the crazy treasure hunters are off on another wild-goose chase, and we drive out and make the pickup."

"What do we do with the stuff once we have it?"

"Nothin'."

"Nothing?"

"After we get back in we do our usual routine: clean up the boat, fix a drink, hang out a while, then lock up and leave. Within twenty-four hours somebody'll get the package off the boat. He didn't say who, how or when; we're just supposed to stay out of sight for a day."

"How about the money?"

"We're to open an account in the bank of our choice. After the delivery has been approved, the cash'll be electronically transferred into the account."

Hink was silent for a moment. "Bobo, that is fucking amazing."

The approaching evening was just beginning to redefine the cool edge of the marsh as Jamison and Charlie entered the dockmaster's office at the Fredericka Marina.

The dockmaster looked up from a stack of papers. "Hi, Cap'n, how long you gonna be with us?"

Eight hours of sun had warmed the metal building and a window air conditioner was going full blast, rustling announcements and boat-for-sale notices pinned to a bulletin board on the wall behind the check-in counter. Texaco oil containers filled the glass display case that formed the top shelf of the counter. There was a cash register to the right, and a desk with a telephone and adding machine to the left. The VHF radio on a shelf in the corner periodically squawked messages from unseen boats.

"Two nights. We've got a little work to do on the boat; then we'll be moving on south day after tomorrow," Jamison replied, as he filled out the check-in form.

"You'll find power and water at each slip. Here's a list of local restaurants and services." The dockmaster slid a canary yellow sheet across the counter. "At the bottom of the page is the combination to the bathrooms and showers." He shoved his cap back on his head revealing a shock of sun-bleached hair. "Oh, we're also havin' a dock party tomorrow night. It's bein' sponsored by one of the restaurants, a bunch of the stores, and a local radio station. It'll be startin' around five-thirty; hope you'll join us. If you need anythin' just let me know."

Once the boat was secured and cleaned up, they grabbed a change of clothes and headed up the dock for the showers.

As Jamison luxuriated in the steaming spray he could hear Charlie singing in the next stall. Jesus, it felt good. Soap, suds and shampoo—the trinity of western hygiene and sacrament of the senses. After three days on a boat, fifteen minutes in a hot shower was a religious experience.

Later, born again, scrubbed down and dressed in clean jeans, sock-less sneakers and fresh tee shirts, they found a restaurant and bar. With a beer and margarita as cushions, they located a table with a view of the water and settled back to Jimmy Buffet and the "Twelve-Volt-Man," while the sun performed its final dance of the day on St. Simons Sound. After dinner, strolling the docks in the magenta half-light, they were feeling pretty satisfied.

The last three days had been a good shakedown, and they were feeling good about themselves and the boat. With the exception of the GPS, all systems and equipment were functioning perfectly. The numbers were looking better to Jamison, and he agreed with Charlie that the adventure was off to a good start.

His brief encounter earlier in the day had been filed away as nothing more than a peculiar but pleasant day dream.

CHAPTER 4

Susan Dunbar swung around the palm-lined curve through a wisp of pink morning shadows and braked her turquoise Toyota to a stop at the Demere Road intersection. She loved the little coupe. It was one of her best friends. Blanche—the car had gotten its name because its turquoise color reminded her of Miami, and Miami reminded her of Blanche, her favorite character on *The Golden Girls* television series—was always there when she needed her, ready for any new and exciting adventure.

The light changed and she turned left, toward the marsh and the Fredericka River. She had driven along this road all her life, but she never tired of the sensation of sweeping off the island, over the marsh and out above the mysterious dark waters of the river. In past years there had been a draw bridge at this point, but its old technology had given way to progress, and the singsong of the metal grating had been replaced with the high speed whir of four lane concrete. *The change was a bummer,* she thought, but at least she had been away at school when it happened and didn't have to watch the dismantling of the old span.

Bursting out onto the bridge from the tunnels of live oak and palmetto always elated her. It was as if the whole world was opening up before her. In the distance was the blue haze of the mainland and in between, an endless sweep of golden marsh. To the right the river wound along the back of St. Simons as it worked its way north, accented by a few docks and an anchored sailboat. To the left, the sound spread out toward Jekyll Island and the Atlantic Ocean. Closer in next to the bridge, was the Fredericka Marina, and across the river tied to their docks were several shrimp boats and a Coast Guard patrol boat.

Susan always counted the boats on the transient dock of the marina when she crossed the bridge. This morning she noted that there were two trawlers, a large power cruiser and a sailboat with a red dinghy floating by its side. The red dinghy had caught her eye when she first started across the bridge. It stood out like a beacon against the dark water and the white hull of the sailboat. Then she was off the bridge and slowing down to make the left turn into the marina's parking lot.

The sky below was about the same scuddy gray as the weathered boards of the dock that arched overhead. A seagull looped into view and settled up on a piling protruding down to Charlie's right. He contemplated some drips and dribbles of yellow paint that floated like stars on the pressure-treated firmament. Beneath an electrical outlet there was a small spider web. Suddenly a head and shoulders popped down from the boat tied to the upper left of the dock. The sleepy eyes on the face swept toward him, then opened in astonishment. Charlie tried to smile and formed a mental "Hi, there." He couldn't move his hands, much less open his mouth. The face registered surprise, confusion and then embarrassment. Then as quickly as he popped down, he popped back up out of sight.

Charlie decided that it was time to come down. Ever so slowly he let his feet drop down to the uneven boards. After a few seconds in the fetal position he extended and rolled over onto his back. The sky swung around to where it should be. Up was up and down was down. The sun would continue to rise in the east and set in the west, and the queen still ruled what little was left of the empire. He breathed deeply and let the pungent fragrance of the marsh and sea float him into the day.

Charlie had been practicing yoga for several years. It had become a refuge, a place of retreat and a space for the rebonding and energizing of an overstressed psyche, exhausted mental, and abused body parts. There had been mornings when he was sure that it was the only thing that kept him from being shipped off to the chicken factory in a body bag. Yoga was also a bridge between art and the everyday world; a way to move back and forth between the tangible and the intangible. Now he had a problem: there wasn't enough room on the boat to do the postures, and after this morning's experience, he didn't think that he wanted to become a public attraction, so it looked like he would be giving it up for the rest of the trip. He would just have to operate on the assumption that there was sufficient prana in this fresh, natural environment to soak into his system by osmosis.

A gentle mist of rain began to fall as Charlie climbed back aboard *September Song*. His father had gone in search of a grocery store, so Charlie decided to fix a cup of tea and then explore the marina and see if he could track down a marine supply store. They needed a fuel filter, and poking around in a boat store seemed the perfect way to spend a rainy morning.

Susan Dunbar was checking the inventory database in the back room that served as an office for Kilkinny Marine, when she heard the ringing of the ship's bell that was attached to the front door. She pushed back from her desk and stepped into the store. A tall, broad-shouldered young man in a windbreaker and blue running shorts had just entered and was thumbing through the chart books that were displayed along the far wall between the foul-weather gear and sailboat hardware. His back was to her, but there was something familiar about the easy stance and the dark, slightly unruly hair that curled down over the top of his collar. She felt a tiny flutter of recognition, like an electric butterfly, take flight in her breast. She stepped around the check-out counter.

"May I help you with something?"

He turned toward her.

The fluttering rose to her throat."

"Oh, my..."

Their eyes held for a long heartbeat and her optical nerves confirmed the tremulous flight in her heart.

"Susan?" he inquired tentatively.

The butterfly circled up and settled on the petals of her Pineal Chakra.

"Charlie?" she acknowledged.

Then the quivering insect shoved its proboscis into the flower of her being and Susan's tongue came unglued.

"Three years. It's been three years because Blanche will be three years old the third of June."

The words tumbled out of a memory bank that had long been shut down and put under lock and key. *Oh, God, where did that come from?* she thought. *He'll think I've lost my mind.*

"Blanche?" He looked bewildered.

"Blanche. My car."

She could see a flicker of recognition in his eyes.

"I remember, it was green, wasn't it?" he volunteered.

"Turquoise," she corrected.

"Right, turquoise." A slow smile played with his face. "But green was pretty close."

"Close enough." The color flooded back into her cheeks.

"Your parents gave it to you at graduation. Remember? I was there."

"That's right. It was three years ago."

There was a long pause and the energy between them shifted.

"Damn, Susan, you look wonderful."

She felt him reaching out for her.

"You've held up pretty well yourself, amico."

The butterfly took a deep drag, the circuit between them closed, and she was in Rome dancing in the evening shadows in front of Trevi Fountain with Charlie Jamison one more time.

He moved a step closer to her.

"How have you been?"

She slipped out of the purple sunset.

"Okay. I've been okay."

He paused. "I thought you were in Charleston."

"I was."

"How's Hink?"

She hesitated. "I don't know. I haven't seen him in a year." The words caught in her throat. "It didn't work out."

"I'm sorry."

He looked embarrassed.

"It was my mistake. I guess we're allowed one mistake, don't you think?"

He nodded. "Sure, I guess we are."

She brushed a sudden film of moisture from her eyes.

"I thought about trying to get in touch, but I didn't want to intrude," he said.

The butterfly sipped nectar as she smoothed her blouse and reached for a modicum of composure.

"What in the world are you doing here?"

"I'm on a sailboat with my dad, headed south."

Susan remembered the red dinghy against the white hull of the sailboat tied at the marina dock.

"You don't by any chance have a red dinghy, do you?"

"Why yes, but how did you know?"

"Don't you remember? I'm magic."

The first hint of a smile teased her lips. The butterfly sucked it up one final time, popped off into nirvana, and she flowed out like a wave and engulfed Charlie.

He caught a long-suppressed vision of her on top of him, breasts swaying in rhythm, hair washing his face and eyes flashing like sparklers. The memory took him completely by surprise.

43

Her smile continued to tease.

Oh, God, he thought. *I must be totally transparent.* He shifted gears heading for safer ground.

"What about you?" He looked around the store.

She followed his lead. "The store belongs to my parents. They bought it when my father retired. After Hink and I divorced, I left Charleston and moved back to the island. I help them run it. Among other things I'm the computer person, if you can believe that."

Charlie laughed. "That's hard to believe. I'm impressed!"

"Only one little computer. It's amazing what you can do when you have to."

He smiled. "I know. I've been working in a chicken factory. Part of the time I drove a truck, the rest you don't want to know about, believe me."

A shadow crossed her face and a note of concern entered her voice.

"You haven't quit painting...."

"Oh no, harvesting chicken parts was just a means to an end."

He double-clutched and changed gears again.

"Where are your parents? I'd love to see them."

"They're on vacation. Went to Europe to see if they could rekindle the fire. I gave them a few suggestions." Her smile teased again.

"I'll bet you did."

The vision popped back. They were both damp with perspiration. Her tongue exploring his ear. This time he made no attempt to run for cover and a boyish grin danced across his tanned face.

A slight blush crept up her neck.

"So, I've got the store to myself for another week."

While they were talking, two men in foul weather jackets entered. "Hi, Susan," the taller of the two greeted her, as he unzipped his coat.

"Hi, Alan. What can I do for you?" she answered.

"We need a Charleston to Cape Canaveral chart. You got one by any chance?"

"I think so."

She touched Charlie's arm. Her fingers lingered. "Please, don't leave."

Then she broke away and stepped across the room to the chart cabinet followed by Alan and his companion. "I should have one here someplace."

Charlie headed over to a shelf and some bins where he had seen fuel filters stacked. He felt a little breathless. He was caught in the fragile plume of her perfume. The scent was just there, barely tinting her space—it was the fragrance of summer love, the tall cedars of Rome and innocence. Charlie had tried to forget, put the passion of their summer behind him and throw himself into painting, but there had been many dark nights when the creative fires burned low and he had to admit that he had been only partially successful.

He leaned against the shelf to steady himself and pulled a rumpled piece of yellow paper from his pocket. He studied the number scrawled on it, then started sorting through the filters looking for the matching product code. His mind was such a jumble of conflicting emotions that he could hardly focus.

Susan had found the chart that her friends needed and was ringing up the purchase.

Charlie was having no luck. He was just about to give up, when there it was, the last one in the stack. He picked it up and started back to the check-out counter just as the two customers opened the door to leave.

"See you later, Susan."

"Be careful in the rain," she called after them.

She turned to Charlie as he approached her.

"I...need this filter."

He handed her the poly bag with the filter in it. It made a crinkling sound.

She took the bag.

"Okay."

She turned to the cash register, then stopped.

"I don't want you to go away."

"I know."

His mind raced. This was ridiculous. They were pulling out tomorrow. He couldn't just walk out the door and never see her again. Then it came to him.

"Look, there's going to be a dock party tonight. Would you like to go with me? We could have dinner and drinks and catch up. I could show you the boat."

"And the red dinghy?"

"How did you know about the red dinghy?"

"I told you, magic."

The sparkle was back in her eyes.

He smiled. "What time do you close up?"

"Usually at six o'clock, but what if I close early and meet you back here at six?"

"That would be great."

He grinned. "I want to meet Blanche."

"You'll meet Blanche."

He backed toward the door.

"I'll be here at six."

She held up the poly bag.

"Wasn't this what you came in for, Mr. Jamison?"

Charlie smiled. "Yeah, I guess it was."

The rain had become a gentle sprinkle as he left the store. It dampened his hair and ran down his neck as he headed down the dock to *September Song*. The trees on St. Simons were emerging from the mist, and he felt as if he could leap the river and dance along the edge that their top-most branches made against the patchwork blue of the clearing sky. It would make a great painting: Charlie Jamison, seized by surprise, slow-dancing in the sky.

There wasn't much in the way of a grocery store in the Fredericka Marina complex, so Jamison had called a cab to take him into the village of St. Simons. As much as anything else, going into town was an excuse to get a little space and stretch his legs. All they really needed was some bread and maybe some fruit and cheese. The fact of the matter was they could have gotten along a few more days without either, but it was raining and he couldn't do the repair work he wanted to, so bread was as good a reason as any to get off the boat.

The cab dropped him off at the corner where the village's two main streets intersected. Most of the town's stores and shops were along Mallory Street, which ran south toward the water and ended at a pier that jutted out into the sound toward Jekyll Island. Watching over the small community was a black and white lighthouse that rose above the trees a few hundred yards to the east. *The village is charming and timeless*, he thought. He had been here once, years ago, and it seemed to him that nothing had changed. It was a comforting feeling.

Jamison worked his way along the street of shops and quaint restaurants until a book in the window of a small book seller caught his eye. *Cruising The Southeast Coast—A Guide to the Golden Isles of Georgia and South Carolina* was displayed among books of local interest and regional lore. He turned the antique brass doorknob and went in.

He was greeted by a middle-aged woman with reading glasses suspended by a purple Crokie around her neck. "Good morning, if I can be of any help just let me know."

"Thank you. I'm interested in the cruising book that you have in the window," he replied.

"Oh, of course, it's right back here." She came out from behind the counter and led the way to the back of the store. "Are you a sailor?"

"Why yes, how did you know?" Her question had caught him by surprise.

"Well, the foul weather jacket and the boat shoes, but really, it's your eyes."

"My eyes?" His curiosity was piqued.

"It's in your eyes. My husband was a sailor and he had the same look in his eyes. I got where I could pick sailors out in a crowd. It always amazed him."

"You speak of him in the past tense."

"Yes, he passed away eighteen months ago. That's when I bought this store."

"Oh, I'm sorry." He felt as if he had invaded her privacy.

"That's all right. We had a good life together." She smiled. "Now I have the store and a new life." She picked the book off a crowded shelf and handed it to him. "I think this is the book you are looking for." It was the one he had seen in the window.

"Yes, this is it. Thanks." He thumbed through a few pages.

"Can I show you anything else?" She was still smiling. She had crystal blue eyes.

"Did you sail with him?"

"Yes, I did."

Jamison returned her smile. "I think you're right about the eyes."

Her smile broadened.

"I think I'll browse around a little bit."

"Take your time."

Jamison wandered over to a table of gift and art books that he had noticed when he first came in. He was attracted to a small book with a medallion containing two dolphins on its dark blue cover. He picked it up and discovered that the dolphins circled a compass rose centered within a golden ring that caught the light and changed color as he viewed it from different angles. The medallion was embossed and gold-stamped so it shone with a three-dimensional reality that he found breathtaking. The device was centered vertically and horizontally; there was nothing else on the cover. He was taken by its beauty and simplicity. He estimated it to be about seven by nine inches and about an inch thick. Jamison ran his fingers over its surface. It had an almost undetectable texture that he decided was somewhere between an eggshell and a vellum finish. It felt inviting to his touch. He opened it and was delighted to find that the inside cover and endsheets were marbled paper.

What a wonderful little book, he thought. He turned to the title page; it was blank. He flipped through several more pages. All the pages were blank. *Of course,* he mused, *it's a sketchbook or perhaps a journal.* He closed it and looked at the cover again.

"Isn't that a lovely little book?" the store owner asked. She had been watching him as he examined the small volume.

"Yes it is, lovely and unusual. How much is it?"

"Twelve-fifty. I couldn't bring myself to put a sticker on it."

"I'll take it." He turned and walked back to the counter. "There's no publisher or company name on it, where did you find it?"

She rang up the two books. "I don't know, it's sort of a one-of-a-kind. It was included in a recent shipment of orders, but it didn't show up on the shipping receipt. I started to send it back, but I just fell in love with it so I decided to put it out and see how it would do. I'm glad that you found it." She put on her reading glasses. "Let's see, that will be thirty-seven-fifty."

Jamison handed her his Visa card. She ran it through the machine and handed him the charge slip. He signed it and took the receipt.

She considered him for a minute. "Do you believe in coincidence?"

He looked up into her eyes. "Why no. I believe you control your destiny." He was bemused. "Why do you ask?"

She slipped the books into a silver paper bag. "I was just thinking about the dolphin book. It just appeared, sort of out of nowhere; then I almost sent it back, but at the last minute decided to keep it. Then, the morning I put it on display, you walk in thirty minutes later and buy it. It's almost like it was intended for you."

He nodded. "Do you think that was coincidence?"

She smiled. "I believe coincidence is the way angels have of working things out. Some people call it serendipity, others call it providence." She handed him the silver bag.

He returned her smile. "I'll have to give that some thought." He started to leave, then turned back. "Oh, there is one other thing you could possibility help me with."

"Of course, what's that?"

"I need to get some bread. Is there a grocery or bakery nearby?"

She directed him to a delicatessen a few doors away where they made their own bread. He thanked her and went back out into the rain. He tucked his new books under his jacket to keep them from getting wet. *What a charming person,* he thought. As he started down the street he realized that he didn't know the name of the store. He turned to look for the sign. It was there, hanging above a blue and silver awning. *A Touch Of Fantasy* the oval carving proclaimed. The bracket that supported it was a gold dolphin.

The showers had stopped when the Brunswick Taxi Service delivered Jamison back to the marina. A fresh breeze was blowing the clouds away and the sun was beginning to break through, causing a mist of steam to rise off the parking lot. The docks bustled with activity. A band was setting up under a blue and white awning that sheltered an outdoor pub, while a bartender wiped down the bar and waiters arranged tables along a deck overlooking the water. High above, a radio station was assembling a DJ's booth on the bridge that connected the upper deck of stores. A bright red and gold banner proclaimed WBCH Soft Rock "The Voice Of The Golden Isles."

It's going to be quite a party, Jamison thought as he weaved through the happy confusion to the ramp that led down to the boats. As he started down he ran into Charlie coming up. He had a towel and his shave kit under his arm.

"Hi, thought I'd take a shower," Charlie greeted him.

"Got a heavy date?" Jamison called as they passed.

"As a matter of fact I do." Charlie grinned over his shoulder. "Tell you about it later."

This could turn out to be an interesting day, Jamison thought, as he lifted the shopping bag filled with bread and his two new books onto *September Song's* deck.

CHAPTER 5

Jamison sat on a railing that kept the boisterous crowd from tumbling headlong into the black sticky mud of the marsh ten feet below. The dock party was well on its way to being a big success. The lead singer of the band was directing cheers. He waved a magic marker sign over his head—ARE, and the crowd shouted *ARE!* Next up was WE, and the crowd responded *WE!* Then HAVING, *HAVING!* FUN, *FUN!* Followed by a great cheer, and the drummer did a roll-down into "Tequila Sunrise" to a roar of approval.

The restaurants had thrown open their doors and were serving on the decks. Waitresses in "It's A Deck Of A Party" tee shirts had the bartender under the blue and white awning jumping, and the DJ in the red and gold WBCH sky booth on the upper deck was revving up his boosters to leave the planet. Jamison hooked his feet behind the second rung of the railing and took another sip of his Island Kamikaze.

Charlie and Susan appeared out of the crowd. "Dad, I'd like you to meet Susan Dunbar."

Jamison slipped off the railing. A very pretty blonde with an open, engaging smile extended her hand. She wore a black tee shirt, white shorts, and a bright floral baseball cap. A gold dolphin on a chain hung from her neck. It shone against the tee shirt.

He smiled and took her hand. "So you're the young lady I've heard so much about over the last few hours! It's a pleasure to meet you."

She made no effort to let go of his hand. "Charlie told me what a great time you two are having."

Jamison reluctantly released her. "Whatever he's told you is all true." He smiled at Charlie. He had to lean close and raise his voice to be heard over the band's loudspeakers. "Would you two join me for a drink?"

"Thanks, but we've just finished dinner and we're on the way to meet Blanche, a friend of Susan's," Charlie shouted over the pounding base guitar. Susan laughed up at him and he gave her a squeeze. "Maybe if we get back in time."

"I'm probably not going to hang around much longer." Jamison raised his glass. "Another one of these and we won't be leaving tomorrow. Give my regards to Blanche."

"Thanks, Dad, see you later."

"Bye, Mr. Jamison, maybe I'll see you tomorrow."

"Everybody calls me Jamison, Susan."

Susan blessed him with a big smile. "Jamison it is."

Jamison gave them a little salute with the pink umbrella from the Kamikaze. "Have a good time."

"I really like your father," Susan said, once they worked their way free of the crowd.

"Yeah, he's a great guy. I haven't seen much of him the last few years, what with school and painting, so this trip is like renewing an old friendship." He squeezed her hand. "If you know what I mean."

She pulled his arm around her. "You must have a lot to talk about."

"We got a good start before we left." He thought for a moment. "But one of the interesting things about sailing is that it's more about *being* than talking. Everything is pretty much in the moment: the shared pleasures and discomforts, the frustrations, even ecstasy, and sometimes fear. You develop a bond and a form of communication that goes beyond words. I think you could sail a few hundred miles with a person and never speak a word, yet end up knowing them better than if you sat next to that same individual in an office for a year."

Susan smiled. "I like that."

"On a trip like this you get away from all the noise and talking heads. It's like going out in the desert to find something you lost in the city, only we've chosen the ocean. In a way, Dad and I are sailing our way back together again."

"Sounds a little like Zen."

Charlie grinned. "Yeah, that too."

They were crossing the crowded parking lot. Away from the party it was cool and quiet. The tree frogs provided accompaniment to the distant beat of the band.

"Charlie Jamison, I would like for you to meet Miss Blanche Boudreaux." Even in the dark it was apparent the car was turquoise—it seemed to generate its own light.

He ran his hand along the shiny fender. "Blanche, I can tell you're a fine lady."

Susan was opening the driver's door. "Would you like to go for a ride?"

"How can I resist two such inviting women?" Charlie slid into the seat next to Susan. "Boudreaux? Did you say Boudreaux?" He laughed.

"It's southern gothic. You do speak southern gothic don't you?" Her eyes smiled through the darkness.

"Well, no, ma'am, you see I'm from the big city—"

"Well, city boy, I'm just the girl to teach you southern gothic." She leaned across and playfully kissed his ear.

He turned and his lips brushed against hers. They lingered for a long moment; then she slowly pulled away, turned on the ignition and opened the sunroof. The stars were bright overhead. Blanche's engine purred to life.

"How long has it been since you were on the island?" she asked, as they pulled out of the parking lot.

"Oh, it's been years. The family came here for a vacation when I was about twelve."

"Not much has changed; that's one of the things that I love about this place. The bridge is new, and there's some development, mostly out the Fredericka Road, but for the most part the island has been able to keep its charm."

"How about the Coast Guard Station?"

"The Coast Guard has moved out, but the building's still there. We'll run out that way. Would you like to take a walk on the beach?"

"That would be nice."

They crossed the bridge and took the turn that led toward the village. The night was black southern velvet, and it felt as if they were being sucked through it by some mystical force. Charlie wasn't sure that the engine was even running, it was so smooth. He was convinced that they were airborne, suspended just above the pavement.

A string of blue lights appeared to their left; Charlie recognized them immediately. "That's the airport. I remember there were a lot of antique planes on the island for a fly-in when we were here. I would be out on the beach when they would fly over in formation. There were bi-planes and some old World War II fighters. It was really great stuff for a twelve-year-old boy."

"I can imagine." Susan was slowing for the traffic light in the village.

"It kind of runs in the family. I think Dad wanted to fly, but he was never able to do it. But sailing is like flying in many ways, so all in all, things seem to have worked out pretty well."

They passed the lights of the village and Susan made a right turn onto a street that ran parallel to the beach. Charlie could hear the surf and see the winking red and green lights of the St.

Simons channel buoys. Then the water was gone and they drove between warm lights in the windows of homes and beach cottages.

"I like *September Song*. You've done a good job on her—very comfortable and cozy. You don't need another crew member, do you?" They were passing the tennis courts of the King and Prince Hotel.

"Hmm, I don't know. Where would you sleep?"

The soft light from the dashboard created an intimate glow. Her eyes caught his. "I think we could find a way to work that out."

Charlie's fingers brushed across the back of her neck and rested on her shoulder. She felt a familiar tingling sensation. The night creatures created a symphony as Susan laid her head back on his arm and let the warmth spread up through her body. She made a left turn and a moment later came to a stop at a corner in front of a group of small shops and a restaurant. A neon sign announced The Crab Trap. The salty fragrance of seafood permeated the intersection. The door of the restaurant opened and a family came out. Susan turned right. For a moment the sounds of music and laughter caught up with Blanche, and then she accelerated and they were out of the neon and gone into the darkness. They drove in silence, enraptured by the night and the ecstasy of touching, each one reliving shared joys, traveling in their separate time capsules.

"Here we are."

Susan braked Blanche to a stop in the darkened parking lot and turned off the engine. With a click the lights faded. The smell of the ocean blew into the car, and the rustling of sea oats replaced the chorus of crickets and frogs. They didn't move for a moment, not wanting to leave the memories. Then Charlie leaned over and pulled Susan to him. His lips caressed her eyes, then played with her nose, and finally found her lips. They parted, and her tongue explored his as she pressed toward him. He reached down and fumbled with the seatbelts until they finally unsnapped and their bodies were free. His fingers moved up her body and traced the shape of her breast. He explored the lace of her bra and she felt herself harden against the palm of his hand. She arched her back and pulled his head down and buried her face in his hair.

"Charlie Jamison, I think I could get back into you," she whispered, as she traced his ear with the tip of her tongue.

The day following Hink and Bobo's meeting at Las Chitas, a telephone rang in a softly lit second floor office a block west of Ocean Drive in Miami's South Beach. The blond caller heard three rings, then a click followed by a long pause, then the familiar sensual nightingale voice.

"This is the front office."

"This is the director of player personnel. It looks a good day for a baseball game," he replied.

"The manager will be pleased to hear that. How was your scouting trip?" she asked.

The mix of authority and control coasting on the undercurrent of her voice turned him on. In his fantasies she was always dominant.

"Very successful. The two prospects have signed and will report within the week."

"Outstanding. Do they understand the signals?"

"Completely."

"What is the risk factor?"

Although he was sure the conversation was being recorded, he could hear the clicking of computer keys and suspected she was typing into a database.

"Risk: low to moderate."

"Are they good for extra innings?"

"Only time will tell how long they'll last."

"When do you expect to put them into the lineup?"

"As soon as we can schedule a game. There are several open dates coming up."

"Keep them on a tight leash until they have a few games under their belt, but the sooner the better." Her tone was firm.

"I understand." He liked the idea of a tight leash.

There was an almost imperceptible shift in her voice. "How are the cigars holding out?" she asked.

He smiled. When the front office was pleased they sent cigars. Always good. Always Cuban.

"The bullpen's running a little low."

"We just got in a shipment of Hoyo De Monterreys."

"That should get us through batting practice."

"You've earned them." Then there was a click, a pause, three beeps, and she was gone.

Jamison finished his Kamikaze and sat through a few more sets by the band, then decided to head back to the boat. He enjoyed watching the people around him, but it was frustrating being alone in a crowd that was having so much fun. It seemed to him that there were attractive women everywhere, which only reinforced the feeling that he was a lone ranger. Maybe it was the effect of the drink, but the party was beginning to make him feel a little melancholy. He thought about calling Tommy, but a look at his watch told him that it was too late; she would be asleep. Besides, he had called her yesterday when they got in. As he edged past a couple in a body-lock he understood why sailors raised so much hell when they got in port—anything to ease the pain.

September Song's lines seemed to be in order. The bow line and aft spring line were stretched tight by the current but securely attached. The dinghy appeared to be in good shape. It hadn't decided to take off on its own, so after a walk around the deck, Jamison unlocked the companionway and went below. Charlie wasn't back; he would have been surprised if he was. Jamison lit the stove and put on the tea kettle.

He really liked what he had seen of Susan Dunbar. From what Charlie had told him about her, there was a lot of history and a lot to like. *She wouldn't be bad to have around*, he thought, as he poured the boiling water over one of Charlie's herbal tea bags. He rummaged through a cabinet and found a tin of biscotti. He picked out two of the biscuits and settled down on the settee with the cup of tea.

Jamison had been reading about St. Simons in the cruising book he bought in town before he left for the party. It was still on the table, so he opened it with the intention of picking up where he had left off. He thumbed through a few pages but couldn't seem to get back into it, so he put it down and picked up the small volume with the gold dolphin medallion embossed on its cover. *It really is a magical little book,* he thought. He opened it and inspected the marbled paper. When he held it at just the right angle he could see tiny gold flecks in the swirling red, maroon and black pattern. *I believe it's French,* he thought. He remembered the swatches of French papers he had carefully filed at the agency.

He dipped a piece of biscotti in the tea, and pondered the empty pages that were open before him. He had the feeling that he was looking into the future. It was as if the pages were made not of paper, but the essence of time.

CHAPTER 6

The Dolphin Chronicle #2

Eden is a state of mind. A framework of being. It dances in the eyes of the very young child still damp with its memory, and sings like a siren in the dim recollections of the aging. It is the place before places, the time before time, the dream that returns when the mind is asleep. Eden is pure sensation, pure joy, pure love, pure beauty, pure acceptance, and complete powerlessness. There are no straight lines in Eden. No calculations. No analyses. No deductions. No left brains.

In the "Garden" the dawning of linear reality in the minds of Adam and Eve was the snake too beguiling to resist, the apple too satisfying to deny. In choosing reason over wonder, they rewrote the rules of reality. It was the "Big Bang" of consciousness, the beginning of time, the final curtain in Paradise. From then on they were on their own, refugees in a strange new world, dancing the fine, rational line of mortal gods. For the first time they had to live by their wits. In the business of survival, "doing" became the name of the game. "Being" was lost in the shuffle. Eden became a legend, a poignant myth to be passed along to the tribe around campfires and to the assembled faithful in the cavernous echo chambers of great cathedrals. Theirs was the initial salvo in the struggle of left and right cranial hemispheres. The birth of ego. The loss of innocence. The genesis of the Memory. The ghost in the soul.

Jamison was the first to awaken. He could hear Charlie's deep, rhythmic breathing resonating from the aft cabin. *I must have been out like a light. I never heard him come in,* he thought. He squinted at his watch: 8:30:29 the digital seconds blinked back. He needed to get going. With a sigh he slid out of the bunk and pulled on a pair of shorts and a sleeveless shirt. He was pleased to note the effect of the Kamikaze had almost worn off. It looked as if he was going to have a smooth landing.

As quietly as possible Jamison made his way into the galley. He gently closed the door to the aft cabin, lit the stove and put on the coffee pot. He found the bag of pastries he had bought at the deli in town and took out two Danish. One he put on a folded paper towel along with Charlie's mug, and the other he munched as he poured his coffee.

His two new books were on the table where he had left them when he went to bed. He sat down on the settee and opened the *Cruising Guide* to the chapter on Georgia and flipped through the pages to Cumberland Island. The island was a preservation legend, and he had been looking forward to visiting it for years. He hoped the guide would offer some insight into dock access and anchorages. Their schedule called for them to arrive there the next day.

He had just found the reference when he was interrupted by someone knocking on the cabin top. Jamison closed the book and opened the companionway hatch. He poked his head through and was greeted by Susan Dunbar's smiling face.

"Hi, Jamison, I was on my way to open the store and I thought I'd see if you two were up."

Jamison raised a finger to his mouth. "I'm into my first cup, but your friend is still sacked out. I thought I'd let him sleep a while longer."

"We were pretty late getting back. What time are you pulling out?" she whispered.

"Sometime after lunch. I need to repair a hole in the in the stern of the boat. Would you like some coffee?"

"Oh, I appreciate it, but I really do have to get to the store. Just tell Charlie I dropped by. Maybe we could have lunch."

There was that dazzling smile. She looked as if she had been in bed at nine o'clock. *This woman was born to make every day one to remember,* Jamison thought.

"I'll be glad to. Thanks for looking in on us."

"See you later." She stepped off the boat onto the dock, and started up the ramp. Jamison was still standing in the companionway when she got to the top. She stopped and waved, and he raised his mug in reply.

"Jamison, it's time for you to get to work," he said. He felt energized.

An hour later Charlie found Jamison hanging upside down over the stern. "I wondered where you were. Thanks for the coffee and Danish." He leaned over the rail. "How's it going?"

"I've about got it." He paused for a minute and wiped the perspiration off his forehead. "This epoxy's a pain in the ass to work with."

Charlie nodded. "Can I help?"

"Thanks, but it's pretty much a one man job." Jamison pulled himself back into the cockpit. "I'll let that cure and then sand it. Oh, Susan came by to see you about an hour ago. She was on her way to the store."

"She did? I thought that I'd go by and see her." Charlie was obviously pleased.

"She thought that you two might have lunch."

"Just what I was thinking. What time do you want to leave?"

"How about 1:30? I should have this little project finished by then."

"You're sure you don't need any help?"

"No it's in good shape."

"I'll get everything in order below." There was a sparkle in Charlie's eyes as he disappeared into the cabin.

Jamison smiled, picked up a sheet of sandpaper and squeezed back through the stern rail.

At 1:30 Jamison turned *September Song's* diesel over. It didn't catch the first time so he advanced the throttle and punched the starter button again. He caught a whiff of exhaust when it took hold and coughed out a cloud of hydro-carbons.

Charlie was on the dock with Susan. He was disconnecting the shore power cable and she was standing by the spring lines. It was clear to Jamison that they were both concentrating on being busy. Charlie passed the coiled cable up to Jamison, who stowed it in the seat hatch. Susan undid the bow spring line and tossed it onto the deck. Charlie did the same with the aft line and they were set to go.

"Write me, okay?" she blurted out.

Charlie took her in his arms. "And I'll call you whenever we get on land."

"If I'm not there leave a message on the machine."

"I will. Think about Nassau."

"Let me know as soon as you have an idea about time." She gave him a quick kiss.

"Gotta go."

"I know."

They broke away and Charlie climbed aboard. "Toss me the bow line; we'll slip the stern."

Susan uncleated the line and tossed it to him as Jamison swung the boat away from the dock. When Charlie had finished coiling the line and looked back, they were already several hundred yards out in mid-channel. She was still there in the same spot. The next time he looked she was gone. He searched the docks and the ramp, then he found her—she had climbed to the upper deck of the complex. He picked up the binoculars and lifted them to his eyes. She was waving. Then they rounded a bend and she was out of sight.

It was calm and they were getting off too late to go outside, so they decided to run the Waterway until night caught up with them and then go into Cumberland the next day. They re-entered St. Simons Sound and passed beneath the stern of a large freighter anchored in the fairway. Following the shipping channel southwest to the entrance of Jekyll Creek, they left the sound and wound in behind Jekyll Island.

Charlie took the binoculars from around his neck and hung them over the steering pedestal grabrail. He hadn't said a word since they had pulled out of St. Simons.

Jamison broke the silence. "Charlie, you want to navigate?"

"Sure." Charlie picked up the chart. "Where are we?"

"Just past the entrance channel. There's a shoal to port."

Charlie traced his finger along the plastic covered page until he found their location.

"I really enjoyed meeting Susan," Jamison said.

"I thought you'd like her." He turned the chart, orienting it to their course.

"Did I hear you talking about Nassau when you were on the dock?"

Charlie looked chagrined. "God, I forgot to mention that to you. I invited her over when we get there. Damn, I hope that's okay."

"I think that's a great idea." Jamison was searching the water ahead. "What am I looking for?"

Charlie pointed. "A green marker. Just off the port bow."

Jamison nodded. "I see it." He paused. "I'm sure Mom will like her."

"I hope so." Charlie thought for a moment. "We really put this together at the last minute. I'll have to find her a place to stay."

"I think we can handle that." They were approaching the day beacon Charlie had pointed out. Jamison could just make out the number. "Green thirteen?"

Charlie checked the chart. "Right, thirteen. There's shoaling just out past it."

Jamison steered a little more to the center of the stream. "And this was the first time you've been with her since graduation?" he asked.

"Really since Italy. I ran into her and her family at graduation but we were just passing in the night. She was getting married the next day."

"You mentioned she was married."

"Yeah, but definitely past tense. From what Susan says, the guy was false advertising. He couldn't commit for the long haul. It got to be a mess, so she pulled the plug." Charlie suddenly pointed ahead. "Watch out for that patch of grass."

"Where? Oh, I see it." Jamison edged to the left to avoid the floating clump of marsh grass. "Did you know the fellow?"

"Hink? No, not really." He paused. "We traveled in different circles. He came from an old Charleston banking family. Majored in business. The contract with Susan was negotiated long before I came into the picture."

"Did he know about your relationship with Susan?"

"Are you kidding? He'd have gone crazy. As it is, nobody seems to know what happened to him. The last Susan heard he was somewhere in Florida chasing sunken treasure."

Jamison thought about the young woman he had just met. "Son, from what I've seen, she deserves better than that."

Charlie nodded. "Dad, I couldn't agree with you more."

Jamison studied his son. "You know, there may have been more to that summer than either one of you realized."

Charlie pondered the idea. "Yeah, you could be right."

They were both silent while Jamison cruised the back roads of his long lost summers looking for road signs of seasons yet to come.

"We have a bridge ahead." Charlie interrupted his reverie. The high-bridge from the mainland to Jekyll Island spanned the Waterway about a quarter of a mile ahead. The bridge was well above the top of *September Song's* mast, and there was no oncoming traffic, so Jamison nudged the throttle and they passed under with plenty of room to spare.

Charlie wondered aloud, "How many people sitting in their cars up there wish they were headed south with us, do you imagine?"

"Most of them," Jamison guessed.

A couple of miles later they entered Jekyll Sound and turned southeast into St. Andrews Sound. The shore breeze had picked up, and they bucked a light chop as they worked their way across open water toward Little Cumberland Island. Off the point of the island, just past land's end, Jamison turned back to the southwest and Charlie raised the sails. There was a perfect ten-knot breeze.

They sailed close past the deserted beach with its abandoned lighthouse still watchful on the high ground above the sea oats, and entered the broad purple-deep still waters of the Cumberland River. The sails were tinted saffron by the sun as they left the beaches behind and glided effortlessly into the golden wilderness. The light dissolved into translucent particles. Jamison felt a tingling sensation.

"Jamison, I like what you said about my hair."

He heard her voice first, somewhere inside his head; then it was as if she began to emerge from her words. It reminded him of the movie editing technique where you hear the sound before you see the next scene.

"I don't understand what's going on here."

"Why do you have to understand?"

She had completely materialized now. The effect was holographic, but fully incarnate and in living color.

"I don't know. It's just that I'm not used to talking to a hallucination."

But he wasn't really talking, at least not out loud. No sound ever got past his pineal gland. In time they would laugh and call it the Walkman effect.

"Oh, you think you're hallucinating?"

"You're not a hallucination?"

"Hallucination is such a…" She paused. *"Difficult word."*

"All right, how about fantasy?"

She nodded. *"Fantasy is nice."*
"So you're a fantasy?"
"If that makes you comfortable."
Jamison decided to go with the flow.
"I'll settle for fantasy."
She smiled. *"My face, tell me about my face."*
"Well, it's a lovely face."
"Lovely?"
The light molded her high cheekbones and caught the delicate turn of her chin. She was beguiling.
"Okay, beautiful."
"That's much better. My skin?"
"Your skin is transparent, luminous, with hints of green and blue in the shadows."
"Is it smooth?"
He saw his fingers brush across her face.
"Yes, like fresh cream."
"My eyes."
"Like two windows on the universe."
"Your universe or mine?"
"I'm not sure."
"What do you see through them?"
"Passion, joy, wonder, peace...pain."
"My lips."
"Soft, inviting, the prelude to a song."
"My tongue."
"Fire."
From high above the light, slicing the moment, came the piercing cry of a hawk.
"Jamison, come with me."
She was just a circling speck in the twilight sky, but the call was crystal clear. One dream merged into another, and for a flash they were one—merged by the alchemy of wind and water, feather, fantasy, and flesh. For just an instant he could see with hawks' eyes the green of the islands and, far below, the golden sails of a boat sweeping through the darkening waters

into the night of an emerald Eden. For an imperceptible moment Jamison was free.

September Song's sails dipped with the changing rhythms of the wind as they blew past Terrapin Point and into the narrows of the Waterway at Shellbine Creek. They rounded the bend at Cabin Bluff, and Charlie dropped the sails as the wind hardened on their bow. A few minutes later they turned west into the Crooked River, folded their wings and settled down in twelve feet of water for the night.

CHAPTER 7

Damn, Jamison thought, as he threw the covers off, *it's getting worse.* It was 3:00 a.m., it was blowing like hell, and he and Charlie were headed back on deck for the third time. The wind gnawed at their exposed flesh and the water boiled like a cauldron. The last time out they had set the second anchor and now they had a serious problem. Somehow in the melee the two anchor lines had gotten crossed.

Jamison was on his knees in the bow pulpit following the lines with his flashlight. "Charlie, these things will chew through each other if we don't do something pretty quick." Losing both anchors on a night like this would really screw up the balance sheet.

Charlie was checking the tension on both lines. "The right one has some slack; maybe we can work a switch."

But they both knew that switching the lines would be not be easy with the wind and current beating up on them this hard. They huddled in the bow pulpit trying to get what shelter they could from each other's bodies while they tried to determine a course of action. Even though they were practically in each other's ears, they had to shout to make themselves heard over the howling wind and the waves pounding against the hull.

After considerable debate, they decided to release the downwind line, walk it around the stern and reattach it on the upwind side. They would then release the upwind line, pass it around the bow and cleat it on the downwind side. It seemed like a workable plan, so Jamison released the downwind line and Charlie started it around the deck. When Jamison shined his flashlight down into the surging water to check its progress, he couldn't believe his eyes.

"Charlie, pull up on the line!" he shouted.

Charlie gave it a heave. It flipped completely out of the water. "Oh shit," he exclaimed.

They were both stunned. There *was no line*; it had been cut in two. There had been about a hundred and twenty feet out, but all that was left was the deck coil and about ten feet dangling from Charlie's hand.

After examining the frayed strands, all they could figure was that during the last tidal change the line must have been severed by the keel. A careful check of the other anchor line revealed that it was in good shape. The plastic chaff guard was in place and there was no evidence of wear or abrasion. The other anchor was holding like Gibraltar, and *September Song* was holding her own, so they decided to leave it like that for the night.

That was close, Jamison thought. He didn't want to admit he was shaken. He had been cool and focused while they were on deck, just like always, but afterwards he realized that losing the anchor had scratched a raw nerve that he didn't know existed.

"I've got to stay on top of this," he said to himself as he shoved the hatch closed.

"Did you say something?" Charlie asked as he pulled his jacket off.

"I was just thinking about losing the anchor."

"We can probably replace it in St. Augustine." Charlie was already in his bunk.

"Yeah, I guess we can."

Jamison turned off the light. What was going on? Why was he feeling so damned insecure? It was as if he had momentarily lost his bearings. He slipped out of his shoes, climbed into bed and pulled the sheet up around his shoulders. He finally dozed off, but he couldn't seem to get comfortable and he tossed most of the night.

Hinkley Prescott's father could never forgive him for being born with a club foot. It didn't make any difference that an orthopedic surgeon was able to correct the deformity; Hink was damaged goods, and in his father's carefully crafted universe, there was no room for anything but perfection. He wore it like a resplendent suit of armor, a shield against the world, but in fact it was his Maginot Line, for Henry Drayton Prescott was a coward.

The tradition within the Charleston branch of the Prescott clan required all male offspring to attend the Citadel. The precedent was started by Henry's great-grandfather who graduated from the Citadel and went on to a brilliant career killing Yankees in the First South Carolina Regiment of Cavalry during the Civil War. His battle experiences sharpened his predatory instinct and when the hostilities were over, the colonel, as he came to be known, parlayed a modest family inheritance and a sharp eye for profit into a banking empire by financing reconstruction efforts throughout South Carolina and the low country.

Drayton Almstead Prescott was a power to be reckoned with as he sat in his second story office at Prescott Bank and Trust on King Street, where he manipulated the fortunes of countless businesses, families and political power brokers who depended on his good will for their prosperity and well being. He was a ruthless autocrat who established a stern regimen for the men who were blessed, or cursed, to bear the Prescott name.

The colonel's marching orders for keeping the Prescott banking interests preeminent in South Carolina came to be known in the family as *The Tradition*. It was a two-step process: four years at the Citadel for attitude modification, then into the capitalist trenches at the bank to slug it out for the spoils of commerce. The strategy worked remarkably well as three generations of Prescotts lifted the banner and followed the Spartan calling of the colonel, building a financial empire that was unchallenged in the state.

The thread began to unravel when it became Henry's turn to leave the tea olive scented balconies on South Battery and join the ranks of his forebears. Henry lived in fear of *The Tradition*, of the day he would be marched off to the Citadel and be inducted into the fraternity of Prescott manhood.

Henry wasn't sure when his life started to go wrong. All he knew was that somewhere around his fifteenth birthday it dawned on him that he wanted no part of a life dominated by black suits, starched collars and the bare knuckles of high finance. He wanted to be a physician, but it was already too late, for whatever free-will he possessed had long ago been appropriated by *The Tradition*. No matter how intensely the rebel flame burned, he knew when the moment of decision came he would deny the desires of his heart and put on the uniform of a Prescott soldier.

The day he marched through the gate of the Citadel he committed an act of cowardice that robbed him of his soul. It was the ultimate sacrifice to the tyranny of his genealogy.

To compensate for his shame and to conceal his spiritual disfigurement, he wrapped himself in the protective mantle of perfection. He was driven to excel. Henry examined every thought, every idea, and every action by the light of the merciless discipline that drove him, until in time, the memory of that infamous day was purged from the working program of his consciousness. Banished, that is, until the birth of his first son, when he looked down and saw Hinkley's bent right leg. In that moment an emotional dam burst, and the memory of his own twisted psyche came rushing back in a lava flow of self-hate.

Hinkley Prescott's future was sealed in that moment. From the first day of his life he would bear the mark of his father's self-loathing. Hinkley could never measure up. No matter how he excelled, it was never enough. His father drove him as he had driven himself, until one day, in a flash of revelation, Hinkley discovered a niche in Henry's armor. It dawned on him that he could drive his father crazy by failing. In that moment he drew a sword that would assuage his pain and level the battlefield that had become the devastated garden of his childhood.

If his father was Attila the Hun, Hinkley's mother was Florence Nightingale. After a day of slash and burn, she would come to him and bind up his wounds. She was his balm, an angel that brought him whatever healing he was capable of accepting, and in time, his ticket out of the carnage. In Hinkley's thirteenth year, Mary Durell Prescott had had enough. She sued Henry for divorce, took her son and moved to St. Simons Island, Georgia.

The move saved Hinkley's life, but the years of guerrilla warfare had left deep and irreversible scars. He had become so adept at the craft of failure that it had become his second nature. His strategy for besting his father on the battlefield of familial survival became a blueprint for losing on the playing fields of life, where he desperately wanted to win. It began to look as if the taste of victory was, in reality, the bitter cup of defeat. His father had won the war. The realization was a spear thrust through his heart, and what had begun as fear of Henry turned to hate.

The first thing Jamison did when he awakened the next morning was to check the anchor line. It was reassuring to see it intact and, after checking the creek banks, confirm that it had not dragged. At 9:15 the anchor was secured in the anchor well, and they re-entered the Waterway for the seven-mile ride to the Park Service docks on Cumberland. An hour and a half later *September Song* slipped into the green reflections of palmettos and live oak on Cumberland's western shore.

Some Park Service personnel on a small dock pointed them on their way, and they soon arrived at the public dock. There was but one finger available for visiting boaters, but they were in luck; there was a single runabout tied up with room for them in front. The rest of the docking facilities were for park boats and the ferry that provided transportation to the island. Once they were secured and had the fenders set, Charlie fixed a picnic lunch and Jamison packed it in a small backpack with their cameras, suntan lotion, and a bottle of water.

"Don't forget the OFF." Charlie tossed the green can of insect repellent from the head across the cabin to Jamison.

Jamison one-handed it behind his back and flipped it into the pack.

"Nice catch!" Charlie exclaimed.

Jamison laughed. "My lad, when you're hot, you're hot."

They had docked at Sea Camp landing. After checking the bulletin boards and maps of the island at the visitors' center, they picked up a trail that would take them across the island to the beach. The path led through a semi-tropical woodland of live oak. Their gnarled, twisting trunks and limbs formed a sculptured umbrella that filtered sun and sound.

As they walked along the sandy trail, Jamison could feel the day dissolving in the hushed tranquility. The wind sighed over the tree tops, and flecks of sunlight seemed to sway in the air before him, creating a kaleidoscope effect. A rustling in the leaves to his left revealed an armadillo in an Eocene ritual search for lunch. Did Jamison still have a pulse? He was sure his cardiovascular system had already left for the Bahamas.

This time he felt her presence before she spoke.

"Hi, Jamison."

She coalesced out of the flecks of sunlight.

"Oh, God."

"I hope that you're not getting used to me."

"Can you do this anytime you want to?"

"You mean appear to you? Yes, when it suits me."

"Do I have any say in it?"

"No, not really."

"I was afraid of that."

"Are you afraid of me?"

"Well, no. At least I don't think so. Can Charlie see you?"

"No, he doesn't need to see me—he has his own sirens. Besides, this is just between you and me."

"You and me?"

"Just us."

"That's cozy."

She smiled. "When we were interrupted yesterday, you were telling me about my tongue."

"Come on, not now."

"Why not now?"

"Because it's very hard to watch where I'm going and look at you at the same time."

"Why do you care where you're going?"

"I said watch where I'm going."

"Sometimes you can lose your way because you're so busy watching where you're going; besides, once you get to know me you may not care where you're going."

"That's comforting."

"Umm-humm. Can you still see me?"

He nodded.

"Am I really pretty?"

"Yes."

"How do you like my neck?"

He gave up. "You win."

She chuckled.

"It's graceful and slender like a swan."

"Oh, that's nice."

"The hollows where it joins your body…"

"Yes?"

"Cool, secret grottos."

"My shoulders."

"Inviting, sun-fresh knolls."

She smiled. *"Now see, while we've been talking, you've let where you're going take care of itself, and you haven't so much as stumbled."*

He sighed. *"You're a hard woman."*

Her eyes teased.

"My arms."

"Flowing and strong. Comforting. I can see a gentle breeze stirring on the lightness of their soft hair."

"Would you like to feel them around you?"

There was a sudden burst of light from above. "Hey, Dad, we're almost there."

The trees, pruned by the constant action of the salt spray and wind, had become shorter and the foliage denser. The dunes formed a wall that led them up toward the bright light flooding through an archway in the forest's ceiling.

"Have fun on the beach, Jamison."

"Charlie, watch where…No, forget it."

Charlie turned and flashed Jamison a big smile then vanished through the light. Jamison took a deep breath and dived through behind him.

The view on the other side was breathtaking. The dunes spread out in an unbroken line to the north and south. Beyond them, the ocean, bluer than the sky, raced to the horizon. A protective, sand-dusted boardwalk, built well above the fragile dunes and sea oats, led to the beach. Only a few distant figures broke the sense of isolation.

The cool breeze crystallized the air. The sun warmed his skin and whispered "come on," so he chased Charlie across the boardwalk and down to the beach where they wandered along the edge of the surf for a while before returning to the shelter of the forest to eat lunch.

After resting in the tangled arms of a giant live oak they decided to visit Dungeness, the ruins of the Carnegie estate at the south end of the island. Thomas Carnegie had once owned Cumberland, and Dungeness had been the focus of life and activity for the family and their guests. The Carnegies had long since departed, but the mark of their presence still remained in the crumbling stone and mortar of their great manor house.

From the giant live oak Dungeness was about a two-mile hike down the only north-south road on this part of the island. Away from the breeze the air was pleasantly warm and the dirt road beneath Jamison's feet comfortably soft. An occasional park service vehicle passed by, kicking up a small cloud of fine dust. They finally arrived at the gates to the estate, along with some young people who had been exploring the south beach.

Dungeness stood exposed, in the open, with the sun slightly behind it. With its detail lost in shadow, it loomed as the brooding memory of a faded dream. Jamison was uneasy as they wandered the grounds. His feet were tired and his back itched from a light film of perspiration. The hulk was like a giant time machine holding the laughter, passion, pain, and joy that once animated it deep within its brick and stone. Standing in the shadows listening to the wind explore the crumbling hopes of the past he caught, for a fleeting moment, a vision of lost splendor and glory. But it was a fantasy that quickly faded in the heat of the noonday sun. The fairy tale was gone, leaving only lizards to dance in the halls, squirrels and mice to feast and copulate in the great rooms, and wild horses to manicure the lawn. The itch worked its way up the back of his neck. He felt as if he were standing on a grave.

An hour later, Charlie and Jamison threaded their way through the backpacks and bags the campers and day-visitors had piled on Sea Camp dock awaiting the ferry. Everyone was laid-back and easy, lounging in the shade or propped up against the dock railing lost in quiet conversation.

They kicked the sand off their sneakers and climbed aboard *September Song*. After a long cold drink and a look at the charts, Jamison started the diesel. Charlie cast off the lines, and they headed for Florida.

PART II

CHAPTER 8

The Dolphin Chronicle #3

In the post Eden state we create our own reality. Our tradition (habit) is straight lines. Our method — rational, analytical, scientific. Our practice has been one of predictability, control and power. If someone or something is "out of line" it is a threat to the carefully constructed status quo. Even our spiritual lives are judged on a continuum of cause and effect. Prayer and worship are something you do instead of something you are.

In Adam and Eve's new creation, Caesar is god. He is the personification of linear reality, the prince of power, the regent of respectability. In the linear event, we traded a home in Eden for citizenship in Rome. We are caught in a self-limiting geometry of our own creation: a structure where meaning is defined by straight thinking, order is maintained by straight shooters, and our dreams held captive by straight arrows.

Jamison couldn't put his finger on it. There was something going on and he wasn't sure what it was. He was having feelings that he hadn't felt in a long time. They caught up with him again as he and Charlie pulled out of Cumberland.

At first he tried to ignore them. When that didn't work, he interpreted their persistence as a manifestation of his sudden change of environment over the last week—a sort of progressive disorientation accompanied by a heightened awareness, and a vaguely pleasing sense of anticipation. But he still couldn't get his emotions focused. There were so many new stimuli that he was having trouble arranging his emotional impulses into a recognizable pattern. When he was busy with Charlie and the boat, they were crowded out to the periphery of his consciousness, but they were always there just out of reach, teasing, waiting for him to let down, lower the barrier. What bothered him the most was their familiarity, but everything was out of context. He couldn't make anything fit.

He tried to remember when they had first begun. There was nothing before St. Simons, he was sure of that. Or was he? He backtracked for a moment. Yeah, he was sure. So it must have been somewhere between St. Simons and Cumberland. That was it. In his mind he replayed their course behind Jekyll Island and under the high bridge. He made the turn in St. Andrews Sound and saw Charlie raise the sails as they entered the Cumberland River; then it began.

It was like a tingle, an electric vibration from the farthest edge of an inner universe. It quivered like a resonating violin string in his solar plexus. Then it broke loose and spun up his central nervous system, arced from synapse to synapse, and bloomed somewhere in his right cerebral hemisphere.

"Jamison, I like what you said."

Her voice came floating back to him on the wind, splitting open his soul. His optical nerves blossomed. Her face materialized out of a thousand sparkling molecules and he knew, oh, God he knew, that he was falling in love.

At about the same time Jamison realized that he was

probably losing what was left of his mind, *September Song* left Georgia and entered Florida waters. He tried to pull himself together and bring the scene into focus. It was not a pretty picture.

After the primitive beauty of Cumberland Island, the mills and industry of Amelia Island and Fernandina came as an assault to his fragile senses. The first hint of their presence was the unmistakable odor of cooking paper, followed shortly by white clouds of exhaust erupting from skyscraper-high smokestacks that seemed to have burst up through the fragile mantle of the marsh. Finally, the entire structure of a mill elbowed its way into view—cement blocks and corrugated metal, conveyer belts, pipes and windowless walls. It was nouveau post industrial revolution architecture at its accidental, linear worst. The emotional impact was akin to a loss of innocence, a re-entry into a world that he thought they had left behind.

Sometime during Jamison and Charlie's reality check the knotmeter ceased to function. Jamison tapped the blank instrument.

"Charlie, we've got zeroes on the knotmeter. Could be electrical or maybe the paddlewheel is fouled."

Charlie nodded. "I'll go down and check it."

"Flip it on and off a few times. Let's see if that will help."

Charlie went below to the aft cabin where the backs of the instruments protruded through a bulkhead.

"OK, I'm switching off and on. Anything happen?"

The knotmeter blinked but still read zeroes. "No, nothing.

"I'll double-check the power."

Jamison could hear Charlie moving to the main control panel. "Ah, Dad, it looks like we've lost battery two. The meter shows battery one charging, but we're getting nothing from two."

Jamison sighed. *Damn boat's falling apart*, he thought. It was as if they had entered a time warp and all systems were shutting down.

After checking the electrical system Jamison climbed back into the cockpit.

"I think the 'black hole' is probably in the battery selection switch," he said. "As long as we're motoring we won't have a problem. The alternator will keep the remaining battery charged and the electronics functioning, but if we do any long-distance sailing we'll have to be careful not to drain all our power."

They could live without the knotmeter, estimating their speed through the water pretty accurately by using the engine tachometer or eyeballing *September Song's* wake, but they needed help. Charlie dug out the charts and the *Waterway Guide* in search of the nearest source for marine electronics repair.

"It looks like our best bet is going to be St. Augustine. We can find just about anything we need there."

"How far?"

"Hang on a minute." Charlie was hunched over the chart in the nav station. "I'd say about a day south. If we can average five to five and a half knots, we could be in there tomorrow night."

They were both bushed. To Paradise and back in one day was becoming an odyssey.

"Charlie, it's been a tough day. How about checking the chart again and see if you can find us a place to anchor."

"Sounds like a great idea." Charlie disappeared into the nav station and returned a few minutes later with the chartbook. "There's not much for the next few miles—Alligator Creek is about it. It's open and shallow."

"That's appropriate. Up to our chainplates in alligators." Jamison managed a weary smile. "How's the bottom?"

Charlie studied the enigmatic symbols. "It ought to hold us."

"Then that's it."

Thirty minutes later, Jamison backed down hard and set the anchor in the shallow, windswept waters of Alligator Creek.

His skin was salt-dried, his clothes clung like shrink-wrap and he had a splitting headache.

Later that evening, before falling asleep, he thought back over the day. *What the hell is happening?* he wondered. *I'm falling in love with a damned ghost, or maybe it's normal to have an exotic woman who talks kung fu, show movies in your head. If it were thirty years ago I'd swear it was funny mushrooms. Oh, dear God, has it been thirty years? I am so tired, please be gentle with me.* He felt as if he had been traveling for a lifetime.

CHAPTER 9

Dear Susan,
It's Sunday morning and the sun is tinting the high cirrus clouds pink over the palmetto and mangrove. Dad's still asleep, so I have the cockpit to myself except for a dragonfly that is balanced about a foot away on the lifeline. It is very quiet and peaceful, and Rome seems only a breath away, as if the years since then were only a heartbeat, as if you had just gone shopping for bread and I had run out for a bottle of wine and now, minutes later, we've returned, the table is set, the bread warmed, the wine poured and the evening is before us...

Sometime during the night the wind eased up. Jamison didn't know when, but his subconscious must have picked up on the changed motion of the hull, for it released him into a deep, peaceful, dreamless sleep. He didn't even wake up for his usual three a.m. anchor check but slept through until the sun, angling through the hatch, warmed his face and the aroma of coffee brewing aroused his senses.

It was just a little past seven but Charlie had been up for some time. Jamison rolled over as Charlie came down the companionway for another cup of coffee.

"How long have you been up?" Jamison asked, as he swung his feet out of the bunk.

"Hi, Captain. About forty-five minutes. It was so calm I decided to sit outside, watch the sun come up and drop Susan a note. How'd you sleep?"

"Best night's sleep I've had so far."

"Yeah, me too. I think we both needed it." Charlie refilled his mug and poured one for Jamison. "Coffee's ready. I'll have breakfast on the table by the time you're through shaving."

"Great. How's the weather?" Jamison maneuvered past Charlie into the head.

"Beautiful. I think we're going to have a good day."

"It couldn't come at a better time." The shaving cream was like a healing balm to Jamison. The warm water and the soothing lather bathed his face in a fragrant cloud that restored his being.

It *was* a beautiful day. After cleaning up the breakfast dishes and getting underway, they were able to raise the jib and motor sail. Within an hour the breeze had picked up, so they added the mainsail and turned off the engine. Sailing was a bit of a risk since they still had use of only the one battery, but as Charlie said, "What the hell, let's enjoy the sail and the peace and quiet." So they slid south toward Mayport, each lost in his own thoughts.

It was the sort of peaceful Sunday morning that Jamison remembered as a child — stretching awake between cool sheets, the smell of bacon and sweetbreads cooking and the soft singing of his mother as she moved effortlessly about the kitchen. For the moment, the events of yesterday had been left behind in the lavender shadows and deep lagoons of a mysterious island.

Art was natural for Jamison. It was all around him. He grew up surrounded by his mother's conte crayon figure drawings and his father's scripts. He drew easily and deciphered perspective and the secrets of color early on. He was performing and had learned the two-step by the time he was eight. It was almost too easy. Perhaps that's why he wanted to be an engineer. More specifically, he wanted to be an aeronautical engineer. Maybe the urge came from all the model airplanes he built and he and his father flew in the center of the dusty riding rink not far from their home.

His great dream was to design and fly swift, agile pursuit planes that could carry him through the majestic cloud canyons that formed every summer afternoon high above his tree—the giant tulip poplar in his backyard. Or perhaps the urge originated in the stars, from some distant galaxy beyond the edge of time. He didn't know; all he knew was that, for him, it was a natural step from pursuit planes to rockets. When he wasn't designing them, he was drawing pictures of spacemen exploring the outer reaches of the solar system.

On warm summer nights when the family had gone to bed, he would slip out, lie in the tall grass behind his house, and dream of being the first man to walk among the stars that formed the crown of his beloved tulip poplar.

When he was fifteen, his father bought a sailboat. It was the beginning of a lifelong love affair for Jamison. He was a water person. He had played some football, with modest success, but when he attended tryouts for the high school swimming team he knew that he would never put on pads again. He swam backstroke and butterfly. His specialties were the relays and the hundred meters. He wasn't a star, but he was good at what he did, and before it was over he earned a letter.

On the weekends he raced sailboats. He raced anything that he could get his hands on. When his parents were racing the family boat, Jamison was to be found walking the docks looking for a ride as a skipper or crew. As he became an accomplished skipper, boat owners began to seek him out to race their boats. Thistles, Snipes, Penguins, Y-Flyers, he raced them all, and if he didn't win, he usually finished in the top three.

He could thank sailing for Tommy. He had seen her on the docks at the sailing club, but it took a racing accident to bring them together. They were competing skippers in a weekend regatta. It was the fourth and final race; she was in the lead and should have had him beat fair and square. It was a blustery day, and her boat was just ahead of him as they approached the finish line. She had just taken a hard gust and was pulling up into the wind when her mast snapped off three feet above the deck.

It was chaos: mast, boom, sails, rigging, and crew everywhere. Jamison went through the carnage so fast that he didn't grasp what had happened until he looked back and saw Tommy's boat dead in the water. At that moment the finish cannon on the committee launch went off practically in his ear. He had won the race and the regatta.

After the awards presentation he found Tommy sitting alone by the water's edge. She smiled up at him and he sat down next to her. He told her how sorry he was for her misfortune. How she should have won, and how bad he felt winning the way that he had. She took his hand, looked at him with the deepest, most beautiful brown eyes that he had ever seen and said that it was alright. He couldn't remember anything else. Except somehow, he was able to blurt out that he would like for her to go on the club's moonlight sail with him that evening, and from somewhere far off in the distance, he heard her say yes. That night, on a moon-painted lake in north Georgia, with Dave Wengard playing his string base in the boat ghosting along off their stern, the earth shifted on its axis for Peter McKinzie Jamison Jr. and Tommy Delancy Whitfield.

Three weeks after that fateful evening he flunked algebra for the second time, and he knew that he would never swoop through summer afternoon cloud canyons in a pursuit plane of his own design, or create a rocket that would carry him to the stars.

Traffic was beginning to get heavy as they approached the St. Johns River. "Looks like everybody is out for a Sunday drive," Charlie observed.

Jamison reached down and switched on the ignition. "Let's get the sails down. I think we'd better run under power in this crowd."

The quiet solitude of the morning gave way to the whine and snarl of high speed motors and the amplified sounds of dockside revelry. At one fish camp a sizable fleet of small boats had anchored, and the party flowed in waves from the shore to the boats. Back and forth, in and out of the water, beer, bikinis and beach music defined the afternoon.

Jamison became so involved trying to avoid party boats that he ran aground twice. The first time they were able to plow through the soft bottom and work free, but the second was a harder bump, and Charlie had to raise the jib to catch a freshening breeze and tilt *September Song* off the shoal. Once they were back in the channel they were able to motor sail under a darkening sky. Houses were now further apart; the wind had become chilly, and the sky more threatening. The party fleets had vanished, and except for a few pelicans and an occasional osprey, they had the Waterway to themselves.

"How much further to St. Augustine?" Jamison asked, as he pulled on a light windbreaker.

"Couldn't be more than three or four miles. North Point Cove Marina is just north of town, and they have most of the facilities we need," Charlie answered.

Forty-five minutes later *September Song* turned into the North Point entrance channel. Ten minutes later a dock hand caught their lines as the sun poked back through the clouds.

Later, after dinner, Charlie went for a walk while Jamison cleaned up the nav station. As he was rearranging the cruising guides the dolphin book caught his eye. It was tucked in between a Waterway directory and a set of navigation data tables where he had put it before they left St. Simons. The past few days had been so eventful that he had completely forgotten it was there.

He smiled, carefully lifted it from the shelf and ran his fingers over the cover. The embossed dolphins felt alive beneath his touch. He sat down and thumbed through the blank pages. It's been ages since I kept a sketch book or journal, he mused. He recalled a cruise book that the captain of a South African sailboat had shown him. It was the loving compilation of a year under sail: notes, drawings, photos, and memorabilia.

After a moment he closed the small volume and turned back to the cover. As he held it, the early evening sun coming through the companionway illuminated the dolphin medallion. *Why not?* he thought. He took a ball point pen from the pencil rack, opened the book to the first page, thought for a moment then carefully inscribed precisely in the center of the page: *The Dolphin Chronicle*. As he studied the inscription, he felt a movement in the air and a kiss on his forehead.

Months later, when he looked back through its pages, he would add: *A Testament*.

CHAPTER 10

Hink rolled over and hit the snooze alarm for the third time. "Jesus, I really have to get up," he muttered, as he pulled the sheet over his head.

This was the big day, well, actually tomorrow was the big hit. Today Bobo would check the tanks and the gear and then they would pull out in the afternoon. This morning he would go to work like always; then after lunch he would explain that he had a dive scheduled and needed to take a couple of days off. Jake would bitch and moan for a few minutes, but then he would lighten up, wish him good luck and call Ed Dent to fill in for him.

Jake had half jokingly told him that he owed SouthCoast Yacht Services half of what he dragged out of the ocean, and he was more than half right. Jake had given him a place to land when no one else seemed to give a damn. He sure as hell couldn't go home. His father had signed off on him years ago after he refused to join the bank, and he had broken his mother's heart when he screwed up his marriage to Susan. The divorce was one thing, but to be the first Prescott in three generations to disappoint the board of directors of Prescott Bank and Trust, well, there are some things you just don't do in low country society and live to see the next cotillion.

The phone rang as Hink's feet hit the floor. "Up and at 'em, my man," Jake's voice reverberated in his ear. "I've got a sailboat in here that can't tell where it is, how fast it's going or where the juice is coming from to get there."

"GPS's busted, knotmeter's out and the batteries died," guessed Hink.

"My man, you are a genius. When can you get here?"

"I'll stop by McDonald's. Be there in thirty minutes."

"Boat's name is *September Song*, in F3. I'll be out in the yard. I know you haven't seen it yet, my man, but it's another beautiful day in Paradise." The phone clicked and went dead.

Goddamn, it's impossible not to love that son-of-a-bitch, Hink thought, as he stumbled into the bathroom.

Seven minutes later Hink washed the shaving cream off his face and examined a razor nick on his chin. There was a trickle of blood oozing from the cut. He tore off a small piece of toilet paper and pressed it to the wound. The paper immediately turned red but it stuck to the cut. *Should be dried up by the time I leave,* he thought.

The last four months *had* been amazing. There had been eight drops, and with the exception of one trip, the pickups went just as planned. The one exception was trip three. The drop was in deeper water than the others and the current was stronger than Hink had anticipated. Before the packages with their anchor reached the bottom, they were swept a hundred yards south of their GPS position into an outcropping of coral. It took him thirty minutes of searching before he found them in a shallow cave.

After each trip they did just as they had been instructed. They would return to the dock and follow their usual clean up procedure, then fix a drink and hang out and trade stories with anybody who happened by. On two occasions they slipped aboard some junk they recovered on an earlier expedition, then unloaded it onto the dock after the pickup—just a little extra touch to add to their cover story. They had never seen the two South Beach "dudes" again.

All the contacts had been as they were told they would be: brief messages always left on their answering machines. Sometimes on Bobo's machine and sometimes on Hink's. There were three voices that alternated, all male, never the same one twice in a row. Bobo was sure one of them was the blond. The other two neither one of them recognized. It disturbed Hink that the contacts were always on the answering machines. It was either coincidental or someone knew when they were out. He had a feeling that it wasn't coincidental. If it were his operation he would keep an eye on all the players.

Hink pulled on a pair of faded jeans and a pink polo shirt with "SouthCoast Yacht Services" embroidered in teal over the pocket. If he was going to meet customers, Jake wanted him to look professional. When the shirt went on over his head it knocked the bloodstained toilet paper off his chin. He was pleased to see that the cut had stopped bleeding.

Before leaving, he stood at the front window and looked up and down the street. Maybe he was becoming paranoid, but the answering machine thing had started to get to him. He didn't know what he expected to see. Maybe a strange car parked in the alley across the way. Or maybe a blond-haired dude in a flamingo shirt and reflective sunglasses slouching in a doorway pretending to read a newspaper. Since he had made the decision to take the money and run, he felt like he had been living in a B-grade movie.

It didn't take an act of genius to figure out what was in the sealed containers he and Bobo retrieved from the ocean floor. The packages had to be cocaine. They were too small and light to be anything else. They had been instructed not to open them, and they understood the danger in doing so. In a way they felt better not knowing. But somebody knew, and Hink knew that the gravy train wouldn't last forever. At some point the movers would decide to change carriers and he and Bobo would become expendable. Before he got that midnight call it was going to be "hasta la vista, baby" with the money and the final shipment. Everything was ready except for Bobo. He couldn't make up his mind what to do about Bobo, but this Bud was for Hink and there wasn't room for anyone else.

He took one last look around the apartment. He had been careful not to change any patterns. He even left some dirty dishes in the sink, just like always, just as if he intended to be back in a couple of days. He had called the bank and arranged for the transfer of their account. He could live on what he had in his pocket until then.

He locked the door, went down the steps and tossed his boat duffel into the aging red Corvette Stingray. The engine rumbled to life; Hink adjusted his sunglasses and pulled out into traffic. At the next corner he turned left and headed for the marina. He didn't notice the tanned young man leaning against a lamp post studying a city map.

The young man watched Hink turn the corner, then took a final drag on his skinny little cigar, flipped it into the street, and pulled a cell phone out of his pocket.

"How much chain do you need?" The clerk was pulling anchor chain from a tub.

"Ten feet ought to do it," Charlie said, "and I'll need a couple of shackles."

"They're on the end of the shelf next to the bow rollers."

"Need any help with those cutters?" Charlie asked. The clerk finished measuring the chain and reached for a large pair of bolt cutters.

"No thanks, I've done it a million times."

"I'll just carry the rest of this stuff up to the counter." Charlie picked up an anchor and a roll of anchor line, found the shackles he needed, and headed for the check-out counter.

"That will be one hundred fifty-two dollars and twenty-two cents."

"Travelers checks?"

"Sure. Which way you headed?" The clerk was bagging the chain and line.

"We're bucking the trend—south by southeast."

"The road less traveled. It's been pretty quiet around here since all the snow-birds came through headed north." The clerk handed him the receipt. "Have a safe trip."

"Thanks." *She was pretty cute,* Charlie thought, as he pushed through the door. Her smile reminded him of Susan, but then every woman reminded him of Susan. *Charlie, my boy, you have got it bad and that is good,* he thought, as he started out the dock to the boat.

Jamison was cleaning up the cockpit when Charlie arrived. "I see you had a successful trip."

"They have a very complete ship's store. Just about everything you'd ever need," Charlie said, as he handed the anchor and ground tackle up to Jamison.

"We're in luck on the electronics. I talked to the owner of SouthCoast Yacht Services, a nice fellow named Jake Dupree, and he's going to have his electronics man check the GPS and battery before lunch. Thought he would have us up and running in no time."

"Fantastic. Do we have to hang around for him?" Charlie was still standing on the dock. He had been looking forward to poking around St. Augustine.

Jamison grinned. "I gave him the combination to the lock. He said we could settle up with him this afternoon or tomorrow before we pull out. Why don't you call a cab at the dockmaster's office. I'll get some money and lock up."

CHAPTER 11

Johnny Dash had been watching the red '85 Stingray in his rearview mirror and thinking: *Is this guy in a hurry or what?* The car had pulled up behind him at a stoplight just after Johnny had received a call to rendezvous with two fares at North Point Cove Marina, and the guy had been on his bumper ever since.

Johnny had been driving for the All American Taxi Company for five years and he considered himself the Top Gun of the fleet. He was the best: considerate to old ladies, kind to children, an encyclopedia of information for tourists, a credit to his profession and the city that he loved. There was only one thing that unraveled him. It really pissed him off to be tailgated. To a professional like himself it seemed dangerous, inconsiderate, and arrogant; evidence that amateur drivers just don't give a damn. The sky was full of them these days.

Well, he thought, *I can't let this guy get under my skin. I am, after all, Johnny Dash, the best of the best. But damn, this hot-dog is glued to me.* The Stingray was so close he could almost read the words embroidered on the driver's pink polo shirt. Not for much longer though.

The marina complex was just ahead on the left—flaps down, blinkers on, airspeed dropping. Johnny made the turn into the double drive and jigged to the right past the unmanned security booth, then jigged back to the left. He glanced in his left mirror. The Stingray was still with him. He looked again and it was gone. He checked his right mirror and saw that it had turned into SouthCoast Yacht Services. He smiled. *That last maneuver was too much for him.* He felt a sudden rush of satisfaction. He had managed to shake off the offending bogey and he was cleared for landing. He was, without a doubt, the best.

The fares were waiting under a palm tree next to the dockmaster's office. His trained eye appraised them. One in his twenties, the other in his fifties. The young one looked to be a little over six feet tall and was dressed in a tee shirt, blue shorts, fanny pack and running shoes. A shock of unruly hair fell across his forehead. His companion was a little shorter and had on a navy polo shirt, tan cargo shorts, and sneakers. His hair was graying around the temples. Both were slim and in obvious good shape. They were laughing about something. *Sailors, no question about it. Father and son,* he guessed. *Easy going. Good guys. This is going to be a pleasant mission.*

He pulled to a stop and stepped out of the car. "You gentlemen call for a cab?" He touched two fingers to the bill of his baseball cap in a casual salute. He was, after all, a professional.

"Sure did," the father responded. Senior officer to senior officer. Johnny liked the protocol.

"I'm Johnny Dash. Welcome aboard." The two men climbed into the back seat and Johnny slipped back into the cockpit. "Where can I take you?"

"Well, we're not sure. We're having some electronics work done on our boat, so we decided to take a day and see your fair city. Perhaps you could suggest some places," the father said.

Intelligence briefing. Johnny was delighted. "What do you do for a living?" he asked.

"I'm an artist," the son answered.

"I'm a creative director in an advertising agency." This from the father.

Interesting. Mission upgrade, Johnny thought. "What kind of food do you like?"

"We're pretty flexible." The father looked at his son. "Charlie, you in the mood for anything in particular?"

"Mexican would be a good change of pace. I could go for a margarita. How about you?"

The father nodded. "Sounds good to me."

Johnny ran through the mission maps in his mind, sorting targeting data. It took but a moment to identify the perfect objectives.

He switched to his briefing mode. "Your first destination will be the Lightner Museum. It's in a portion of what used to be a grand hotel built by Henry Flagler in 1887. You'll love the architecture, and the museum is good for two to four hours. The city government offices are in the same complex, and there are several shops and a small restaurant for lunch. After that I suggest you walk down King Street, past Government House, and turn left on St. George Street where you can shop and catch the flavor of the old town. Two-thirds of the way down St. George is the Las Chitas Restaurant and Cantina. It's a bit touristy, but they serve good Mexican food and great, and I do mean great, margaritas. That should be about all you can handle in one day. When you are ready to return to the marina give me a call. I'll be on duty until midnight."

Johnny leaned over the seat and handed Jamison his card. He was the only driver at All American who had a business card. He had them printed himself. They were red, white, and blue with an American flag at the top of the card, just to the left of the company logo. His name was centered, and neatly positioned beneath it were the words "Top Gun" in gold.

The two men were clearly impressed. The father and son looked at each other. "Sounds good to me," the son said.

"Lead on, Johnny," the father said. "By the way, my name's Jamison."

"I'm Charlie. Nice to meet you, Johnny."

Johnny touched his cap again. "Couldn't ask for a better crew. Fasten your seat belts and we'll be off."

He flipped on the meter. "I'll point out the Fountain of Youth and Ripley's Believe It Or Not Museum on the way, so you can say that you saw them."

He swung around out of the drive, noticed that the Stingray was still on the tarmac at SouthCoast, and turned right onto Highway A1A. Thirty, thirty-five, forty, forty-five, rotation—it felt great to be back in the air again. *Johnny,* he thought, *you're hot today.* He scanned the sky. *No bogeys. A perfect mission. It just doesn't get any better than this.*

The Lightner Museum was a delight. It held the eclectic private collection of publisher Otto Lightner. Everything from music boxes and player pianos, to 19th century French paintings and art nouveau vases tinkled, honked, sparkled and glowed in the intimate card rooms and gathering spaces that had once been the Hotel Alcazar. When combined with the Spanish/Castilian style of the enormous building, with its tile roofs, arched porticos and lush, tropical courtyard, no whimsy seemed too fanciful and no fancy too exotic.

Jamison found his way into what the plaque on the wall identified as the Steam Room. There was no art here, only artifacts of what appeared to be a 1920's science-fiction film. The monochromatic tones made him feel as if he had been absorbed into a black-and-white movie set. At any moment he expected to see Wallace Beery step through the door, turn a valve on one of the bizarre water therapy devices and send him to the moon.

This building and museum are a memorial to a time and lifestyle that was an art form in itself, mused Jamison. He felt as if he had discovered a lost civilization.

As he left the baths and stepped into a connecting hall, he bumped into Charlie. "Don't miss the Steam Room." Jamison nodded toward the door he had just come through.

"Interesting?"

Jamison smiled. "It'll change your life."

"There's a nice Rubenesque painting across the hall."

"It's almost one-thirty. Are you about ready for lunch?" Jamison asked.

"Is it that late already?" Charlie looked at his watch. "Sure, I could eat a bite."

"Meet you back here in ten minutes."

Charlie nodded. "Ten minutes."

"I'll check out the painting." Jamison headed in the direction that Charlie had indicated.

He found the painting in a small chapel-like room with doors on either side. It occupied the end wall to Jamison's right as he entered. It was centered between two enormous 18th century urns decorated with frolicking baroque figures, and immediately above an ornately carved 19th century storage bench.

The painting was oil, about forty-eight by thirty-six inches, with an ornate gold frame that added another twelve inches to its dimensions. It was not just the focal point of the room, it was the purpose of the room.

Jamison was transfixed. He immediately became aware of every sensation he was experiencing. The Liszt piano concerto playing in the background stirred air currents that were creating eddies around the urns and a stream around his body. The light in the room seemed to be quanta-fying itself, changing from particle to wave and back to particle, breathing life into the colors that formed the figures in the painting. The eyes glistened, the fingers caressed tenderly, the weathered lips suckled hungrily at the plump breast. She, the giver of life, the messenger of hope, the angel of freedom. He, the aging warrior, the fallen hero, the prisoner of circumstance. They were Cimon and Para.

Jamison remembered the story from art history. Cimon had been a heroic Greek general, but when his enemies came to power he had fallen from grace and been imprisoned. He was ordered held without food in the belief that he would soon die. The only person who was allowed to visit him was his daughter, Para, who had recently given birth. She was thoroughly searched each time she arrived, to be sure that she was not smuggling food; however, Cimon's captors were unaware of the recent birth and so did not realize that she carried the milk of life within her own body. Once they were left alone, Para would suckle her father at her breast. To the amazement of his tormentors, Cimon flourished, leading them to believe that he was favored by the gods. Fearful of divine retribution, his captors set him free.

Jamison leaned across the velvet rope that separated him from the painting. The molecules of pigment, linseed oil and varnish throbbed with energy.

"What are you thinking, Jamison?"

She emerged from the painting.

Somehow, he wasn't surprised.

"I wondered when I'd see you again."

"Do you like the painting?"

"It's a wonderful painting."

"Do you think it's erotic?"

Jamison examined the painting.

"I don't know, I have conflicting emotions."

"She has nice breasts."

"Yes, she does."

"Are they as nice as mine?"

She had on a blue gown that matched the one Para wore in the painting. She released a clasp and allowed it to fall from her shoulders. Jamison's heart almost stopped. He took a deep breath.

"Perhaps it would be easier for you to see them if I were a little closer."

She moved toward him.

Jamison studied her breasts; they were no more than twelve inches in front of his face, so close that he could feel the aura of their warmth. An indefinable, lightly flowered fragrance emanated from her body. As she breathed, her blushing nipples swayed gently from side to side.

"It really is a nice painting, isn't it?" Charlie was standing right beside him.

Jamison's blood pressure topped out. He had been totally absorbed in the moment, all of his senses caught up in a passion that he hadn't experienced in years.

"I'll leave you a little gift, Jamison."

She raised her fingers to her lips in a kiss as she disappeared.

He managed to find his voice. "How long have you been standing there?" he asked.

"Only a couple of minutes. I hated to interrupt; you were so caught up in the painting." Charlie looked concerned. "Are you alright? You look a little flushed."

"I'm fine. All I need is a drink of water."

Jamison realized that he was feeling an unexpected twinge of guilt in the pleasurable rush of his surging libido.

"I think there's a water fountain on the way out. Let's get some lunch."

They ate in the restaurant that faced the verdant courtyard of the old hotel. Charlie was in an expansive mood. The building reminded him of Europe, and the museum brought back fond memories of artistic discoveries in Italy and France. His conversation jumped from Rome and Florence to Paris, from Donatello and Leonardo to Degas, and then to the marble Cleopatra that had knocked him on his ass thirty minutes earlier in the Lightner. It was such a beautiful use of the material and so damned sensual. He swore that the sculpture was right up there with Botticelli. She had made his day. Now, if he just had a good margarita, he could die happy.

Jamison was thankful for Charlie's exuberance. It gave him a chance to come down unnoticed from his own sensual apocalypse. He was pretty sure that his flustered state in the museum had been forgotten in the enthusiasm of the moment.

By the time they were through eating he had his feet pretty much back on the ground, and he could carry on the pretext of an intelligent conversation.

After lunch they followed Johnny's itinerary and wandered down King Street toward the bay. The sea breeze that blew off the water and up through Sandy Park freshened the pleasantly warm afternoon. They turned left on St. George Street at the western end of the park and soon found themselves in the historic old town. The tourist season had barely begun, so the narrow streets were not too crowded, allowing them to explore at their leisure the shops that lined the street.

Jamison was poking around in the back of a gift shop when his eye was caught by small, blue glass and silver perfume bottle. He picked it up and held it up to the light. The glass was his favorite shade of blue, a deep ultramarine that defined the silver filigree that contained it. It reminded him of a similar perfume bottle that his mother had owned when he was a child. The memory was one of his fondest treasures. She kept the bottle on a small table in front of a window in her bedroom. He would walk around the table until the light was behind it and the stained glass shone like a jewel. The light and color always filled him with a sense of wonder and peace.

"Open it, Jamison."

Jamison carefully removed the stopper and instinctively raised it to his nose. Her lightly flowered fragrance enveloped him.

"This is my gift, for when you want me close."

The childhood feelings of wonder and peace mingled with the adult sensations of passion and mystery. Jamison was beyond words.

"You don't have to say anything."

He closed the bottle and let the light shine through it again. His mind raced back to his mother's bedroom.

"How did you know?"

He felt her smile, and then she was gone.

"That's a beautiful perfume bottle. Where did you find it,

Dad?" Jamison and Charlie were standing at the cash register. "May I see it?"

Jamison handed the bottle to Charlie. "I found it on that little shelf of old bottles along the wall."

Charlie raised it to the light. "Ultramarine blue. It's wonderful." He removed the stopper and sniffed it. "I guess it would be too much to ask for it to still have perfume in it."

"No perfume?" Jamison attempted to cover his surprise.

"Not that I can smell. Here." He handed it to Jamison.

Jamison took a whiff, and his nostrils tingled with her fragrance.

"I told you this was just between you and me, Jamison."

"I would think that anything in that bottle would have been pretty exotic," observed Charlie.

Jamison nodded. "Pretty exotic."

He put the stopper back in its place and stepped up to the cash register.

The sun had set and the lights of the city were beginning to sparkle along the waterfront, as Johnny Dash banked left onto the Bridge of Lions from Anastasia Island and headed across the harbor toward the city. He had just received a call from air traffic control that he had two passengers who were leaving the Las Chitas Restaurant and would meet him at the Old City Gate. He glanced at his watch. *They're about on schedule*, he thought.

As he climbed out over the bridge, his eye was caught by a cloud of dark smoke rising against the evening sky north of the Castillo De San Marco. *Bearing nine-zero degrees. That would put the fire in the vicinity of North Point Cove.* He reached down and punched on his police scanner.

Christ Almighty, something big is going on. Everything was being called in: the cops, medics and fire department were either already at North Point or on the way. From what he could decipher from the urgent and somewhat garbled messages, there had been an explosion of some kind in the marina area.

Damn, sounds like a flight of unfriendlies slipped past me and blew the place sky-high. Shit, how could that happen? He was the best of the best. *How could I have missed them?*

He re-played the day's missions. *I was patrolling to the south, so they must have come in from the north, probably right on the deck,* he thought. *Of course, that was it. Had I been north they would have never made it. I would have blasted them out of the sky, cleaned their clocks, had them for lunch.* He felt a wave of relief. Johnny Dash, All American Top Gun, was still number one in the sky over America's oldest city.

He approached the Old City Gate. There they were, standing at the corner of Orange and St. George. They had spotted him. Charlie, the son, waved. Damn nice guys. Were they in for a surprise when they found out that somebody had raided their home base. He lowered his flaps and switched off the police scanner.

"Welcome back aboard, gentlemen. I hope you had a pleasant day."

"Thanks to you, Johnny, we've had a memorable day," the father answered.

"Everything up to your expectations?"

"Couldn't have been better," the son replied.

"Then I guess it's back to the marina?"

The father nodded.

Johnny released the brake, checked the taxiways for traffic and applied power. They were soon airborne, headed north on A1A again.

"From what I hear on the radio, there was a little excitement out your way this evening." Johnny glanced at them in the rearview mirror.

"Oh really, what happened?" The father was looking out the window at the water.

"There was an explosion and fire of some sort. Every cop and emergency vehicle in town seemed to be headed that way."

"Really? How long ago?"

He had their attention.

"I would guess about thirty or forty minutes."

"Anybody have any idea what it was?" The son leaned forward to hear better.

"There was a lot of confusion and not much information. Maybe somebody will know something when we get there."

"How much longer?"

"Only five or ten minutes. Looks like traffic is already slowing down."

They saw the blue lights from a half-mile away. Patrol cars were on both sides of the highway at the entrance to North Point Cove. A police officer tried to keep the traffic moving, but a few rubberneckers slowed the flow.

"Looks like we're busy up ahead." Johnny slowed down, easing into the pattern. "I don't see any smoke. They must have it under control."

As they inched closer, they could see that the night sky was clear of smoke. There was no sign of fire, but red, yellow and blue lights danced like fireflies in the marina complex. Johnny put on his left blinker as he pulled up to the entrance.

"Sorry, pal, no turns; you'll have to keep moving." The officer was polite, but all business.

Johnny recognized the patrolman. "Billy, it's Johnny. Got a couple of fares that live here. What the hell is going on?"

"Johnny! Damned if I know. They think some acetylene tanks blew. I've been out here on the highway ever since I got here. You need to get in?"

"Sure do, buddy."

"I think we can handle you. Stay to the left of the guard house and away from the emergency vehicles." He raised his hand to stop the oncoming traffic.

"Thanks, pal. You've got a free lift anytime you need one."

"How 'bout a beer tomorrow night?"

"You're on."

The traffic came to a stop and Billy waved them through. Johnny passed to the left of the guard house and slowed to a crawl. From what he could make out, the explosion must have occurred in the SouthCoast Yacht Services yard. Patrol cars and fire and rescue trucks filled the parking area. Off to one side, a television news van was parked with its satellite dish aimed at the sky. A young woman was interviewing a fireman in the harsh glare of quartz-halogen lights. The wet pavement transformed the scene into a strobing kaleidoscope. While they watched, an ambulance, with red lights flashing, pulled past them and headed for town.

"Not good. Let's hope whoever that is, isn't injured too badly." Johnny maneuvered past the last patrol car and coasted to a stop in the marina parking lot.

"Well, gentlemen, safely home." He climbed out of the cockpit and opened the back door.

Jamison was the first out. "It's been an eventful day, thanks to your good services, Johnny. How much do we owe you?"

"Ten-fifty. It was a pleasure having you aboard. If I can be of further service, let me know."

Jamison counted out the money and added a tip. "Keep 'em flying." He smiled and raised two fingers in a salute.

Johnny returned the salute. "Have a safe trip, Captain."

He watched Jamison and Charlie turn and head down to the docks. *Damn fine men. The fleet's in good hands*, he thought.

Johnny waited until they were out of sight before slipping back behind the wheel. He sat for a moment thinking, then pulled the door to and slipped the transmission into reverse. He backed around and rolled slowly toward the flashing red and blue lights. When he got to the end of the parking lot, he pulled into a parking place that was screened from the explosion scene by a clump of palm trees. He stepped out of the car and slipped quietly through the darkness to a spot beneath the trees where he had a clear view of the SouthCoast Yacht yard.

It looked as if the activity was winding down. The television crew was packing up as the last fire truck pulled out. The frame of a burned-out car was being winched onto a flat-bed wrecker, while two police officers stretched yellow crime-scene tape across the entrance to the SouthCoast parking area.

Why would they be marking the yard as a crime scene, he wondered, *unless?* He stepped forward to get a better view, and his toe kicked something on the pavement. The object made a sharp scraping sound. He bent down and picked it up. He turned it to the light to get a better look. It was a red, torn piece of fiberglass with part of an embossed shape on it. *It's part of a car,* he thought, *maybe from a quarter panel.* He held the shard so the light fell across it. He looked again at the twisted shell of the burned car being strapped down to the wrecker.

Then the truth began to dawn on him. *Holy shit,* he thought. *It wasn't an acetylene explosion.* He turned the ragged piece of red fiberglass over in his hand. *This came from a car all right—a very special car—the bogey. Somebody blew the Hell out of the red Stingray.*

CHAPTER 12

The Dolphin Chronicle #4

A straight line is hard to walk. It requires concentration and practice. It does not come naturally; we are not made that way. The straight line is the building block of Adam and Eve's reality, but it is not a natural event. It claims to be the shortest distance between two points, but that applies only in the linear environment of our post Eden creation. In the natural state, the shortest distance between two points may be a curve, a circle or an infinite variety of fluid variations. In one reality a calculation, in the other a dance—an exercise in control or going with the flow.

To the extent that the straight and rigid become the reference point for identity and being, to that extent our calculations limit the potential of life. When the boxes of our linear constructions are no longer adequate containers for experience, then our carefully crafted reality begins to collapse. The reference points shatter and dissolve. Straight lines begin to flex and undulate in an attempt to realign with the inspiration, spontaneity and natural rhythms of life. We are caught in an implosion of ego, an earthquake of consciousness, a crisis of faith. It is the darkness at noon and the light at the end of the tunnel.

Susan got up from the table and adjusted the volume on the TV set. She hoped to catch the morning weather report before she headed to the store. She poured a second cup of coffee and got a sweet roll out of the microwave. A karate kick-boxer was chopping prices for a Jacksonville car dealer as she settled back into her chair. The commercial whacked its way to black and the WTCG news team appeared on the screen. As the music theme faded, the screen cut to a close-up of a blond, blue-eyed, "surf's-up" anchor.

"And now to update you on a story that we have been following, we take you to Sandra Beekman who is standing by in St. Augustine."

The picture on the screen cut from the news anchor to an attractive reporter standing in a parking lot cordoned off with yellow crime scene tape.

"Thank you, Dave. I want to take you back to last night. This was the scene at North Point Cove Marina just north of the city."

The screen cut to a night scene of flashing emergency lights, flame and smoke. The camera zoomed in on Sandra interviewing a policeman, then cut to a close-up of the officer; he was in mid-sentence.

"...and there was a large explosion of some kind. It's too early to tell exactly what it was, but we think that several acetylene tanks that were stored in this shed may have been the cause." The camera panned to firemen hosing down a shed and a burning car.

The scene cut back to Sandra in the sunny parking lot. "That was last night. This morning we learned that there may be more to this story than was first reported. According to a source close to the investigation, the explosion was the result of a car bomb and not an accidental acetylene explosion. We have also been informed that the blast claimed a victim. The person's condition and identity are unknown at this time, but the possibility of personal injury, or loss of life, adds a tragic note to this bizarre story. We will continue to follow this story for you as it unfolds. For WTCG, this is Sandra Beekman, live, in St. Augustine."

Susan never heard the weather report. A chill prickled the back of her neck. *North Point Marina—that's where Charlie and Jamison are.* Her mind raced. *Charlie called from there night before last. My God, I hope they're alright. There was no mention of any boats being damaged, but a bomb exploded and somebody was hurt, or even worse, killed.*

She carried her dishes to the sink and looked up at the clock over the door. *Not quite eight; North Point's marina office will probably open in a few minutes,* she thought, as she rinsed the dishes and put them in the dishwasher. She wiped off the counter. *I'm sure they're okay, but damn.* The pictures of the burning building and the flashing emergency lights came back in a rush.

She turned to the telephone stand and began rummaging through a pile of telephone and address books. "I know I put it here somewhere."

Halfway through the stack she pulled out a light blue brochure: *A Guide to Southeastern Marinas.* She opened it to Florida and ran her finger down the listings to St. Augustine—North Point Marina. Susan looked again at the clock: five after eight. She reached for the phone, put the handset to her ear and began to punch in the North Point number. Before she could complete the dialing the call waiting signal beeped. She hesitated, then hit the flash button.

"Hello."

"Hi, sweetheart." Charlie's voice was as clear as if he were standing next to her. "Hoped I'd catch you before you left for work."

Susan's heart leaped. "Oh, God, Charlie, I was just trying to call you." She paused. "Are you okay?"

"Sure, I'm fine—"

"How's Jamison?"

"When I saw him ten minutes ago, he looked pretty good." He hesitated. "What's wrong, Susan?"

"I just saw on the news that there was an explosion at North Point, and I was worried about you."

"It's on the news up there?"

"A Jacksonville station that we get on cable is covering it."

There was a pause, and his voice softened. "You don't have to worry, we're okay. Our slip is a good way from the site of the explosion, and we were in town when it happened. Did they say anything about somebody being injured?"

"Nothing, other than there was a victim. They did say that the explosion was not an accident."

"Not an accident?"

"The authorities think it was a car bomb."

"That's serious shit!"

A dark presence permeated Susan. She was, for the most part, fearless, but in those rare moments when fear invaded her, it came as a swarthy angel casting a shadow over her heart.

"Charlie, you and Jamison be careful."

"We'll be okay, honey," Charlie said reassuringly. "I don't think a car bomb, if it was a car bomb, would have anything to do with us. Nobody knows us. We're just one of hundreds of boats cruising up and down the Waterway. In fact, we'll be leaving just as soon as Dad gets back from paying a repair bill. I don't think there's any threat to us."

"I know I'm being a little irrational, but I just don't like the people I care for being close to violence. I can't bear the thought of anything hurting you." She resisted adding: "Or taking you from me."

There was a long pause, then Charlie replied gently, "I know it's scary, but we'll be all right, there's nothing to be afraid of." His voice brightened. "Besides, I can't think of anything that could keep me away from the greatest ass in the Western world."

He had caught the fear off guard and with one deft stroke

sent it packing. Her heart was liberated. She laughed. "Charlie Jamison, how I miss you. Be careful."

"I will."

Susan hung up the phone. She walked into the bedroom, untied her robe and threw it across the bed. She smiled at her naked body in the mirror, then turned sideways and ran her hands up her thighs and over her stomach. She appraised her profile as the light from a tree-shrouded window illuminated her subtle terrain. *The boy is only half right*, she thought, as she traced her fingers around to her back and down over the firm mounds that capped her upper thighs: *That is the greatest ass in the galaxy*.

Susan loved her body. She could never understand why people were embarrassed by what she perceived as God's most beautiful creation. When she was a small child, and St. Simons was less crowded, she was allowed to roam the beach with her parents, naked as a jay bird. She loved the tingle of the sun; the aroma of suntan lotion; the wind that cast her hair like a net, and the gurgle of the salt foam as the sea rushed between her legs. It was in the sand, with the warm fingers of the Atlantic Ocean caressing her legs, that she first discovered the mysteries of what it would mean to be a woman.

Her childhood excursions were usually in the morning before 11:00 and in the afternoon after 3:00. The only time she wore clothes was during the middle of the day. She absorbed the sun into her very being. It became her sign and marked her with the spirit of life. Her mother taught her that the sun was a source of life and joy, but if its blessings were abused, it could bring suffering and pain. It was all part of a great natural plan laid out for the children and grown-ups of the world. If you understood how it worked and could become part of its rhythms and cycles life would be a wonderful dance that never ended. These were idyllic years for Susan, and they gave her an inner light that would enliven and sustain her when storm clouds formed and threatened to blot out the sun that brought her such joy.

Her father was in the Merchant Marine. He graduated from the Academy with a bright future ahead of him. Everyone agreed that it would be only a matter of time before he had his own command and, true to form, he rose quickly in the ranks. He was a second officer when Susan was born, and her first memories of him were being swept off her feet into his navy-blue arms and being swung around the room by her prince in blue and gold. Her saddest times were his extended periods at sea. During the months when he was away, she would sit among the seagulls and tell them stories about the father-prince who was away on voyages of splendid adventure, slaying sea dragons and rescuing beautiful island princesses.

These were times of great closeness with her mother. Susan helped with the cooking and household chores. Later they would wander the beach together while her mother told her stories of the crab kings and their courts, how the tides moved with the moon, and why the winds changed direction with the passing of storms. Sometimes at night when the moon was full, they took off their clothes and swam naked, out the silver path the moon made on the water. Her mother would hold her close, and Susan wondered at the slipperiness of their warm bodies as they stroked through the shimmering alloy of light and water.

On one such evening, when she was eight, they were approached by a group of dolphins. Her mother began making chirping sounds, and the dolphins began sounding them. Susan felt the sound waves they were emitting as they "sensed" her body. After a few moments of exploring them, the pod continued on its way down the beach, and Susan and her mother turned and swam back toward the shore. But in that high moment, bathed in the enchanted light of the night sun, her understanding of her place in the universe changed forever.

Charlie stood by the phone booth and let the warm morning sun heal the pain of Susan's absence. He tried to hold on to her voice, but he knew it would soon fade into the conversations and background sounds of the day. He was amazed at how much a part of his fiber she had become. Six months ago such a total intrusion would have terrified him. He had never allowed any woman such open access for fear she would consume the passion of his muse, a threat he feared more than any power on the planet. But that was six months ago.

He turned and walked down a few steps to the walkway surrounding the marina and headed for the harbor master's office. *So the explosion was a car bomb. No wonder Susan was concerned,* he thought. *Hell, it's scary just thinking about it. It's the sort of thing you see in Al Pacino movies or read about in the paper, but to have it happen practically in our face, and in a place like St. Augustine for God's sake.* He resisted an impulse to look over his shoulder to see if he was being followed.

The harbor master was on the phone when Charlie stepped through the door of the stucco and terra-cotta building. She raised a hand and mouthed, "Be through in a minute."

Charlie nodded and turned back to look out the window. The sun sparkled on the white and chrome hulls sitting motionless in their berths. There was just enough breeze to turn the wind indicators on the tops of the sailboat masts, but not enough to ruffle a flag. Nothing hinted of the pall of flame, smoke, and violence that had hung over the marina just hours before.

The attendant hung up as Charlie turned back to the counter that divided the room. He pulled out Jamison's Visa card and laid it in the counter. "We're ready to check out," he said.

She opened a record book and flipped through several pages. "Let's see, that's *September Song.*"

Charlie nodded. "That's right, in F3."

"Two nights, electricity, and thirteen gallons of fuel?"

"That's us."

She took the card and ran it through the machine.

"Have you heard anything about the person who was involved in the explosion last night?" he asked.

She looked up. "Oh my, wasn't that just the most awful

thing? I was at home and saw it on television. It made me feel a little uneasy about coming to work this morning."

She pushed the receipt across the counter for him to sign. "I haven't heard any more about the victim, but it makes me want to look under my car before I get in it. You wonder what the world is coming to."

She stapled the Visa carbon to the marina receipt and handed it to Charlie, who folded them and put them in his pocket.

He nodded. "Yeah, you do. I hope they catch whoever did it." He smiled. "We've enjoyed our stay, although you gave us a little more excitement than we expected."

"Which way are you headed?"

"South. We hope to jump over to the Bahamas from Miami."

"Oh, that sounds wonderful. Have a safe trip, and stop in if you're by this way again." She paused. "It's usually pretty quiet around here, really."

Jamison was untying the spring lines when Charlie arrived back at *September Song*. The engine was already running, warming up to operating temperature.

"We're all signed out, free to leave on the tide." Charlie began unhooking the power cable. "Say, did you hear that the explosion last night was a car bomb?"

Jamison concentrated on coiling the lines. "Yeah, I heard."

Charlie laid the cord in the cockpit. "There was somebody in that emergency medical vehicle that passed us when we were in Johnny's cab."

Jamison tossed the line onto the deck. "I know."

"They haven't released a name yet."

Jamison leaned against the boat and looked over at Charlie. "It was Jake Dupree, the owner of SouthCoast Yacht Services."

Charlie realized for the first time that his father was pale. "That's the fellow who repaired the electronics."

"Actually, one of his people did the work."

"How did you find out?"

"I was in SouthCoast paying the bill, when the police came in and told them. They knew that someone had been hurt, but they had no idea who it was. Apparently Jake was the last person to leave last night."

"How is he?"

Jamison hesitated. "He's dead. There wasn't much left of him. The only blessing is that he died instantly."

Charlie took a deep breath and leaned against the hull next to his father. "Do they know why anybody would want to kill him?"

Jamison sighed. "That's the real tragedy. Apparently the bomb was intended for someone else. There were two cars in the parking lot, Jake's and an employee's. The employee's car was blocking a loading ramp at the back of the shed. From what they gather, Jake must have decided to move the car, and boom; that's all she wrote."

"Have they got the employee?"

"No, he's off on a diving expedition, but get this," Jamison paused. "He's the one who repaired our electronics."

"No kidding! Do you know his name?"

"No, about that time the police realized I wasn't an employee and asked me to leave."

Charlie studied his father. "How are you feeling, Dad?"

Jamison thought for a minute. "It's odd, I have a real sense of loss. I only met Jake once, but I feel like I've known him all my life."

Charlie nodded slowly. "There are people like that."

Jamison took one last look around the marina. "I think it's time we got out of here."

Forty-five minutes later Charlie unclipped the VHF microphone and asked for southbound clearance through the Bridge of Lions. At the eastern end of the bridge Anastasia Island formed a barrier against the vagaries of the sea. To the west, St. Augustine decorated the shore like a string of well worn pearls.

CHAPTER 13

Hink adjusted the throttle of the port engine until its RPMs matched the output of its starboard companion. When the heartbeats of the twin turbo diesels were in synch, they created music that released a flood of endorphins somewhere in his pleasure dome. When he felt that perfect rhythm radiating up through the balls of his feet, he forgot his pain and frustration. It was his magic carpet ride, a momentary fix on the endless detour through the agony that had become his life.

"The turbos are runnin' great today." Bobo slipped into the seat next to him on the fly-bridge.

"Fuckin-A, Bobo. They're music to my ears."

"What's the plan?" Bobo opened the chart kit in his lap. They had just left the St. Augustine sea buoy behind and were headed south on a course of 162° at twenty-five knots. The sea was calm, the sun warm, and the wind in Hink's hair felt like it was right off the beach at Paradise Island.

They had been late getting off. After Hink had finished repairing the GPS and checking the batteries and electrical system on the sailboat, *September Song*, he had to check a radio on a large motor yacht. By the time he had it working to his satisfaction and got down to Goldrush, it was three o'clock. When they entered the St. Augustine channel, it was three-thirty and the sun was well into the last half of its afternoon quadrant.

Hink looked over at Bobo. He saw himself looking back. "Jesus, Bobo, where did you get those shades?"

Bobo grinned out from under a pair of mirrored sunglasses with swept back electric blue frames and temples.

"Shit, Hink, I had to go all the way to Ft. Lauderdale for them. The women love 'em."

"Bobo, you damn near scared the pee out of me. For a moment I thought Miami had sent a hit man up here to end my miserable life."

Bobo's smile faded. "Don't say that, Hink."

In spite of himself, Hink was touched by Bobo's concern. "Okay, Bobo, just a figure of speech."

Bobo stared straight ahead. "You know, Hink, you're the only real friend that I've ever had."

Goddamn, Hink thought, *don't make this harder for me than it already is.* He still hadn't figured out how to get Bobo out of the picture once they made the pickup tomorrow. He tweaked the starboard throttle. He had felt a slight change in rhythm and noticed that it had dropped a few RPMs.

"That's hard to believe, Bobo."

"I know." They were silent. The diesels were back in tune.

Hink felt an unexpected twinge of conscience which made him uneasy. He needed to get back on his edge.

"Back to the plan. Since we were so late getting off, I thought we'd run down to Ponce Inlet and anchor in Sheepshead Cut for the night and top off the tanks in New Smyrna Beach before we head out tomorrow." Then as an afterthought, "I love the glasses. Get me a pair the next time you're in Lauderdale."

Bobo's face lit up. "I thought you'd like 'em. They're killer all right."

"Have you had a chance to plot the exact drop position?" Hink asked.

Bobo turned the chart kit to another page. He had noted the position of the sunken wreck they were using for cover. "The Korsholm went down at North 28°12.10′, West 80°29.16′. The drop is just to the south and east of the site in about fifty-four feet of water. I've already programmed the waypoint into the GPS."

"Damn, Bobo, when you're hot, you're fucking incendiary. How much longer to Ponce?"

Bobo punched into the GPS for the Ponce de Leon Inlet waypoint. "Hour and thirty-five minutes."

Hink nodded as his gaze swept the horizon. There was nothing in sight; they owned the ocean. The sun and the turbos worked their magic, and the downer he felt a few moments ago about Bobo passed as quickly as it had come. He was in command. He knew where he was going, and he felt like he could kick ass up Collins Avenue and down Miami Beach.

CHAPTER 14

It was good to be under way again. *September Song* had become a small, familiar world where Jamison felt safe and in control. He felt his spirits lifting as the miles slipped by and the troubling events of the previous night were left further and further behind. The new anchor was rigged and secured in the anchor well, the second battery was back on line, and Charlie was down below tinkering with the GPS. From his running narrative it appeared to be operating up to their expectations at last. According to the repair ticket, the cause of the problem was an antenna connection that had not been soldered when it was initially installed. Knowing that all systems were functional gave Jamison a sense of satisfaction and renewed confidence. A warm gust played with his hair as he adjusted his sunglasses. Things were looking up.

With high school graduation approaching and engineering a lost cause, Jamison had fallen back on what he knew best, drawing pictures. He decided that he would follow the family tradition and become an artist, but he had no idea where to go to college. That is, until an older sailing buddy invited him to a summer fraternity rush party at a large southern university nestled in the cotton fields of southeastern Alabama. Jamison had little interest in the fraternity, but he accepted the invitation because it was offered, and because he had heard that the university had an art department. Looking back on it, he realized that what began as a lark turned out to be serendipity.

The weekend's festivities kicked off on a sweltering Saturday morning on the manicured front lawn of the fraternity's white columned Georgian house. A member in a Confederate cavalry hat marched up to the front porch and read a rambling call for the South to secede from the union. Then everyone stood at attention while the Confederate flag was run up the flagpole. When the limp banner reached the top of the pole, there was a deafening roar as a decrepit cannon blew a wad of packing into a herd of startled goats munching grass in a field across the street.

When the smoke cleared and the rebel yells died away, a group of brothers in gray uniforms formed a facing column, raised sabers, and the lodge sweetheart, Nancy Sue Bryce, was presented by the president, Roland T. Picket, resplendent in a red sash and the gold braid of a Confederate Major. Nancy Sue introduced Mama Batey, the house mother, who welcomed the assembled rushees, and then she and Nancy Sue retired to the relative security of the house to have tea and catch up on the latest campus gossip. Once the ladies were out of sight, the honor guard sheathed their sabers and led the expectant throng around to the patio, where four kegs of beer were rolled out and the weekend got down to serious business.

Jamison hung around until it was obvious that no one would realize he was missing, and then slipped away and drifted over to the campus to see if he could find the art department. It was not hard to find.

The art and architecture building occupied the entrance corner of the university. It was a three-story L-shaped affair with glass windows running the length of each floor. Jamison entered the front door and checked the directory. The art department offices were on the third floor. He started up a flight of stairs, and by the time he reached the second floor, all he had to do was follow his nose. The familiar fragrance of oil paint floated down the stairwell to greet him. He had an immediate sense of well-being when he emerged onto the third floor corridor. Studios lined the left side of the hall, and offices and storage rooms occupied the right. He checked each studio: printmaking, advertising design, figure drawing.

In the painting studio he found the source of the pungent aroma of linseed oil, Damar varnish, turpentine and oil paint. A single student was working on a large canvas. The artist didn't notice the boy watching him from the door, but Jamison never forgot the intensity and passion of the young painter. He would remember the experience years later when he first saw Charlie's paintings. That afternoon Jamison knew that he had found a home.

Two months later, his parents dropped him off on the front porch of a scruffy one story bungalow that would be his first home away from home. It was owned by a Mrs. M. Fontaine, a hunched and wizened French woman in her seventies, who appeared to have been shrunken and freeze-dried. The boys she rented rooms to attributed her physical appearance to the cumulative effect of too many years spent hunched over in the stifling summer heat and humidity, stomping the legions of gigantic cockroaches that cohabited the house with her scholar tenants. It became a principle of survival for Jamison never to get out of bed without first turning on a light to clear the floor of the marauding "palmetto bugs." Within a year he had joined a fraternity to have access to an innerspring mattress and showers where he didn't have to carry a stick and constantly watch his feet.

Jamison became immersed in art. The curriculum and studio work were challenging, and he worked many nights until the custodians locked the building, with only a break to dash across the street to a one-counter diner where he would wolf down a bowl of chili. He discovered the subtle delineations of charcoal lines, the push and pull of light and dark, the illusions of perspective, and the spatial tensions of warm and cool colors. It was a world that he had grown up with, but now was fully discovering for the first time.

By the time he had completed the basic two year program, he had decided to major in advertising design and option as many courses as possible in painting and print-making. He felt that advertising offered a more secure future, but he knew by now that he needed the depth of expression he found in front of an easel and on a litho stone to nurture his soul. He sensed intuitively that his creative health depended ultimately on seeking truth simply for its own beauty and joy. It was an insight that he would later ignore at his own peril.

These were great years for Jamison, filled with personal discovery and self-realization. The third floor was like a corner of the West Bank, dug up in Paris and dropped into the red clay and shotgun shacks of the old South's fading dreams. The reality was closer to Soho than Sylacauga; closer to Zen than old-time religion. In the thin air of the art department, the saints were names unrecognized in the one-room churches and slash pine hamlets: Picasso, Modigliani, Matisse. The new prophets were even more obscure: Roy Lichtenstein, Red Grooms, Paul Rand, but they formed the inspiration and canon of the young believers who had discovered the new faith.

While developing an advertising assignment, he met a young writer who had shaken off the dust of the cotton fields and mill towns to answer the siren call of Hemingway, Faulkner and Dylan Thomas. They became fast friends, and over beer at a watering hole on the Opelika Highway, Peter Jamison, the son of artists from Pittsburgh, and Sandy Langford, the son of a Southern Baptist Minister from Andalusia, Alabama, reached across generations of distrust, misunderstanding, and cannon smoke, and drank to the promise of their future advertising agency.

"What speed are you showing up there?" Charlie called out from the nav station.

Jamison checked the knot meter. "Five and a half knots. What have you got down there?"

Charlie read the numbers off the GPS screen. "Only three and a half over the bottom, according to the GPS."

"We're running into a pretty strong current. The GPS is probably about right. Looks like we won't get as far today." *Disappointing,* Jamison thought, *but at least we have better information to work with.* "Where's our best stopping place for the night?"

Before Charlie could answer, the VHF interrupted. *"Gold Rush, Gold Rush, Gold Rush, this is Coast Guard Mayport. I repeat: Gold Rush, Gold Rush, Gold Rush, this is Coast Guard Mayport. Please answer on channel sixteen."*

"Hey, that boat was in the marina with us." Charlie was standing in the companionway. "I remember it was stern out on the next dock."

Jamison visualized the dock. "You're right. I remember, the lettering was gold foil."

"I wonder—" But before Charlie could finish his sentence the radio interrupted again.

"Gold Rush, Gold Rush, Gold Rush, this is Coast Guard Mayport."

Bobo and Hink were also listening intently to the message. "What do you think, Hink?" Bobo asked nervously.

"Turn the radio down. I don't want anybody to hear it." They were taking on fuel at a boat yard in New Smyrna Beach.

"Why do you think they would be calling us?"

"I don't know, Bobo, but I don't like it." Hink had an immediate sense of foreboding. "Bobo, as soon as the tanks are full, pay the guy and check the oil. I'm going to use their head."

"Hurry, Hink. I wanna get the hell outta here."

Hink nodded. "I'll be right back."

He jumped to the dock and followed the restroom sign

around the side of the building. As he rounded the corner, he bumped into a newspaper box sitting out from the wall. As Hink recovered, he noticed the headline of the *Florida Times Union*: *One Person Dead in Explosion at St. Augustine's North Point Marina.* He bent down to try and read the story. It disappeared under the fold.

"Fuck," he said. "What the hell is going on?"

He fumbled in his pocket for some quarters, found three and put two in the coin slot. The paper in the window was the last one. He pulled it out and hurried down the walk to the men's room, went in and locked the door. He turned on the light, sat down on the toilet, and scanned the article. The person who was killed was not identified, but there were enough details of the car that was destroyed for him to realize it was his Corvette Stingray.

He read the article again and the terrible realization set in. Some poor son-of-a-bitch had been the victim of a bomb that had been meant for him. It was the *midnight call*, and he hadn't been there to take it. Shit, they must have figured out he was ready to split. *Goddamn, I'm in serious trouble,* he thought. Suddenly the collar of his tee shirt was too tight and the palms of his hands began to perspire. The feeling of foreboding turned to genuine fear.

Hink's first impulse was to cut and run. Just walk out the door and disappear. Leave Bobo with the boat; let them blow him up. But he had cut and run all his life. This time he was almost there. If he could just get the shipment, he could afford to lay low for the rest of his life. He could even afford to forget the money in the bank, or at least wait until things had quieted down and then come back for it. What the hell did he have to lose? His life was a disaster anyway.

He pushed the fear aside, folded the newspaper and stuffed it in the restroom's trash can. He wouldn't tell Bobo about the explosion at North Point, and they sure as hell weren't going to answer any Coast Guard calls.

Charlie was at the nav station studying the Waterway chart. The Coast Guard had continued to call *Gold Rush*, but the transmissions were now on the hour. Whatever the people on *Gold Rush* were doing, they either had their radio off, were out of range, or were refusing to answer.

September Song had been running through a series of showers for the last few hours, and Charlie had been in the cockpit enjoying the change of pace. It was a light, windless rain broken by periods of sunshine, the first rain that they had run into, and he and Jamison had pulled on foul weather jackets, even though the Bimini top kept most of the precipitation off them. The air was cool and fresh, and the calm waters were a welcome change to the wind and chop they had been facing most of the trip. Charlie called it sugar rain, a delicate combination of light and moisture that seemed to put a sweet coating on everything.

When the rain lifted and the clouds had blown away, he returned to the charts to find a place to spend the night.

"Any luck?" Jamison called to him.

Charlie folded the chart and climbed into the cockpit. "It's too shallow along here to anchor and there's only one marina in range. That's the bad news," he said.

Jamison frowned. "What's the good news?"

"The marina sounds luxurious: swimming pool, Jacuzzi, hotel, golf course and running trails."

Jamison brightened. "I could get into that."

Charlie grinned. "Yeah, I haven't had a good run in days."

Hink adjusted the starboard throttle for the third time. *Something's wrong,* he thought. The engine was losing RPMs again. His feet told him that the music had shifted down an octave, and he felt an occasional hesitation in its finely tuned rhythm. Even Bobo picked it up.

"What's goin' on with number one, Hink? Sounds a little rough to me."

"I don't know, Bobo. She's been losing power and starting to skip. I first noticed it yesterday." He pushed the throttle forward but this time there was no response. "Shit, we've got problems. Have we got spare fuel filters aboard?"

"Should be some in the engine locker. I'll go check." Bobo slipped out of his chair and climbed down from the fly-bridge.

Hink eased back on both throttles and the bow dropped as the speed decreased. At fifteen knots the engine smoothed out. *Damn, this is going to ruin the day, as if enough hasn't already happened to ruin the day,* he thought.

Bobo reappeared. "We've got filters out the ass."

"Goddamn it, Bobo, how many?" The events of the day were beginning to wear on Hink.

"Six." He was apologetic. "Sorry, Hink. I know we've got problems."

"That's the understatement of the year."

"What're we gonna to do?"

"I'm thinking."

Hink had decided to run down the Waterway instead of going outside, to be less conspicuous in case the Coast Guard was looking for them with helicopters. Now it looked as if they were going to lose another day, and the security of the Waterway was beginning to look pretty good.

"We need to anchor somewhere and change the fuel filters and hope that takes care of it, Bobo."

"How are they doin'? Starboard side sounds better."

"At half throttle we'll never get out and back, and I can guaran-fucking-tee you I'm not going out there with an engine that's fouling out."

Bobo nodded. "I'll check the chart and find a place we can pull over."

"Get us as close to the Canaveral Barge Canal as you can. After we fix it, we'll spend the night and be at the canal as early in the morning as possible."

"How 'bout a marina?"

"No marinas."

The last thing I want to do is sign in at a marina, Hink thought. Going through the bridge in the canal made him nervous enough. He wished he could scrape the name off their stern.

"Maybe we can anchor in the lee of Addison Point."

"See what you can do, Bobo."

The Canaveral Barge Canal ran from the Waterway in the Indian River across Merritt Island, the Banana River and the Canaveral Peninsula to the Atlantic. From the seaward marker in the Canaveral channel, Hank calculated that it was twelve and a half miles to the wreck of the Korsholm and the drop site. If they could get the starboard engine up to speed they should be over the site between 10:00 and 10:30 in the morning. With any luck they should have the shipment on board and be yesterday's news by 11:30.

Jamison settled into the hot Jacuzzi. The bubbles surged up around him, and he felt as if he were floating in a tub of hyperactive champagne.

They had pulled into Palmetto Marina around five-thirty, after being delayed for about an hour by a dredging barge that had the Waterway completely blocked. When a large yacht coming from the other direction was almost hit by a swinging cable, Jamison got on the radio and asked for guidance from the dredge captain. A few minutes later, a yellow runabout appeared and guided them safely around the tangle of pipes and cables that blocked their way. Once in the marina, they were directed to a slip that faced on the swimming pool, restaurant and Jacuzzi. As soon as they had hosed off the boat, stowed the foul weather gear, and made everything shipshape, Charlie took off for a run, and Jamison headed for the bubbly water. They agreed to rendezvous later at the restaurant for dinner.

Jamison let his body be supported by the rushing bubbles as they raced around him to burst in tiny clouds of sparkling mist just above the surface of the water. He closed his eyes and allowed the fragrance of the flower gardens around the pool float him into another world, somewhere between Tahiti and Pango Pango. He hoped that She would find him there. He wasn't disappointed.

She slipped into the water facing him. She was completely nude.

"Damn, you're beautiful."

"Do you like what you see?"

"Yes, I like what I see."

"What do you like?"

Her image glowed in the late afternoon sun.

"Everything. The light in your hair, the reflections in your eyes, the way your breasts seem to float on the water."

"I like what I see, too."

"You've never talked about me. What do you like?"

Her eyes softened.

"The hint of gray in your hair, your clear blue eyes, the tilt of your nose, your sensuous lips. You are a handsome man."

She reached out her hand. Her fingers traced down his chest and disappeared under the water. He could feel her outline his hips and thighs.

"I like your body. It's a very firm body, Jamison."

She leaned toward him.

"I want you to touch my breasts."

She took his hands and cupped them under her breasts. He felt their weight filling his palms. They were firm and perfectly formed. He lifted them gently until they broke the surface of the water. She rose onto her knees so that they were suspended just above the surface of the water and directed his fingers to explore their shape. Her nipples were erect. His forefingers circled them; then his thumbs came up and he gently rolled them between his fingers, pulling slightly along their length.

"Suck them, Jamison. I want you to suck them."

She leaned closer to him and moved a knee between his thighs. His hands slid down her back as his lips found her right breast. Suddenly there was a large wave in the Jacuzzi, and Jamison felt the water rise.

"Hope you don't mind if I join you, friend."

Jamison was greeted by a fleshy, slightly balding man in his fifties who was settling into the tub. He had on colored glasses and a flowered bathing suit, and held a cigar in one hand and the *Wall Street Journal* in the other.

"Fine weather we're having, wouldn't you say?"

"Don't let him bother you, Jamison. Remember, he can't see me."

She leaned closer and shifted her other breast into his mouth.

"Yes, fine weather," Jamison managed to blurt out. The man ground the cigar out on the aqua tile that lined the Jacuzzi and opened the *Journal*.

"I tell you, friend, the world market is going wild. Take my advice: now's the time to be in emerging economies."

Jamison brought his hand up to support her breast; his tongue danced.

"Oh, Jamison, that's wonderful." She let out a tiny moan.

"Anything in emerging economies. With globalization exploding now's the time to jump on board." He looked around the paper at Jamison. "Are you with me, friend?"

"Don't listen to him Jamison. Concentrate on me."

She arched her back and pulled him closer.

The man was focusing on Jamison. "These are great times we live in, friend. Opportunity is knocking, but we must seize the moment, wouldn't you agree?"

Jamison couldn't talk with his mouth full; his psyche was in overdrive. She moved against him. Her hands were silky as they slipped down around his waist.

"Stay with me, Jamison."

His left and right brains were at war, and he was caught in the cerebral crossfire.

"Are you with me, friend? Wouldn't you agree?"

He felt her slipping away.

"Close, Jamison, we were very close."

"The market, don't you agree that now's the time?"

Jamison squinted across the sparkling water at his tormentor. He could see the sun setting in the man's sunglasses, making his eyes glow like hot coals. The bottom of the *Wall Street Journal* was turning into a wet rag and the cigar was disintegrating in a puddle of tobacco-brown juice. He glared him.

"Frankly, friend. I don't give a damn."

CHAPTER 15

"Hi, Johnny, how are the friendly skies?" The pretty blond waitress leaned over the table. A gold cross on a chain teased from her unbuttoned polo shirt. Her white short shorts stopped just at the table top, accenting the summer tan of her long legs. Against the smoky darkness of the tavern, framed by a neon Heineken's sign, she was an angel of light.

Johnny had been secretly in love from the first moment he laid eyes on her. The only problem was the gold band on her left ring finger, and since Johnny was an honorable warrior, he had restricted the expressions of his affection to his fantasies. But he still held out the hope that one day she would join him on an evening patrol through the starry night of St. Augustine.

"Hi, Linda, couldn't be friendlier. How about a Bud and some salsa and chips."

Linda jotted the order on her pad. "You dining alone?"

"No, Billy's due here any minute. Haven't seen him, have you?"

"Not tonight, but I'll keep an eye out for him."

"He'll be in need of an act of mercy."

She laughed. "From the sound of the news it's been pretty tough out there. Back with your beer and chips in a minute."

Johnny leaned back and adjusted his Top Gun cap. It had been an easy day. Nothing like the excitement of the night before. He thought about Jamison and Charlie and wondered how they were doing. He hadn't been back to North Point since he dropped them off. He couldn't get the explosion off his mind, and he was looking forward to hearing about the status of the investigation from Billy.

"One Budweiser, one Coors, salsa, and chips." Linda poured the beers into frosted glasses. "Billy just came in. He's in the bathroom. I told him where you were."

"You're wonderful." He wanted to say: why don't you come live with me?

She smiled. "You're a sweet man, Johnny."

"Hey, guys." Billy gave Linda a squeeze and slid into the booth facing Johnny.

Linda put a hand on Johnny's shoulder. "Anything else I can get you two?"

Billy looked appreciatively at his foaming head of beer. "I'm covered."

Johnny was hanging on to Linda's touch. "I'm fine."

"I'll check back." She disappeared into the darkness.

"How you doin', Captain Midnight?" Billy took a deep pull on his beer.

"Not bad, Dick Tracy. How are things on the street?"

"Could be better, could be worse. Some drunk tried to drive off the Bridge of Lions; a city father beat up his wife; a six-year-old kid kissed another kid and the girl's mother turned the boy in on assault charges. All in all a pretty uninspiring day. How about you?"

"Pretty much the same. A few tourists, a couple of park service guys, and old Mrs. McGowan needed help with her groceries."

"You're a goddamn saint, John. When you fly away and

leave this town, half the winos and widows in St. Augustine are going to starve to death."

Johnny stared into his beer. Compliments embarrassed him. He saw himself as a cross between Tom Cruise and Gary Cooper. He just tried to do the right thing.

"How's the investigation into the explosion going?" He scooped a chip into the salsa.

"Off the record?"

Johnny nodded. "Off the record."

Billy sipped his beer. "You've heard the person who died was Jake Dupree?"

"Jake Dupree? Damn, Billy, he was a nice guy. Why would anybody want to kill him?"

"We don't think anyone wanted to kill him. We think they were after somebody else."

"Mistaken identity?"

"Not exactly. The mistake was Jake's. The bomb was planted in a Corvette Stingray owned by a fellow named Hinkley Prescott. Apparently Jake got in the car, cranked it up and it blew him to hell and back."

The bogey got Jake, Johnny thought. "God, that's awful. How are his wife and kids?"

"They're in a state of shock. She's sedated, and his brother and his wife are flying in from somewhere in Ohio to take care of the kids."

"I can't believe it. I hauled Jake around last month when his car broke down."

"It's a bitch alright. Do you know Hinkley Prescott?"

Johnny thought for a second. "I've heard Jake mention his name. I think he was his electronics man. Maybe did some diving. What have you got on him?"

"Not much more at the moment. It seems that he and a guy named Bobo McHenry are in some kind of a diving business together. They've apparently been hunting for treasure and diving all up and down the coast for the last eight or nine months."

"Have they had any luck?"

"Not from the sounds of things, but it looks like they may have come into some pretty big money lately."

"What do you mean?"

Billy leaned forward. "Well, they bought a new boat a month ago—traded in their old one and paid the balance in cash, which doesn't fit their otherwise modest lifestyle. But the red storm flag is the bomb. There's no doubt that it was a professional job. What does that tell you?"

"Drugs."

Billy nodded, and a note of caution entered his voice. "Yeah, it's got the cartel written all over it. The Feds are already here and they're checking bank account and phone records. We got a court order to search their apartments, and we'll keep their places under surveillance."

"You don't know where they are?" Johnny sounded surprised.

Billy shook his head. "They pulled out on their boat for another diving expedition yesterday and have disappeared. The Coast Guard, the Marine Patrol, everybody is looking for them, but so far no luck. As far as we know, they don't know about the explosion."

"But by now the guys who did it probably know they got the wrong person."

"We haven't released Jake's name yet, but too many people already know, so it's only a matter of time."

"Then they're both at risk."

"Yeah." Billy paused. "I expect whoever did it will try again."

"You're pretty sure it's drugs?" Johnny asked.

"It doesn't match the MO of a pissed-off husband."

They were both silent. Billy took another sip of beer and sat back. Johnny dipped into the salsa.

"So you think the diving expeditions were a cover for picking up drug shipments?"

"Looks that way. The question is: what did they do with the

stuff? From what I understand, their apartments were clean, nothing suspicious at all. Personally, I think they may have been holding a little back, skimming off the top. The bad guys found out and brought in their bomb squad."

"Maybe they suspected the game was up, grabbed their stash and took off," Johnny offered.

"Could be, but maybe they were afraid of getting caught with their hands in the cookie jar, so at the last minute they hid it."

"Where would they hide it?"

"Who knows, maybe in the sofa, maybe in a safe deposit box, maybe in a boat that Prescott had worked on. We're checking his work orders for the past two weeks."

Johnny immediately thought of Jamison and Charlie. He remembered that they were having some electronics work done on their boat.

Billy continued. "Then again maybe none of the above is true. Maybe Prescott is just a happy-go-lucky guy who got mixed up with the wrong people and got his car blown up. Or maybe it was really a mistake to begin with, and somebody smoked the wrong car. Who knows, maybe it was just a bad joke. We won't know for sure until we find him, or until some incriminating evidence turns up. Right now he's clean, but we can't afford to take any chances." He paused. "I think I'll have another beer, how about you, hot shot?"

Johnny drained his glass. "You're on." But he couldn't get his mind of Jamison and Charlie. They could be standing into danger.

After escaping the Wall Street mogul in the Jacuzzi, Jamison changed clothes and met Charlie for dinner in the poolside café. Later, after they turned in, he got out the perfume bottle, contemplated it for a minute, and then removed the stopper. Her fragrance filled the space around him. He felt a kiss on his forehead and felt her movement in the air.

"That was very nice today, Jamison."

It was just her voice.

"*I'm glad you're here. Are you going to appear?*"

"*Not tonight. You've got other things to do.*"

"*I'm disappointed. I'm having a hard time getting you out of my mind since this afternoon.*"

"*Oh, that's good, but there are other things.*"

"*What other things?*"

"*Writing, Jamison, you have to write.*"

"*Write?*"

"*In your Dolphin Chronicle.*"

"*My Dolphin Chronicle?*"

"*You know, the dolphin book you bought. I want you to write what you're feeling.*"

"*My feelings? I'm not sure I know what I'm feeling.*"

"*You have to sort them out, get inside them and figure out what they're telling you. Let go and see what will happen.*"

"*I don't know if I can do that.*"

"*Yes you can, it's just that you don't remember how. Trust yourself. If you can't trust yourself, trust me. I'll show you.*"

"*Why should I trust you?*"

"*I had the impression that you were falling in love with me.*"

"*Yes, something like that, but it's very confusing. Besides, I don't even know who you are.*"

Her eyes pulled him in.

"*Do you remember when you failed advanced algebra your senior year in high school?*"

Jamison caught his breath.

"*Yes, but how do you know about that?*"

"*Do you know why you failed?*"

"*No, why?*"

"*Because you didn't have a choice. You had gotten your linear and non-linear sides confused.*"

"*I had?*"

"*You had the right idea, but you were headed in the wrong direction. It was the only way to get you back on track. If you had passed you would have ended up an engineer, and that's not who you are."*

"You mean I failed intentionally?"

"Let's just say that at the right moment your intuitive side stepped in and saved your life. It was by one point, wasn't it?"

He nodded.

"And all things considered it's worked out pretty well, hasn't it?"

Jamison had often considered what his life would have been like if the outcome of that test had been different.

"Yes it has, but I still don't understand how—"

"Yes you do, you just haven't figured it out yet."

She paused.

"Do you remember the story of Cimon and Para?"

He thought back to the painting in the Lightner Museum.

"Yes."

"Think of me as Para."

Jamison sighed.

"Alright, say I trust you, where would I start?"

"Start at the beginning. Start with what you know. Start with art."

"I haven't done art in a long time."

"I know."

"I've forgotten how it feels."

"You've forgotten a lot, Jamison. Go back. What was the first thing that you learned from art?"

Jamison drifted back to his childhood, to his mother's studio. She was working on a pastel of a nude figure. Her strokes with the chalk were swift and sure. Sweeping curves and arcs that delineated shoulders, breasts and hips—pinks, greens, flesh, lavenders, blue. An undulating line became an arm that flowed into a hand and became fingers that defined the fluid space on the paper.

As she worked, she pointed out to him that there were no straight lines in nature. The human body was meant to dance, sweep, and flow. Its lines and forms were continuously in motion. Even in death the movement never stopped. It was as if life had been molded and pulled from a great plastic glob of clay and was never meant to be forced into straight lines and boxes. She said it was one of the great secrets of the universe that was hard to see until you got a paintbrush or a piece of chalk in your hand, but when you did, and if you could let yourself go, they would reveal to you the wonders, mysteries and truths of this essential principle of creation.

"Start there, Jamison. Trust your mother's words, trace the curves of creation, see where they will take you."

PART III

CHAPTER 16

The Dolphin Chronicle #5

The animating force in Eden is life. In Eden there is no death; there are no ends, there are only beginnings. The constant state is one of being. Everything that is, was, and everything that was, will be forever. The governing power in post-Eden, linear reality is death. Everything that is, sooner or later, will come to an end. The operative state is entropy and the controlling computation is time.

As the memory of Eden fades and we become more adept at creating ourselves in the image of our linear manipulations, the more death becomes the logical result of our calculations. The clocks begin to run down, the lines run out, and in a stupor of arrogance, we mistake the angel of darkness for the seraphim of light; statisticians become priests, the means justify the end, and the bottom line defines the value of existence.

Hink and Bobo anchored to the north of Addison Point, which gave them shelter from the southerly wind. As soon as the anchor was set, Hink started to work changing the fuel filters on the starboard engine. It had a dual in-line system plus a final filter on the engine. Once he had them switched out and the fuel line bled, he took a deep breath, adjusted the throttle, turned on the ignition and hit the starter button. The starter turned over a couple of times, then the diesel caught hold and roared to life. He backed the throttle down to an idle and cranked the other engine. Once they were both warmed up, Bobo raised the anchor and Hink eased *Gold Rush* out into the Indian River channel. There was no traffic, so he turned north and opened the throttles. His feet passed the message up his central nervous system from the engine compartments: right's in tune, left's in tune. The music was back, and the turbos were singing their song.

"You did it, Hink. They're smoother'n silk," Bobo said.

"Fuckin-A, Bobo. We're back in business."

After running up and down the Waterway for a few minutes at different throttle settings, they were satisfied both engines were in sync and they were ready for the next morning. Hink went below for a beer and Bobo maneuvered back in behind Addison Point and dropped anchor for the night.

The sun was breaking through a few morning clouds as Hink took a last look at the chart and glanced at his watch. It was 7:30.

"Bobo, I think we're all set. Now, if nobody picks us up...."

Bobo rinsed his coffee cup and put it in a cabinet. "Hink, I've got an idea."

"Let's hear it."

"We're worried about someone reading *Gold Rush* on the transom, right?"

"Right."

He leaned on the chart table. "Why don't we inflate the dinghy, stand it on the dive platform and tie it to the stern so that it covers up the name?"

Hink looked at him. "Shit, that's a good idea. I think I'll keep you around, Bobo."

"I hope so, Hink. Want me to unpack the dinghy?"

Hink nodded. "I'll give you a hand."

The fact of the matter was that Hink had decided he couldn't get rid of Bobo just yet. With an all-points bulletin out for them, he couldn't afford to have Bobo running around loose, or worse yet, have his body fished out of the ocean or some creek. Everybody knew they were together, and he couldn't run the risk of raising the ante from "We want to ask you a few questions, Mr. Prescott," to "Cuff him, and read Mr. Prescott his rights."

They soon had the dinghy unrolled and inflated. Once in position, its nine foot length completely covered "*Gold Rush.*"

"Stroke of genius, Bobo."

Bobo grinned from ear to ear. "Should I get the dive tanks out yet?"

"No, let's keep them under cover until we clear the canal and we're in open water, but as soon as we get moving, check out the radar and the GPS. I want to make sure everything's up and running."

"Aye, skipper."

"Let's go get it, Bobo."

Bobo meant it when he said Hink was his only real friend. Until Hink came along he had knocked around from one odd job to another on so many docks and islands that they had all begun to look the same. His parents had split up when he was a kid and had made it clear that he was not wanted in their lives. That's when the moving around had begun, from one relative and foster home to the next, until he was seventeen and got a summer job as a deck hand on a small island freighter out of Miami. When the summer was over, he had just stayed with the boat when it pulled out for another run through the Bahamas. He never finished high school but figured that it didn't make any difference when you were on "island time."

He stayed with the *Island Queen* until it was impounded by the Coast Guard in Bimini. It seemed that the captain had concealed a few bales of marijuana in the cargo in the hope that they would help improve his profit margin. Bobo had been ashore and was returning to the ship when he saw the captain and crew being led away in handcuffs. He felt a brief sense of panic, but it quickly passed; he had been there too many times to let it upset his day. Besides, it was his *lucky day* — he wasn't being hauled off to jail.

Bobo checked his pockets. He had his wallet, twenty-five dollars and change, his rigging knife and a Baby Ruth candy bar. He had been in this situation with less. Shit, he was in good shape.

By the end of the day, he had hired on with a small yacht service company, diving and cleaning boat bottoms. By the end of happy hour, the owner of the company had offered him an aging twenty-nine foot sailboat to live on, if he would restore it and take care of it for him. And by the end of the evening, he had met a dark-haired, brown-eyed girl with an outrageous body, who lived two boats down from his new home on the dock. Lying in his bunk that night, he decided that, all things considered, he was the luckiest man in the world.

That was the beginning of several years of lucky days for Bobo. He moved often and always landed on his feet, but as the years passed, the luck turned to loneliness. His history became his story. He had no real friends for he was afraid to let any one get too close and risk the pain of more loss. That all changed when he met Hink.

They met on a diving trip in Nassau. They were drawn to each other by their concealed pain and recognized intuitively the commonality of their experience. They were both refugees from childhood destruction at the hands of a parent or parents, and although they never talked about it, something in their tortured souls recognized a fellow sufferer. They made a good fit: Hink, the more mature, the sophisticate, the one in command; Bobo, the happy-go-lucky, the guileless, the unworldly. Bobo saw Hink as the big brother that he never had. What Bobo failed to perceive, at his peril, was the ruthlessness that had been bred into Hink by the years of mortal combat with his father. Hink saw Bobo as an amiable, if at times bothersome, companion who possessed useful skills and would do anything for him. Hink liked Bobo, but that was as deep as his repressed emotions could take him.

"Gold Rush, Gold Rush, Gold Rush. This is Coast Guard, Mayport calling Gold Rush on Sixteen."
"They're still looking for *Gold Rush*. Wonder where the hell they are?" Jamison called out from the nav station. He was making the 9:00 entry in the log book: 0900, course: southbound on ICW, position: mileage marker 810, speed: 5.5 knts, wind: SE 10 knts, Barometer: 29.9 steady, scattered clouds.
"Makes you wonder what's going on," Charlie answered from the wheel. He had picked up the binoculars and was watching a boy in a skiff about a half mile ahead. The person appeared to be waving at them.
"Dad, there's a fellow in a boat trying to get our attention."
Jamison climbed up the companionway steps. "Where is he?"
"Just ahead on the port bow."
As they approached, the boy continued to wave.
"What's that in the water?" When they had drawn closer, Charlie could see a dark shape. He refocused the binoculars.
"I believe there's a dolphin next to the boat."
"Slow down." Jamison was in the cockpit.
They were now almost alongside, about twenty yards off the beam.
"What's he trying to say?" The boy was calling to them. The dolphin had its head well up out of the water. Charlie throttled back to an idle. Another dolphin appeared next to the first one. The boy was standing waving both arms. His voice floated across the water.
"The dolphins are talking! The dolphins are talking!"

"What did he say?" Jamison was cupping his ears.

They were now past the boy and the dolphins. He still waved his arms and the dolphins were still up out of the water. In the binoculars Charlie could see their mouths moving.

"He said the dolphins are talking."

They were now a hundred yards away. The boy was still waving.

"That's amazing." Charlie lowered the binoculars.

"I wonder what they're saying."

"That fella seems pretty excited."

"I wonder if they know something we don't," Jamison thought aloud.

Gold Rush cleared the Canaveral Barge Canal and entered the shipping channel at 9:30. The passage through the Canal had gone smoothly, and the dinghy covering the name had done its job. As far as Hink could tell, they were still anonymous. He was relieved to see the open Atlantic at last.

"Bobo, I don't want to attract any attention, so we'll run straight out the channel to the end before we turn south. When we get to the sea buoy give me the GPS bearing to the drop site, lock the auto pilot on, and get the tanks and gear out."

"Got it, Hink. God, it's a beautiful day." Bobo adjusted his colored glasses. The air was clean and clear.

"It is that, my man, it is that." *In fact*, Hink thought, *it couldn't be much better*. The forecast was for a ten knot breeze from the southeast with one to two foot waves, scattered clouds and a steady barometer. It was a perfect day to make a fortune.

"Bobo, why don't you go down and check the radar. Let me know if you see anything near the site. Set it on the twenty-four mile range, and don't forget to take off your glasses. No telling what you'd see with those things on."

Bobo grinned. "When we reach the buoy turn to one-six-eight degrees and I'll lock in the autopilot." He disappeared down the ladder.

Thirty-two minutes later the GPS started beeping. Bobo turned to Hink. "One tenth of a mile to target."

Hink pulled back on the throttles. The bow settled and *Gold Rush* rode forward on its overtaking stern wave.

"Two hundred feet...target. We're there." The GPS screen read N 28º12.2', W 80º29.18'.

Hink swung the boat into the wind and held position.

"Drop the anchor, Bobo." The depth sounder read 55'. "That's about as close as we're going to get."

"Right on the fuckin-A money, so to speak." Bobo folded the chart book.

"Couldn't have said it better myself." Hink shut down the engines. "Let's get going, get the stuff, and get out of here. Bobo, get on the radar while I suit up. Set the alarm for ten miles, and if you see anything coming in this direction, let me know. You got me? Anything, and that includes in the sky."

"You mean like helicopters?"

"Helicopters, airplanes, blimps, anything, but particularly helicopters."

"As in Coast Guard?"

"You got it."

Bobo went into the main cabin and adjusted the radar screen. Hink stripped and began pulling on a wet suit.

"Everything looks clear except for some traffic in the Canaveral channel."

Hink slipped on his dive fins. "Good, come on back and get the dinghy in so we can open the transom door, then give me a hand with the tank."

Bobo went to the stern rail and untied the lashings that held the dinghy in place, pulled it over the rail and placed it on the starboard side of the cockpit floor.

"You checked the tank and regulator?" Hink asked, as Bobo lifted them onto his back.

"Filled it and checked everything myself." He handed him his mask. Hink strapped on the weights, knife, and depth gauge.

149

"I guess I'm ready." He waddled out onto the dive platform and turned to face Bobo.

"Good luck, Hink. Be careful."

Hink gave him a thumbs-up and stepped into the blue water.

Bobo watched from the platform until he saw bubbles break the surface. He checked his watch, turned, and went back into the cabin. He had about thirty minutes to get himself ready. He glanced quickly at the radar screen, then hurried down the steps to the forward cabin. In his haste, he failed to notice a new blip that had just appeared at the edge of the screen SSE of their location. It was twenty-four miles away and headed directly for their position.

Bobo lifted the cushion off the vee-berth, and unlocked and opened a storage locker. He removed a roll of bedding, reached into the forward part of the compartment, and took out a long bag wrapped in plastic. He replaced the bedding, closed the locker, and put the cushion back in place. He sat looking at the package for a moment, then he took a deep breath, picked it up, and unrolled the plastic. *Goddamn it, Hink,* he thought, *why did you have to do it?*

The plastic enclosed a black leather case. He set the plastic aside, unzipped the case and removed a stainless steel, eighteen-inch barrel shotgun. He checked the magazine: it held six magnum shells. He worked the pump mechanism and heard a shell snap into the chamber. He held the weapon to the light and checked the chamber. He could see the shiny brass base of the load in position.

After Bobo had listened to the bank's call he was in a state of shock. He realized that the message the account manager left on his answering machine was a mistake. She had meant to call Hink but had gotten Bobo's number from the account record by mistake.

"Mr. Prescott, this is Marcia Danley from The Royal Bahamas Bank. I'm calling to confirm that the transfer of your account to our

bank has been approved. When you are ready to proceed, call my office and I will activate the transaction. The Royal Bahamas Bank of Nassau thanks you for your business, and I look forward to serving you in the future."

Bobo stared at the machine trying to grasp the meaning of the message. Then it struck him like a truck. Hink was taking the money and running out on him.

Bobo carried the shotgun into the main cabin and laid it on the settee. He checked his watch: ten minutes had elapsed. Hink would go down quickly, spend ten to twenty minutes on the bottom, and ten minutes coming up. He had fifteen to twenty minutes. His plan was to wait until Hink had handed him the container, then wham-o. One shot ought to do it. Hink would be shark bait. He hadn't thought beyond that. Bobo wasn't a planner. His whole life had been lived reacting to one situation after another. Whatever happened he just rolled with the punches, one punch at a time. He counted his life by the seconds, minutes and hours in the day, one day at a time. Hink was the planner. He was the one who brought the concept of the future, and with it, a semblance of stability and hope into Bobo's life. If Hink were gone there would be no future, nothing around the bend, nothing to look forward to, nothing to live for.

He would shoot Hink, and then put the barrel of the shotgun in his own mouth. He hadn't done it sooner because he hadn't been able to think of a plan. He was putting it together from one minute to the next, his brain and psyche numbed by the pain of a crushed heart.

"Bobo, where the hell are you?" It was Hink's voice. Bobo had lost track of the time. He grabbed the shotgun and ran to the stern.

"Give me a hand." Hink was trying to lift a white fiberglass canister onto the dive platform.

Bobo put the shotgun behind the stern rail, knelt on the platform and lifted the container out of the water. It was about thirty-six inches long by eighteen inches in diameter. A twelve-inch piece of half-inch braided nylon line was still attached to an eye at one end where Hink had cut the anchor loose. Bobo laid the canister in the cockpit, picked up the shotgun and walked onto the platform.

"Help me with the tank—" Hink looked up and saw the shotgun in Bobo's hands. "What the fuck are you doing with that gun?" Bobo swung the muzzle towards Hink's face. The stainless steel barrel sparkled in the morning sun.

"Bobo, what the hell is going on?"

Before he could answer, the alarm on the radar went off. Bobo swung around to look into the cabin. Something had penetrated the ten-mile warning range, setting off the alarm signal. Bobo was reacting, second by second, minute by minute. He turned and ran into the cabin. There was a blip on the screen to the southeast, just inside the ten-mile range ring, heading directly for their position. *Goddamn, it's coming fast!* he thought. *Shit, I don't like the looks of this. That boat will be here in minutes.* He stood frozen, staring at the screen. *Who the hell could it be? Damn, they're really hauling ass.*

"Bobo, damn it, what's happening?" Hink shouted from the water.

Bobo's head started to clear. There wasn't time, the situation had changed. He threw the shotgun on the settee and ran back to the dive platform.

"Hink, there's a boat coming like hell! We've got to get you out of the water."

"How far away is it?"

"Seven miles and closing."

"Damn, get the tank. What were you doing with the shotgun?" Bobo took the dripping tank and set it in the cockpit.

"I just thought we ought to have it ready," he mumbled.

"We may need it." Hink was out of the water. "Get the engines started and the anchor up."

"What about the drugs?"

"If it's the Feds we'll be in deep shit. I'll get them overboard." He jerked off his fins and mask.

Bobo dashed into the cabin and took a quick look at the radar screen. "Four miles." He started the engines.

Hink opened a hatch and found a mushroom anchor. He tied it to the canister with the remaining anchor line. The container was weighted, but the extra weight of the anchor would help hold it in position on the bottom. He hoped to come back for it.

"Over you go, motherfucker."

It sank like a rock. The turbos were breathing deeply as the anchor windlass reeled in the chain. Hink was back in the cabin, hunched before the radar screen. He unzipped the jacket, but there wasn't time to get the wet suit off.

"Jesus, Bobo, they *are* coming fast. It's got to be a high-speed Cigarette boat or something like that. I've got a bad feeling."

"Anchor's up."

"Let me have the wheel. We'll run things from down here until we see who they are. Get the shotgun ready, but keep it out of sight. If it turns out to be the Coast Guard or Customs get it back into its locker pronto. Either way, stand by on the radio." Hink replaced Bobo in the helmsman's seat.

"What if it isn't the Coast Guard?"

"I don't want to think about it, Bobo. I'm coming up to half throttle. Do you see them yet?"

Bobo scanned the horizon with binoculars. "No. Yes, there they are."

"Can you tell anything about them?'

"They're still pretty far away, and they're bow on; there's a lot of spray."

"What about color?"

"Hard to say, but I think it's red."

"Oh shit. It's not Coast Guard or Customs. We can't outrun them. By the time we turn and get up to speed they'll be on us."

"Who do you think they are, Hink?"

"I hate to say it, Bobo, but the bad guys may be out to get us."

"Oh, God, what are we gonna do?"

Hink pushed the throttles to full open. The bow rose and leveled as *Gold Rush* got up on a plane.

Hink's mind was racing. The adrenaline throbbed in his head. "We'll do a full speed fly-by, head to head. If they are hostile, we'll be a viable target for only a few seconds." He squinted through the windshield. "What do you see now?"

"One driver, two other guys. Oh, goddamn, Hink, they're armed."

"That answers that. Bobo, get on the radio and call the Coast Guard. Tell them that we're being attacked."

"I'm on it." Bobo reached for the VHF.

Hink could see the red boat clearly now. It was an open, Cigarette-style designed solely for speed. Two men were standing, each with an automatic weapon held chest high. As the gap between the two boats closed, Hink could see fire flashing from each weapon.

"Hit the deck, Bobo, we're taking fire!" He instinctively ducked to the right. Three bullet holes appeared in the windshield; then the other boat was past.

"You okay, Bobo?"

Bobo straightened up. "Okay, Hink." He triggered the mike.

"Coast Guard, Mayport, Coast Guard, Mayport, this is Gold Rush. We're being fired on! I repeat, this is Gold Rush. We're being fired on! Our position is approximately twenty-eight degrees, twelve point ten minutes north; eighty degrees, twenty-nine point sixteen minutes west. We are in need of immediate assistance! I repeat we are in need of immediate assistance!"

The two boats had passed. The Cigarette boat was starting to turn.

Hink turned in the seat searching for the red boat, but he had lost sight of it. "Bobo, tell me which way they're turning!"

Bobo was facing aft trying to keep the speeding Cigarette boat in view. "Left, Hink, they're turning left!"

"OK, I'm going to turn into them and try to ram them!"

"Jesus, Hink!"

Hink put the wheel hard over. The turbos roared as *Gold Rush* leaned into the turn. Bobo braced himself against the seat.

"Where are they, Bobo? Where are they?"

"Just finishing their turn. We've turned inside them—eleven o'clock!"

"I've got 'em!" Both boats had turned and were headed back toward each other. The Cigarette driver made a slight adjustment to bring it closer to *Gold Rush*.

"Charlie, did you hear that?" The call for help, and the urgency in the voice immediately separated the message from all the other radio traffic that had sporadically interrupted Jamison and Charlie's day.

"Sounds pretty serious! What the hell could be going on?" Charlie started down the companionway. "I'm going to turn the volume up."

As he adjusted the radio the voice of a Coast Guard radio operator broke the silence.

"Gold Rush, Gold Rush, this is Coast Guard, Mayport. Do I understand that you are taking gunfire?"

"Gold Rush to Coast Guard, that's affirmative. We need immediate assistance. We are under attack! I repeat, we are under attack!" came the panicked answer.

"All stations, all stations, this is Coast Guard, Mayport. This is an emergency. Channel sixteen is to remain clear of traffic until further notice. Gold Rush, can you repeat your position?"

Charlie was in the nav station. "This is hard to believe. *Gold Rush* finally appears and it's being attacked!"

"Can you plot their position?" Jamison throttled back to reduce engine noise.

"Yeah, I'll try." Charlie spread the chart out on the table.

"Gold Rush, we have a helicopter in the area. It should be over your position in seven minutes." The Coast Guard operator was steady as a rock.

"For God's sake tell it to hurry!"

"Gold Rush, can you switch and answer on twenty-two-A?" The measured voice was a refuge in the chaos.

"Roger, switching twenty-two-A."

Charlie reached for the radio. "I'm following them to twenty-two-A." He pushed the channel-up button until the flashing digital numbers stopped at 22.

"Gold Rush, this is Coast Guard, Mayport on twenty-two-A."

"Coast Guard, this is Gold Rush." The words were tightly drawn as the speaker struggled for control.

"Gold Rush, what is your situation? Do you have any injuries?"

"Negative, we have no injuries, but that could change."

"Describe your vessel and the attacking vessel."

"Gold Rush is a white, thirty-eight foot, fly-bridge sport fish. The attacking vessel is a red Cigarette boat with a driver and two armed crewmembers. Oh, shit, here they come again!" the radio operator cried.

A voice of quiet authority broke into the transmissions. *"Mayport, this is Coast Guard copter 6724. We have the vessels in sight. We are three miles north of their position, altitude six hundred feet. We should be over them in thirty seconds."*

"Gold Rush, this is Coast Guard, Mayport. Did you copy the helicopter? They have you in sight and will be over you in thirty seconds."

"Roger, Coast Guard, we copied and we see him."

When the two boats were nearly on each other, Hink jerked *Gold Rush's* bow into the Cigarette boat. "Hang on, Bobo," he shouted. But he was a split second too soon and the red boat three feet too far away. The other driver saw his move and had just enough room to swerve across Hink's bow. The maneuver threw the shooters off balance, but they were still able to get off a short burst as the two boats bounced and crashed through their wakes only inches apart.

"Charlie, have you figured their position yet?" Jamison called from the wheel.

Charlie checked his calculations penciled on the chart. "It looks like they're five miles offshore, about twelve miles south of the Canaveral channel—"

He was interrupted by the strained voice from *Gold Rush*.

"*Coast Guard, do you, oh, God—*"

The voice was drowned out by a deafening series of explosions; then Gold Rush's radio went dead.

"*Gold Rush, Gold Rush, do you copy? I repeat; Gold Rush, do you hear me?*" There was no response. "*Gold Rush, this is Coast Guard Mayport, do you read me?*"

"*Coast Guard copter 6724, this is Mayport. We've lost contact with Gold Rush. What's the situation out there?*"

The helicopter came back on the radio. "*Gold Rush, this is Coast Guard—*"

There was a long pause before contact was reestablished.

"*Affirmative, Gold Rush, you are loud and clear. Mayport, Gold Rush has just reestablished contact with a handheld VHF. Their primary radio has been destroyed. We will maintain contact and relay to you.*"

"*Roger, Coast Guard 6724. You will act as relay.*"

"*Gold Rush, this is Coast Guard 6724. What is your condition?*"

Charlie had moved to the companionway. "Looks like we're going to hear only half the conversation. Their handheld won't broadcast more than about three miles." Jamison nodded.

"*Mayport, this is Coast Guard 6724. We have taken hostile fire from the Cigarette boat. Gold Rush is damaged but operational. The personnel on board report no injury. The aggressors have broken off the action, and are departing on a course of one-five-eight degrees. We are going in pursuit.*"

"*Roger, Coast Guard 6724. Gold Rush operational, reporting no injuries. Inform Gold Rush a rescue vessel is en route to their position and should be on station in thirty minutes.*"

But the report from *Gold Rush* was only half true. The boat was operational, but Bobo wasn't.

"*Coast Guard 6724, this is Gold Rush. I heard Mayport. A rescue*" *vessel is on the way. We will stand by on twenty-two-A. Gold Rush over."*

After he finished the last transmission, Bobo laid the handheld radio on the console and turned around to face Hink. His chest was soaked with blood.

He smiled. "Hink, I'm sorry it didn't turn out any bet—" He never finished the sentence.

CHAPTER 17

Susan sat in the restaurant bar at Fredericka Marina, looking out over St. Simons Sound and sipping a glass of Pinot Grigio. She was holding Charlie's first letter. It was hard to believe that he had been back in her life for only a little over a week. It was as if he had never been gone. He was right; they had picked up right where they left off. Only this time she had moved beyond the infatuation of a summer affair, and she sensed that their passion held the promise of a deeper, more sustaining love. Perhaps it was because she was a little older, wiser, and more appreciative of unexpected blessings. Whatever the reason, she had come to realize what a gift even a moment of love could be, and now that she'd sipped its joy again, she couldn't bear to let it slip away.

There had been few men in her life since the divorce, and she had decided she was going to have to put love and romance on hold until she could get into a more promising market. St. Simons was a great place to live, but the eligible male population was pretty small, unless she wanted a one or two-week stand with the occasional tourist that caught her eye. She had tried that twice, but there had been too many good-byes in her life, and after the second experience, she called it quits. Something was lacking in those relationships, but it hadn't occurred to her that she had left the missing magic in Italy until Charlie Jamison walked, or rather sailed back into her life.

She tasted the delicately tinted wine and re-read the letter. The thought of Rome brought back memories of lazy mornings and Charlie rolling over, kissing her eyes, then burying his face in her hair and mumbling deliriously about being crazy in love. Then *she'd* get crazy, and they'd pull back the curtains, open an early bottle of wine and make love into the afternoon. She didn't know if being crazy made you fall in love, or if falling in love made you crazy. It didn't seem to make much difference; it was hard to have one without the other, and she hadn't felt either in three years. But now both had returned, and her heart told her that this time there would be no goodbye. She folded the letter and slipped it into her bag.

The waiter appeared. "Care for another glass of wine, Susan?"

She smiled and looked south out over the water. "No thanks, Jimmy, I'm doing just fine."

It was calm when Jamison poked his sleepy head through the companionway hatch. The two sailboats that had been anchored with them in Sheepshead Cut had already left, and they were alone except for a vintage motor cruiser anchored off their stern.

"What time is it?" Charlie's voice drifted out of the aft cabin.

Jamison looked at his watch. "Seven-ten. In thirty minutes we'll have the ebb tide."

Charlie yawned, swung out of his bunk and dug through a locker for a pair of shorts. "Sounds like a pretty good time to be moving on. How does it look out there?"

Jamison scanned the sky. "A few cirrus stratus, a hint of air, and the water's as smooth as a cat's ass."

Charlie laughed and stretched. "Damn, what a day to be alive. Think I'll go ahead and shave." He came out of the aft cabin and crossed to the head.

Jamison smiled. "I'll finish up breakfast." He waited for Charlie to pass, then stepped down into the cabin and made his way into the galley.

"I wonder what happened to *Gold Rush,*" Charlie said, as he popped the cap on a can of shaving cream.

"I've been thinking about that, too." Jamison put two scoops of coffee in a filter cone, placed it on a thermos and added hot water.

"Do you think we're talking drugs?"

Jamison nodded. "Could be. There's a lot of that stuff coming in down here." The coffee steamed up releasing its fragrance.

Charlie sighed. "I feel like we've entered a combat zone."

"There's probably more truth to that than we know." Jamison hesitated. "I even dreamed about the damned thing."

"You did?"

Jamison nodded. "But I woke up in the middle of it, and about all I remember is a voice calling for help over and over."

"The same one we heard yesterday?"

"No, it was different." He thought for a moment. "It seemed familiar, but I couldn't place it."

"I really hate dreams like that." Charlie paused, and a note of concern entered his voice. "Dad, this stuff is getting a little close for comfort. Do you think we're in any danger?"

Jamison divided the sections of an orange and placed them in two small bowls. "No, Charlie, I don't think so, but it makes me angry."

"What do you mean?"

"Because paradise is showing an ugly side that makes me want to cover my back."

"Caught between yin and yang."

"Yeah." Jamison smiled ironically. "And one of them's armed and dangerous. But there's no reason to believe that the explosion the other night, and the shootout yesterday are related, or that they could be connected to us any more than to anyone else."

Charlie nodded. "I told Susan the same thing when I called her from St. Augustine."

But despite his assurances, Jamison wasn't so certain. He remembered what the woman in the shop on St. Simons had said about coincidence, and the dream had him on edge. He hoped her angels would be there for him if he ever had to put all of his chips on the table. It was a disturbing thought.

Charlie rinsed his face and reached for a towel. "Sometimes I wonder if we're still in the dark ages."

"I think the jury's still out on that one." Jamison put the bowls of oranges on the table and poured the cereal.

"Well, it's only an illusion anyway, right?" Charlie grinned and pulled on a tee shirt.

"Sure it is." Jamison held up the cereal box. "And this box of Cheerios is the Golden Fleece." He put two bowls on the table. "Come on, let's eat before it vanishes."

Six hours later, Charlie turned the helm over to Jamison and went below to post the log. *September Song* was heeled fifteen degrees, running on a close reach down the middle of the Indian River channel.

"It doesn't get much better than this!" Jamison shouted.

"Well, we'd better enjoy it while we can. The barometer is falling, and the forecast is holding for strong winds and maybe rain," Charlie called from the nav station. "Probably be losing the sun before long."

"While you're down there go ahead and make sure all the ports and hatches are dogged down; one less thing to worry about later on."

But for now Jamison was enjoying the liberation of sailing after days of noise and fumes from the throbbing diesel. The anxiety he had experienced at breakfast had burned off with the morning mist.

162

At 6:00 Charlie tied a reef in the mainsail. The sky had completely clouded over and the Indian River was building a chop, so they pulled on foul weather gear to fend off spray from the occasional wave that broke against the hull.

Jamison had handed the wheel off to Charlie and was in the cabin studying the chart. He hoped to make it to Melbourne, where they could shop for groceries and maybe find a pump to change the engine oil.

"What was the last marker we passed?" he called out.

Charlie looked back over his shoulder. "Red 80."

Jamison found R80 on the chart and measured the distance to the entrance channel for the Downtown Marina, which appeared to be right in the town of Melbourne.

"A little over fifteen miles, at least three hours," he muttered. He checked his watch: 6:15. *Damn, we'll be nine-thirty getting in there,* he thought. He didn't like to run the Waterway after dark, but it was pretty straight forward here. They just had to steer a compass course, stay in the channel, and use the spotlight to pick up the markers.

When Jamison explained his idea, Charlie readily agreed. Being close in town appealed to him also. While Jamison had been below, the wind had continued to increase, blowing banks of dark angry clouds before it. In the fading light it was becoming increasingly difficult to follow the channel.

Charlie was braced on the windward side holding the wheel with both hands. "It's getting nasty."

Jamison nodded. "I'm going to take the jib down while we can still see what we're doing. Crank up the engine. I think we'd better motor sail to have plenty of control and power for the spotlight once daylight is gone."

"Go ahead. It'll make running the markers a lot easier." Charlie reached for the ignition switch and pushed the starter button.

"Pull into the wind on my signal."

"OK, but make it quick, the channel isn't very wide."

Charlie pulled his cap off and threw it below to keep it from being blown away.

Jamison released the jib halyard, climbed onto the deck, and ran forward to pull the sail down. "Now!"

Charlie turned into the wind, and Jamison caught the thrashing sail and hauled it down hand over hand.

"She's down," he shouted.

Charlie put the wheel back, and they were once again on course. The whole operation had taken less than twenty seconds. *Damn, that was beautiful,* Jamison thought. Their movements were so automatic they seemed to be extensions of each other.

At 9:25 Jamison laid the helm over and they turned from the storm-tossed waves of the Indian River and entered the calm approach to the Downtown Marina. Soon they were gliding slowly through the dark, off the sterns of boats tied to finger docks along the edge of the harbor. Their running lights reflected off the black water, turning the hulls red and green as they passed. They rounded a bend, and a red light identified the fuel dock projecting out into the marina's main basin.

"Let's tie up and look around," Jamison said.

When they arrived at the dock, Charlie jumped off and made their lines fast, while Jamison killed the engine.

"Looks like the place has closed down for the night. I don't see anyone around," Jamison observed, as he and Charlie walked together toward the Dockmaster's office.

When they reached the boardwalk ringing the marina, they turned and looked back over the water. Reflections sparkled from lights in a few boats, a restaurant, and several buildings along the shore. The wind still howled overhead, but the marina basin was sheltered by a bluff that rose toward the town and was calm. *September Song* lay peacefully at the end of the dock.

Caught in the quiet of safe harbor, Jamison felt a sudden rush of fondness for the young man standing next to him in the dark. "I enjoyed sailing with you tonight, son," he said.

Charlie looked over and smiled. "Yeah, Dad." He moved closer and reached out for his father. "We're good together."

Jamison felt the strength of Charlie's arm around him, and in that instant he knew, beyond all doubt, he could trust this still-fresh man with his life. He reached up and gripped Charlie's shoulder. And they remained that way, arm in arm, with the storm raging above, as Jamison pondered with newborn courage the cryptic murmurs of his heart.

CHAPTER 18

Johnny folded his newspaper and laid it on the seat as Billy slid into the booth. The early morning sun filtered through the window of the Copper Skillet and bounced off the top of the stainless steel coffee urn, illuminating the surrounding booths with a soft, forgiving light that took the edge off the overhead fluorescents.

Billy took off his cap, pushed his sunglasses up and rubbed his eyes. "God, it was a long night."

Johnny shoved a cup of coffee toward him. "You have to work late?"

"No." He hesitated. "Mazie got sick and I had to take her to the emergency room, and when I finally got home it was 2:32. That's a.m. By then I was all wired and couldn't get to sleep."

He leaned menacingly across the table. "Do you know that *Gilligan's Island* is on TV at 3:00 in morning? Can you even imagine what Gilligan, whatever his name is, is like at 3:00 in the morning?" He waited for Johnny's reaction. Johnny leaned back and grinned in amusement.

Billy threw his hands up in despair. "No, of course you can't, nobody in their right mind can." He squinted around the room. "Damn, there's a lot of light in here." He pulled his glasses back down. "I finally got to sleep at four-thirty; then the alarm went off at 6:30." He slumped back in the booth. "And now it's 7:30 and here I am."

Johnny tried his best to look serious. "You better let me have your weapon, Tracy. The streets won't be safe with you carrying that thing around."

"Shit, I feel like Rambo." Billy glared squinty-eyed around the room.

"My point exactly." Johnny grinned and opened a menu.

"How's Mazie doing?" he asked carefully, not looking up.

Billy let out a deep breath. He leaned against the table and frowned into his coffee.

"The vet thinks she has cancer." He paused. "I'll probably have to put her to sleep before much longer."

Johnny put the menu down and considered his friend. "I'm sorry to hear that, Billy. I'll miss her too."

Billy looked up at his boyhood pal and smiled. "Thanks, Johnny."

Johnny remembered the day that Billy's dad brought Mazie home. She was just a squirt of a mongrel puppy, but all the neighborhood children had fallen in love with her. Now the children had grown up, and Mazie had grown old and feeble and blind in one eye. She had been losing ground for months, but every time the vet suggested that Billy put her to sleep, he had refused, postponing the painful decision. Now it appeared he wouldn't have a choice. Their time was running out.

"Are you two gentlemen ready to order?" A waitress in a starched yellow dress and white apron was standing behind the counter at the end of the table.

Johnny looked up. "Sure, Marge. What'll it be, Billy?"

Billy glanced at the menu. "Number two, sunny side up, with a large orange juice."

Johnny handed her his menu. "I'll have buttermilk pancakes with sausage and a small tomato juice."

The waitress jotted down the order and then leaned over Billy. "Are you feeling all right, Billy?"

"Yeah, just had a long night. Thanks for asking."

"This may help." She refilled their coffee cups. "Your breakfasts will be right up."

After she turned away to place their order, Billy closed his eyes and took a long sip of his coffee. "The coffee bean is a gift from God." He sighed and held the warm cup against his face.

"Speaking of Columbian produce, I hear there was some sort of drug shootout down near Canaveral yesterday." Johnny stirred his coffee and watched the little whirlpool disappear into its depths.

Billy's energy immediately changed. He put his cup down and shifted forward on his elbows. "I have some late-breaking news for you. It was *Gold Rush* and our friends Prescott and McHenry versus the bad guys." The beans were doing their job.

"Holy moly! Who won?"

"The big loser was McHenry. He was dead when the Coast Guard boat got to them—chest wounds from automatic fire. Prescott was nowhere to be found. Their boat was drifting near the Canaveral channel."

"He wasn't on the boat?"

"No, he either fell overboard or he abandoned ship. We're operating on the premise that he left in an inflatable dinghy that a Coast Guard pilot saw in *Gold Rush's* cockpit during the action. It's missing, too, so abandoning ship seems to be a pretty good guess."

"What about the bad guys?"

"There were three of them in a Cigarette boat. From the radio transmissions it's clear that they were the aggressors. What's interesting is that they seemed to know right where Prescott and McHenry were, and came in with guns blazing."

"So they were set up?"

"Setup or ambushed. We hope to have the answer to that soon."

"What do you mean?"

Before Billy could answer, Marge appeared. "Well, you two seem to have come to life." She put their orders on the table.

"A Number Two, sunny-side up, and buttermilk pancakes. Anything else I can get for you?"

"I could use a little more butter," Johnny said.

She smiled at Billy.

"I'm fine, thanks, Marge."

"Be right back with your butter, Johnny."

Billy peppered his eggs and broke the yokes. "The only reason that *Gold Rush* was still afloat is the Coast Guard had a helicopter in the vicinity that was able to get to the scene of the attack in a matter of minutes. They weren't in time to save McHenry, but they were able to drive the shooters off before they got Prescott, assuming he wasn't critically wounded and is still alive."

"You mentioned you hoped to have some answers soon." Johnny put a lump of butter on the center of his pancakes and surrounded it with syrup.

"Yep, the Coast Guard has the bad guys."

Johnny looked up in surprise. "How did they do that?"

"Well, a Cigarette boat is fast, but it can't outrun a helicopter. After they broke off the attack, the chopper stayed with them down to Lauderdale, where the Coast Guard had a couple of Cutters with plenty of firepower waiting for them. They were completely outgunned, so it was over pretty quickly. They threw up their hands and landed in the brig; the Coast Guard got a new Cigarette boat for drug interdiction, and we'll have the shooters as soon as the CG and Feds get through with them. The odd thing is the chopper pilot reported that *Gold Rush* reported no injuries, when it's clear that McHenry was seriously wounded. It goes without saying that we would love to get our hands on Prescott."

"So the big question is whether Prescott is alive, and if so, where is he?"

"That's the big question, and he has all the answers."

Johnny cut into his pancakes and Billy took a forkful of eggs and grits.

"Were there any drugs on *Gold Rush?*" Johnny sipped his coffee.

"No drugs, but there were diving tanks in the cockpit and one of them was half-full."

"Firearms?"

"No firearms. Except for the missing dinghy, there was nothing we couldn't account for."

Johnny was lost in thought while Billy finished up his plate. "Are you still looking for the boat that Prescott had worked on?"

Billy wiped his mouth with his napkin. "Low priority, at least until we've had a talk with the shooters. The Coast Guard has a description of their boat, and if they spot them they'll pick them up for a safety check and search, but they're not doing a radio call or anything like that."

"You don't think they're at risk?"

"Hard to say, but at the moment we think any risk is minimal. Something on your mind?"

Johnny thought for a moment, then decided to tell Billy about Jamison and Charlie. "The night of the car bomb, my fares were on a sailboat that I think Prescott had worked on, and I'm concerned about them."

Billy smiled. "I don't think you have to worry; they're probably perfectly safe, but if we get anything that changes my opinion, I'll let you know. What was the name of their boat?"

"I don't know." But Johnny decided he would drop by North Point and get the name and see if anybody knew where they were headed. He was still upset that bandits had been able to invade the skies of his city, wreak destruction and kill a truly nice guy and friend. He didn't want to see it happen again.

He picked up the check. "Breakfast's on me."

Tommy sighed and started sorting through the morning mail piled on her desk. It was her first task in what was going to be a busy day. There was the usual assortment of circulars, along with a few invoices that would need her approval and another free software package from an on-line service. She pulled a trade journal out of the bottom of the heap and a postcard fell in her lap. When she picked it up a smile brightened her face. The photo on the front was of a pretty girl in a bikini stretched out beside a swimming pool, oblivious to the large alligator that was swimming toward her outstretched hand. Inscribed in blue ball-point pen over the girl was the word "Tommy," with an arrow pointing to the voluptuous figure. Over the pool, with an arrow pointing to the alligator, were the words "Harry O. circling his prey!" She broke into laughter and flipped the card over.

> *Hi Honey,*
> *Thinking what a great time you must be having at work while we're wasting away here in paradise. Hope Harry isn't driving you crazy. As I mentioned, it was a little explosive in St. Augustine, but we're safely back on the "road." Weather's been good the last few days—much easier traveling. Starting to feel close to Charlie again. Makes all the effort worthwhile. Nice marina here at Palmetto Coast—all the comforts, even a Jacuzzi. Talk soon.*
> *Love You, Jamey*

She smiled and turned the card over. Harry Oliver was a client that drove the whole department nuts. He was demanding, impatient, and overbearing, just to name a few of his more endearing qualities.

I think I'll put the card on the bulletin board in the break room. Everybody will get a kick out of it, she thought. She leaned the card against her coffee mug. *How much longer?* She flipped through her calendar. *Nineteen days until I board the plane for Nassau. God, I can hardly wait.*

From the phone calls Jamison had made along the way, it sounded like the trip was becoming a real adventure. She thought about the time when Charlie was thirteen and the three of them had gone camping and mountain climbing in Colorado. They had camped at ten thousand feet, then drove the van up an old logging road until they crossed a blazed trail that they had been told would lead them up to the tree line, where they could climb to the top of the mountain range.

The climb started easily in a deep forest and became progressively steeper and more difficult as they worked their way up through thinning trees, icy streams, and boulders. Charlie and Jamison eventually made it to the snow line at the summit, where they ran out of time and had to descend to where she was waiting beneath a low shrub just above the tree line. It was so steep that they had to lie on their backs in the sun-bleached and wind-blasted grass to keep from sliding down the slope, while they ate the chocolate and energy bars that Charlie carried in his pack.

The sky was a deep indigo blue. The wind howled about them, and she could see for miles along the rugged spine of the Sangre de Cristo Mountains. She never forgot the closeness of that moment, and the three of them hanging on the roof of the world as if it were the most natural thing for a family to be doing. It became one of their defining moments, a time and place they used to measure the state of their relationship.

The memory made her realize how much she missed those years when everything was fresh and new, and every day seemed like an adventure. She wasn't working then and had the time and energy to devote to exploring life with Charlie. And, even though Jamison was deeply involved with establishing the ad agency, there always seemed to be time for the three of them to enjoy the wonder of growing up together. Since Charlie had left for college, though, it hadn't been the same. She started back to work when he was a freshman in high school. She wasn't sure if that was a contributing factor, but in the last few years she and Jamison had begun to drift apart. It was as if their internal compasses had shifted and they were off on different courses.

Jamison had begun to devote more and more time to the running of the business, and less time to the creative department, which had always been his heart and soul. The bottom line had become more important than ideas, and although he still acted out the creative role, the shift began to impact him in ways both subtle and profound.

As he became more deeply involved in the details of commerce, the openness and spontaneity of their relationship began to diminish, and there seemed to be fewer and fewer hours just to enjoy being together. Sex was still pretty good, but it had lost the ecstasy that stirred the deep rivers of joy and passion that had bound them together in moments of crisis, and animated their lives when the going was easy. For a fleeting moment she had even wished that he would have an affair, in the hope that it might break him loose and get him back in touch with himself, but she realized that would probably be too big a risk for him. Also, she wasn't sure if she could deal with an affair. They still loved each other, she was sure of that, but she had begun to wonder if love was going to be enough.

Then Jamison had the automobile accident, and she became aware how fragile the thread that wove the fabric of her life really was. That realization revived in her all the memories of their early years, and she longed to feel the electricity between them once again. In the midst of her reawakening, Jamison had announced the sailing trip. It caught her totally off guard. She wasn't ready for a separation, and although she supported the idea of him and Charlie getting back together, she was too vulnerable to embrace the venture with the enthusiasm that she knew Jamison hoped for.

But as the plans progressed, she began to see the adventure as an opportunity for a breakthrough in their relationship. It was a chance to be back on the creative edge again where anything was possible. It reminded her of Colorado and the feeling she had when they broke through the tree line and she caught her first glimpse of the snow-capped mountain towering above her. She was thrilled, frightened, and invigorated all at the same time. During the last few weeks she had begun to feel the old tingle, and thought that maybe, just maybe, she might be breaking out of the tree line once again.

She took another look at the card. Just nineteen days and she could kiss Harry O. good-bye for a couple of weeks. She rummaged in her desk for a push pin, picked up the card and headed for the break room. *Sticking Harry O., the alligator, and Tommy J., the bikini bombshell, on the bulletin board isn't exactly a mountaintop experience,* she thought, *but it's a step in the right direction.*

CHAPTER 19

A thin ray of sunlight traced its way across the room from a slit between the curtains. It was as if a laser had sliced through the dark and taken a one-inch wide sampling of whatever it illuminated. The light raced across the carpet, up a chair, over a crumpled tee shirt and disheveled blue jeans, back down to the carpet, and along a bed with wrinkled sheets where it dissected a naked leg. It then climbed the wall to a mirror, and ricocheted back across the room to reveal an unshaven face half buried beneath a pillow.

The warmth of the sunlight became magnified in the troubled dream that had turned into a nightmare in Hink's feverish mind. High-speed red boats, carrying demons dressed in black, raced at him from all directions; no matter which way he turned he could not escape from them. When they closed in on him, the scream of their engines became amplified explosions of automatic gunfire. He would duck and twist, only to be overcome by a red wave, out of which emerged the blood-washed face of Bobo, who looked at him for a moment and then smiled, and Hink heard him say: "I'm really sorry it didn't turn out better, Hink, I really am." Then it began again.

Hink threw the pillow off and sat up on the edge of the bed. The ray of sunlight hit him right between the eyes. He put his hand up to deflect the offending beam and felt his sweat-drenched face. *Damn, I'm soaking wet,* he thought. He felt his way to the bathroom, stripped off his shorts and turned on the shower in the darkness. When the temperature was lukewarm, he stepped in and let the cooling water pour down over him. He slowly turned until he was completely soaked, then stood with his face in the spray until the agony of his dream was purged from his system.

He turned again, fumbled for the soap in the tray and peeled off its soggy wrapper. Slowly he washed his hair, then began to methodically scrub every inch of his body. He followed the same procedure as he did with his hair: scrub then rinse, until he had completely washed himself three times. When he finally finished, he turned off the water, reached outside the shower curtain for a towel and carefully dried himself. As he stepped out of the tub, it was if he was emerging from one dream, only to return to another.

When Bobo collapsed in front of him, Hink was blasted out of hyper-drive into shock. Blood was everywhere except on him: on the windshield, the console, the other seat. *How the hell did Bobo keep standing?* he wondered. He felt the thump, thump, thump as the Coast Guard helicopter swept over and saw the red Cigarette boat swerve away and dash for the horizon. He heard the Coast Guard pilot announce his intention to pursue the attackers, but the message seemed to come to him from miles away through a haze of red fog. He could only stare in disbelief at Bobo's face smiling up at him from an ever-widening crimson pool on the teak floorboards.

After eons, the rhythm coming up through his backside from the twin turbos began to blow the mist away, and Hink slid back into consciousness. *Gold Rush* was still at full bore, running like a scared rabbit. His eyes jumped to the compass—300 degrees NNW—then scanned the horizon and sky: all clear, nothing in sight, not even the chopper. He pulled back on the throttles, and when the bow settled, shifted into neutral.

Hink sat for a moment and tried to gather his wits. With the roar of the engines muted, it was strangely serene. Waves lapped against the hull as *Gold Rush* rocked gently in the following seas. A breeze blew through the cabin, and for the first time, he realized the starboard windows were shattered. He took a deep breath, slipped out of his seat, carefully maneuvered around the pool of blood and knelt beside Bobo.

There was no doubt in Hink's mind that Bobo was dead, but he had to check. Bobo's flesh was still warm and damp with perspiration. As Hink's fingers searched for the artery in Bobo's neck, he was overwhelmed by a sense of forbidden intimacy. It welled up from a long-lost spring somewhere deep in a walled-off corner of his childhood, surged up through his heart, and pooled behind his eyes. He felt the long suppressed release of a tear, but it lasted only a moment before his early warning system went on red alert and closed down his psychic circuits before his defense mechanism was completely breached. He quickly quashed the offending emotion, but the damage was already done.

Hink had been right; there was no pulse. *Jesus, Bobo, I'm sorry it didn't work out better, too. I hope to hell you're on Paradise Island,* he thought, as he stepped back. He was feeling sick and fought to hold the nausea down as he looked around the splintered cabin.

"I've got to get away from this mess before the Coast Guard gets here," he muttered.

He felt himself shifting back into gear, running on reflex. He turned and went out into the cockpit. The inflatable dinghy was still where they had left it. He knelt and checked the tubes and bottom. *Thank God it's in one piece and holding air,* he thought.

A plan began to form in his shell-shocked mind. He grabbed the safety line attached to the tubes, lifted the rubber boat over the stern rail, and laid it on the dive platform. Then he returned to the cockpit and wrestled the outboard from its rail behind the cabin. Once it was mounted on the dinghy, he got the fuel can and oars out of a cockpit locker and set them in the small boat. Next he attached the fuel lines, and slipped the oar locks in place. He then tied the dinghy to the platform, returned to the cabin, carefully avoiding Bobo's body, and went down the two steps into the forward cabin. He unzipped his duffel bag and took out a pair of shorts and a tee shirt, then peeled off the wet suit and stuffed it in the bag. The shotgun case was still lying on the bunk, so he quickly folded it and squeezed it in beside the wet suit.

A moment later he returned to the cabin; threw the duffel on the settee away from the bloodstains, and climbed back into the helmsman's seat. He was beginning to get his confidence back. He pulled on his sunglasses and pushed the throttles forward. The turbos sucked it up, and *Gold Rush* rose out of the water and leaped forward.

Twelve minutes later Hink estimated that he was about a mile offshore and a mile and a half south of the Canaveral Channel. He backed down and watched the RPMs fall. When the tachometers settled at 800, he stopped the engines and removed the ignition key. He hesitated and put it back in the ignition. *I might as well make it easy for them to get Bobo ashore,* he thought. It seemed the least he could do, since he wouldn't be around to help. He searched the horizon. There was still no sight of the Coast Guard, but he knew they couldn't be far away.

He went to the settee and picked up the shotgun, stepped into the cockpit, took it by the barrel, and threw it as far as he could out over the sparkling water. If he were picked up, he didn't want to be caught with it, but more than anything, he didn't want to be involved in another gun battle. He'd seen enough for one day. He was fucked up, but after today, Hink knew that he wasn't a killer.

He waited for the splash and then went back into the cabin. The blood was beginning to dry on Bobo's clothes and the floor. Hink tried to think about his next steps. He pulled out his wallet to check the cash. He had seven hundred and thirty-six dollars and a Visa card. The card was useless—he didn't want to be tracked. *I wonder how much money Bobo has on him,* he thought. He bent over the prostrate form, but when he touched Bobo's lifeless body he felt the nausea rising again.

"Goddamn, Hinkley, you're taking money from a dead man." His voice was hoarse. He stepped back. He couldn't bring himself to inflict one more offense on the shattered body that lay before him.

"OK, Bobo, rest in peace. God knows, you deserve it." He could barely speak. Then, as an afterthought, "It would be nice if they would bury you at sea. I think you'd like that," he whispered.

He stood looking down at the lifeless form for a moment longer. Then he turned, gathered up his duffel and, without looking back, hurried across the cockpit to the dinghy.

Jamison lay forward and reached out over the water to scrape off the beard of grass growing on *September Song's* waterline. It was hot work. The red dinghy offered good support, but it bobbed around as he scrubbed, and he had to hold himself and the little inflatable boat in position with a suction-cup handle that he stuck on the larger hull as he moved along.

Charlie had gone for a run. Jamison hoped to have the job done by the time he got back so they could go grocery shopping, but the stuff was hard to get off, and he was beginning to wonder if he had underestimated the difficulty of the project.

He paused to catch his breath and realized that the dinghy had stopped drifting. *That's odd,* he thought, *it feels like I'm aground.* He felt a movement beneath the surface and suddenly he and the dinghy were lifted out of the water. He grabbed for the hand lines as the boat splashed back down; then, snorting and swooshing, a huge whiskered head burst out of the water no more than twelve inches in front of his face. Two large, gentle, feminine eyes stared at him, her whiskers twitched and the creature sneezed, enveloping him in its pungent breath. Jamison was dumbfounded. Then it dawned on him that he was face to face with a manatee.

Almost by reflex Jamison reached out and placed his hand on the large leathery head. He felt an instant connection. The animal continued to stare into his eyes, then slowly rolled over on her back and reached out a flipper to him. He took the flipper with his left hand to steady the portly body and began to scratch her stomach with his right hand. She seemed completely comfortable, almost in a state of bliss as he stroked her body.

"Oh, Jamison, you have a wonderful touch."

The manatee transformed before his eyes. The pebbly hide became silky flesh and the milkweed eyes dissolved into pale emeralds with a touch of aquamarine. Her golden, translucent hair spread out to form a lacy fan on the surface of the water around her head and a lustrous delta between her legs. He held her hand as his fingers caressed her flat, firmly contoured belly.

"You never cease to amaze me," he said.

"I don't like to be predictable."

"Do you need more support? I could put my arm under you."

"No, I float very easily."

"But a manatee?"

"Sailors used to think manatees were mermaids."

"Looks like they may have been right."

He traced a circle around her breasts and was pleased to see her body respond to his touch.

"How are you doing, Jamison?"

"What do you mean?"

His fingers caressed her face and picked up the curve of her neck.

"You and me. Our relationship."

"Other than feeling a little guilty and wondering if I'm crazy?"

He followed the line of her throat back down and out over her shoulders.

"Do you think you're crazy?"

"You make me crazy."

She held his hand and guided it down her body. A tremor passed through him.

"It's okay to let go, Jamison."

"I've never been unfaithful to Tommy."

"Is there a difference between being faithful to Tommy and being faithful to yourself?"

He thought for a minute.

"I don't know. It helps that you're not real."

"What is reality, Jamison?"

She laid his fingers over the mound between her legs.

"How do I feel?"

He took a deep breath.

"You feel wet, and slippery. Soft and sexy...real, like a woman."

She pulled him closer.

"Then kiss me."

He leaned over the dinghy and found her lips. They opened and her tongue teased with a slow probing motion. Her legs parted and his fingers began to explore the delicate bloom of her body. She unfolded like a flower beneath his touch.

"I love you, Jamison. Dance with me. Let me teach you a new song."

She began to tremble, then sighed and was gone.

The manatee was still on her back luxuriating in the warm sun and Jamison's ministrations. He felt the connection fading. He stroked her for a moment longer, then with a tug of her flipper she slipped out of his grasp, turned upright, gave him one long last look, and disappeared into the dark water.

Jamison tried to get a grasp on his emotions. He was like a Roman candle firing balls of blazing energy in every direction. When he had felt her orgasm beneath his fingers, an erotic spark ignited in a locked chamber somewhere deep within his psyche. It was as if they had shared the same body. Her ecstasy had become his. The spark had become a flame, and he sensed, in the heat of her passion, the key that could unlock the hidden closet. The Roman candle blew out. He was thrilled and terrified at the same time.

The double amputee rolled his wheelchair up to his table at the Early Edition Café and looked out over Loomis Park. It was going to be a beautiful day. The sun sparkled on the beach, there wasn't a cloud in the sky, and the palms rustled with a gentle southeast breeze. *It's a good day to be alive, and if it's a good day to be alive, it will be a good day for business,* he thought.

"Morning, China. *Miami Herald, Wall Street Journal* or the *New York Times*?" An olive-skinned waitress with smoky eyes put a Singapore Sling and a slice of cheesecake before him.

"Mornin', Gloria." He sat back and adjusted his baseball cap. "How about the *Times* today." *See what's happening in the National League,* he thought.

"Hot off the press—coming right up."

His eyes followed the liquid movement of her body as she maneuvered through the tables that were arranged beneath the dark teal awning. *Nice ass,* he observed for the hundredth time that month. There were only a few other customers this early in the morning. A couple of regulars and some tourists, probably European from the art deco hotels that lined Miami Beach's Ocean Drive were randomly seated among the plants and palms that adorned the chic sidewalk café. Later in the day the tempo would pick up as the "beautiful people" and wannabees joined the tourists and locals parading and hanging out. That's when China's business would shift into high gear.

"All the news that's fit to print." Gloria laid the *New York Times* on the table. "Anything else I can do for you?"

"Someday we'll talk about that, honey." He winked at her.

"You know the number." She patted him on the shoulder.

Fred T. "China" Beach cut off a bite of cheesecake, chased it with a sip of the Sling, and turned to the sports page. He started to look for the National League standings but was interrupted by an electronic beeping. He put the paper down, reached into his shirt pocket and pulled out a cell phone.

"I'm here."

"The office put me directly through to you," said the voice of the director of player personnel. "The score in the ballgame is one to zero."

"I see. Who's still on base?"

"Prescott."

"Is he still on the team?"

"I'm not sure."

He frowned. "Not sure?"

"He didn't come on the field for the ninth inning, but his name is still in the lineup. He may be heading home to collect his bonus."

There was a long pause. "I understand. Let me know if the roster changes."

China punched the phone off and jammed it back into his pocket.

"Shit," he fumed. *This has been an expensive fiasco—one Cigarette boat and three men lost. The op wasn't worth it, and on top of that it looks as if I'm going to have to bat clean-up.*

"Goddamn." He attacked the cheesecake. *I hope this screw-up doesn't cost me the franchise. So much for a beautiful day.*

CHAPTER 20

The Dolphin Chronicle #6

There is no fear in Eden. Fear is a linear concept; it is dependent on death for its power. It is the premonition that at any moment, in any place, the linear construct of reality might collapse, whether it be a carefully crafted persona, a precisely delineated relationship, a meticulously designed vision of the future, or the very system that has come to define life itself.

In the linear landscape, death is the serpent and fear is the poisoned apple. It is the juice that paralyzes the will, destroys the heart and embalms the spirit. If fear is the poison, then love is the antidote. Love is the memory of Eden that Adam and Eve carried with them when they left the garden. It is the non-linear lodestone that points the way to hope in the convoluted maze of our analytical structures.

Love is the alien in the linear universe. It comes from another time, another place and bears witness to another reality — a reality that is not defined by boundaries or manipulated by calculations. It is the source of joy, wonder and miracles; the muse of justice, compassion, and freedom. Love is the fly in the ointment of predictability. The horse of a different color. The moose that flies.

Charlie passed Begonia Street and slowed his pace. As he approached downtown Melbourne the sidewalks were becoming more crowded. From the feeling of his legs and his heart rate, he figured he must have covered about six miles. After leaving the marina he had headed north on US1 for about half a mile and then turned left on Hibiscus Boulevard until he came to a large shopping mall, where he turned south over a canal for a block before turning east on New Haven Avenue back toward town and the marina. He had broken a sweat four miles back and his body was in a state of celebration.

Two of the things he missed when on the boat were yoga in the morning and running in the afternoon. Running dated back to high school, where he had run cross country and track. He loved the wind in his face, the perspiration cooling his skin, and the mystic cross-over when the endorphins boosted him past the pain threshold into ecstasy. Today was just a light workout, an appetizer, but it didn't make any difference; his legs never felt better, he was cruising, and hey, the scenery was all new. *The only thing that can possibly top this is running through la-la-land on Miami Beach,* he thought. He had been looking forward to it ever since they hit Florida. He could hardly wait.

He was down to a jog as he entered the semi-tropical, tree-lined downtown area. *This is a charming town,* he mused, as he passed quaint shops, restaurants, stores, and a tattoo parlor. He noted a small grocery and hardware for shopping later, then crossed US1 and turned down through the parking lot of the Lighthouse Hotel. Below, across a small park, the marina basin and broad expanse of the Indian River spread out before him. Across the river was Indialantic and Melbourne Beach and, beyond them, the Atlantic Ocean.

Hink pulled back the curtain and let light flood into the room. The demons had taken a break, and he hoped the brightness of the morning would hold them at bay. At least it beat hiding in the bathroom wondering when the next assault would come. From his window he could see the sky-blue expanse of the Indian River and directly below, just over a grove of trees, the sparkling white hulls of boats decorating a marina. An occasional car passed on the street behind the trees, and here and there on the docks people were at work on their boats.

While he watched, a runner passed down through the hotel parking lot and disappeared beneath the trees, only to emerge a moment later in the marina. If he didn't have other things on his mind, he might have been taken by the beauty and tranquility of the scene. His gaze turned back to the river and the causeway bridge that arched out to the far shore. He followed the near shoreline on the south side of the bridge and carefully examined the water out to the Waterway channel where he had scuttled the dinghy. He was probably too far away to tell, but from his vantage point nothing looked amiss. *Nobody's found it so far,* he thought, *but I'd better be out of Melbourne tonight.*

He turned away from the window. The morning light was having a clarifying effect, and he was beginning to feel rejuvenated. He sat down on the bed, called room service and ordered breakfast, then opened his duffel and pulled out a fresh pair of jeans and a faded print shirt. The image of Bobo returned for an encore, but this time it was a smiling, laughing Bobo from an earlier, less complicated time. *Shit, we did have some great times,* he thought.

It began to dawn on him that Bobo was the closest thing to a friend that he'd ever had, and wittingly or not, Bobo had made the ultimate sacrifice by blocking Hink from the shooters. Otherwise it would have been Hink lying in a pool of blood staring at the sky. *Goddamn, Bobo, we're two lost souls, two fucking lost souls.* The realization swept over him like a tidal wave. The crack that had begun to open when he touched Bobo's dead body burst, and burning rivers from the years of humiliation, pain, and anguish poured down his cheeks.

When the deluge was over, he found his way back to the bathroom and cooled his face with a damp washcloth. When he looked in the mirror, he knew the demons were gone. He wasn't free, but he had opened a window of possibility. It was a beginning. He heard a knock at the door; "room service," a voice called out.

That night Hink checked out of the hotel, threw his duffel over his shoulder, walked up US1 to the Greyhound station, and caught a bus for Miami.

After the manatee disappeared, Jamison lay in the dinghy and let the sun warm his body and settle his psyche. He realized he could no longer avoid the depth of his attraction and the complexity of his feelings for Her. He had decided he could handle the idea of falling in love. That was something he had some experience with. It had happened a couple of times over the years, but he'd learned he could control it by closing down the emotional switches. By keeping the love object at a distance, the attraction, given time, would cool, and he could spare himself the painful risk of uncertain adventures. But this didn't fit his experience or his management technique. He was in deep water, and he sensed that, at some point, he was going to have to choose between swimming for safety or allowing himself to drown in the mysterious deep seas of her passion. It had not occurred to him that in drowning, he might save his life.

Johnny checked the wind direction as he entered the pattern for North Point Marina. *Out of the north—from the looks of the flags near the entrance—perfect for the north-south runway,* he thought. He lowered the landing gear and flaps, eased back on the power and turned into the parking area. The wheels didn't even bump when they hit the tarmac.

He taxied past a palm tree into a parking place overlooking

the marina. "Another perfect landing. You are hot, hot, hot." He nodded with satisfaction and killed the engine.

He sat for a minute looking out over the boats and the sparkling reflections they made on the water. *Damn, the fleet looks beautiful,* he thought. He enjoyed the view for another minute, then opened the door, climbed out of the cockpit, and went down the steps to the marina basin.

The harbor master was sorting a new shipment of charts when the front door opened. She looked up and was greeted by a well-built, six-foot, forty-ish man with a mustache, wearing starched blue jeans, a dark navy polo shirt, aviator sunglasses, and a navy ball cap with "Top Gun" embroidered in gold across the front. She was immediately taken by his easy smile.

"Hi, may I help you?" she asked.

"I hope so," he replied. "I'm looking for two friends who were here on a sailboat a few days ago." He walked across the room and leaned against the counter.

The closer he got, the more she saw to like. "Do you know the name of their boat?"

"No, but they were here the night of the bomb explosion. Their names were Charlie and—"

"Charlie and Peter Jamison." She finished the sentence.

"Why, yes, that's right." He appeared surprised by her quick response.

She smiled. "They were the only transients here that night, and they were such nice men. The name of their boat is *September Song.*"

He nodded. "That's them. By any chance did they say where they were headed? I want to try and get in touch with them."

She thought for a moment. "I think Charlie mentioned they were headed for Miami, then over to the Bahamas."

"Of course," he mused. "They're off on a grand adventure." He handed her his card. "You've been so much help. If you ever need a taxi, the ride's on the house."

She read the card and looked up. "Thank you, Johnny. I may take you up on that." She reached in the drawer and gave him her marina card. "If you need to know anything about boats, give me a ring."

Johnny studied the card, then touched the bill of his cap. "Thanks, Cindy." He started for the door then stopped. "Just ask for me when you call." He smiled and went out.

Cindy watched him leave, read his card again and reached for her purse. She felt a small thrill as she slipped it into her wallet.

CHAPTER 21

"I've changed my mind. You do scare me a little. No, make that a lot. Sometimes you scare me a lot."

Jamison mixed diced onions into a bowl of tuna fish salad. He had sliced a tomato and laid out four pieces of bread for sandwiches. In the background the engine murmured effortlessly as they reeled off the miles somewhere north of Vero Beach.

"Does being scared make you angry?"

She was sitting on the companionway steps.

"Angry?"

She nodded.

"Why would it make me angry?"

"It's about control, Jamison. Besides, are you sure it's me you're afraid of?"

"Who else?"

He spread tuna on the bread and began garnishing it with the tomato slices.

She smiled at him.

He looked up.

"What are you smiling about?"

"You, Jamison."

"What does that mean?"

She sighed, and then leaned forward.

"Do you still love me?"

He followed the light as it sculpted the curve of her neck and shoulder.

"Yes. Too much."

"Are you afraid of love, or afraid of me?"

Her iridescent shadow floated across him.

"Your love."

"My love?"

He nodded.

"Afraid of where it might take me."

"I see. Have you had this problem before?"

"No."

"Why do you think that is?"

Jamison pondered the question.

"Because I've never let it go this far."

"Oh, so love is okay as long as you're in control?"

"It's safer that way."

"What is safe about love, Jamison?"

She reached out and traced the outline of his lips with her finger.

"Who are you really afraid of, Peter?"

Without waiting for an answer, she stood up, drifted over and whispered in his ear.

"You'd better finish lunch. Charlie'll think you've died and left the planet."

The fullness of her body pressed against his arm.

"Don't leave."

He started to turn to her.

"I never leave. I'm closer than you can possibly imagine."

Then she dissolved into the weightless light surrounding him.

Jamison stood staring into her empty space. The moment passed; then he realized he still held a slice of tomato in one hand and a piece of lettuce in the other. *I must look ridiculous,* he thought. *I'm glad Charlie can't see me.* He grinned. Suddenly the scene seemed terribly amusing. Jamison could see the headline: "Screwed Up Old Geezer Fatally Smitten While Making Tuna Fish Sandwich." He chuckled and plopped the tomato and lettuce in place.

"Lunch coming up," he shouted.

"While you're down there, call the Vero Beach Bridge and tell them we're coming through," Charlie called back.

"How far away are we?" Jamison passed the lunch through the companionway. "Here are the plates."

"About half a mile."

"I'll give them a call."

A few minutes later they passed through the bridge and followed the Waterway around to the west.

"Wow, look at that!" Charlie suddenly exclaimed.

Coming up the channel toward them was a large ketch under full sail, wrung out, before the wind. She looked like a giant sea bird with her huge spread of white canvas against the blue sky and green trees. They could see a person moving about on the deck as the vessel began a slow turn into wind to drop sails before going through the bridge. Just as the boat was abeam the wind, it took a hard gust that knocked it on its side.

"Oh, my God!" Charlie cried.

The skipper lost control as the vessel surged forward out of the channel, sails and sheets flapping wildly, dragging its main boom in the water as it drove up on a shoal. Another gust hit, and she skewed around and came to a halt—hard aground with her keel half exposed. Two crew members were struggling to get the thrashing sails down and onto the steeply slanted deck. Two others leaped into the water and tried to push the bow into the wind, but to no avail. The boat was too big and the wind too strong. It was a disaster.

Jamison and Charlie were stunned. "My God, what can we do to help?" Charlie had throttled back.

"It's too shallow, we can't get within fifty yards of them. I'll get on the radio." Jamison started for the nav station.

"No, wait, there's a motorboat." A runabout with three men aboard pulled up beside the beached vessel.

Jamison crouched under the boom in the companionway. "They're too small to pull them off, but at least they can help."

Charlie frowned. "There's not much tide. I'm afraid they're going to be there for a while."

They watched in silence as the crew and their rescuers manhandled the sails and did what they could to secure the stranded boat. The hull, rolled on its side, looked like a beached whale, helpless, its sleek form useless out of its element. It was a sobering reminder of the occasional wrecks they had seen along the way: sun-bleached bones of once loved and proud vessels rotting in the marsh or strewn on a desolate beach. They watched until the last sail was down, then Charlie reluctantly advanced the throttle and they turned south.

As they rounded the next bend, Jamison took one last look at the grounded vessel. Another power boat had pulled up and was taking the shipwrecked crew aboard. As he watched, he couldn't shake off the image of the ketch going out of control. When he finally turned away, he wasn't sure if it was a cool breath of wind or a shiver that explored his body.

"I've got the balloons." Linda emerged out of the neon Heineken light with a colorful bunch of balloons tugging at the strings she held tightly in her right hand.

"Great. We'll tie them to the napkin holder," Johnny exclaimed, as he pulled the heavy metal napkin container to the front of the table. "Here, let me do it."

He took the strings and tied them tightly around the black metal case. While he was rigging up the balloons, Linda got on her knees in the seat opposite him and scotch taped one end of a "CONGRATULATIONS" banner to the wall behind the table.

Johnny thought her legs never looked better. He had to look away to keep his feelings from showing.

She leaned across the table holding the other end of the crepe-framed proclamation. "Here, can you tape this end up over there?"

"Sure." He held it up. "Straight, or at an angle?" He slid his end up and down the partition.

"I think an angle is more fun, what do you think?"

He would have agreed to anything. "Definitely an angle. How about here?" He adjusted it at about a thirty degree pitch.

She nodded. "Perfect."

Johnny stuck it to the wall and they stepped back to admire their work. "Looks great. What time is he due here?" she asked.

He checked his watch. It read 5:45. "Any minute. Is the cake ready?"

"It's behind the counter. Fritz is going to bring it out when I give the signal."

Johnny sat down in the booth. "I hope this will cheer him up."

"I'm sorry about Mazie." She sat next to him. "Was it tough?"

Johnny shoved his cap back on his head and his hair fell across his forehead. He sighed. "Yeah, we were at the vet for about an hour, and the whole time you could tell Mazie knew what was coming. She just sat on the examining table with her head pressed against Billy's chest, trying to get as close to him as she could, while he held and rubbed her. I'm sure it took all her strength; she was little more than a sack of bones, but she didn't move until they carried her away. It damn near killed me, so you can imagine what Billy must have been feeling."

Linda listened quietly, then put her arm around him and laid her head on his shoulder. Johnny hesitated, and then cautiously slipped his arm around her waist and they held each other for a moment, before she slowly pulled away.

"Guess I'd better get the beer." She smiled at him and slid out of the booth.

He fumbled with his watch. "Yeah...be here any minute," he stammered.

"You guys better hurry. He just pulled into the parking lot," a waiter stationed at the door called out.

"Beers up!" the bartender shouted, as Linda hurried over with a tray. She was back, had everything in place and was seated by the time Billy walked through the door.

"Hey, what's going on?" Billy surveyed the booth. The balloons and colorful crepe paper glowed like fluorescent beacons in the dim light.

Johnny leaned back, sipped his beer, then stood up and saluted. "Hi, Detective, glad you could make it."

Before Billy could answer, Linda got up and gave him a hug. "Sit right here, Detective Sparks."

She guided him into the booth, then turned toward the bar and raised her hands as if conducting an orchestra. On her downbeat the entire room burst into "For He's a Jolly Good Fellow," as Fritz, the owner, marched forward and placed a beautifully decorated cake on the table in front of Billy.

"Congratulations, pal, I'm glad you finally made it." He shook Billy's hand.

Inscribed in script on the cake were the words: "The City is Safe at Last! Billy Sparks, St. Augustine's Newest Detective."

Billy was overwhelmed. He returned greetings and shook hands with the crowd of well-wishers gathered around the table. Then he cut the cake and distributed pieces to everyone in the room. Finally, he worked his way back to the booth and sat down with his two friends. Linda poured his beer.

"How you doin', Tracy?" Johnny asked.

Billy raised his glass. "Thanks to you two, this is the best day of my life."

CHAPTER 22

The Royal Palm Hotel was just below 4th Street on Ocean Drive at the south end of the art deco district of Miami Beach. It was a modest, two-story structure finished in pink stucco and shaded by a half-dozen palm trees. Its entrance opened off a sheltered patio that was screened from the street by large, pink-blossomed hibiscus plants in white pots that matched the trim on the building. Although it did not have the ambiance and star power of its more exclusive cousins two blocks to the north, The Royal Palm was off the beaten path and presented the low-profile, unassuming appearance that Hink was looking for. Plus, the price was right, and he was within walking distance of the bank that he was using for the money transfer.

The bus ride from Melbourne had been uneventful, and Hink had checked into the Palm under an assumed name just after lunch. He requested a street-side room on the second floor, which gave him an unobstructed view for several blocks up and down Ocean Drive, as well as a short distance down 4th Street. *Not bad,* he thought, as he carefully checked a street map of the area. There would be plenty of time and money for pricey, beach-view rooms once the next few days were behind him. He slid the map across the desk, closer to the window, and picked up a pen. The South Beach branch of the Miami International Bank was on Alton north of 7th Street. He traced a line west on 4th to Alton then north to 7th. That seemed the most direct and inconspicuous route.

Most of the South Beach restoration had occurred north of 5th Street. The area south was still a work in progress, with some new construction and a few remodeled structures scattered among the existing buildings and vacant lots. Over the next couple of days he planned to walk several different routes to the bank so he would have a thorough knowledge of the neighborhood and a variety of escape options if everything blew up in his face again.

He was sure he hadn't been followed to Miami, but it disturbed him that someone had been able to figure out what he was up to and had tried to cut him off at the Canaveral drop site. His plan was to lay low and watch the streets and the bank until he felt it was safe to go for the money. He didn't know what to look for, but felt that if he saw trouble he would know it.

He checked his watch. It was time to call the Bahamas and get the money moving, then he could kick back and take a walk on the beach to relax. His head was clear, the demons had been left behind in Melbourne, and he felt a tantalizing breath of peace for the first time in his troubled life.

"How's business, Marco?" China rolled past the wall-sized photos of a dozen semi-naked women arranged in increasingly provocative poses, each more beautiful and alluring than the last. The photography was gorgeous—China prided himself on quality touches.

Marco hustled his huge form along behind China, down the erotic tunnel. "A little slow at lunch, but it started picking up about an hour ago, Mr. Beach."

He caught up with China just in time to step past and push open an imposing polished brass and glass door, framed in faux bamboo and white and lime stucco. Marco was amazingly agile for his size.

China didn't miss a beat as he wheeled into the semi-darkness and tantalizing music electrifying the "Living Room" of The Miss Saigon Club. He looked around the space. It was divided by a runway down the middle, which, in turn, split into additional runways that followed the walls around to the front. The girls made their entrances through double, mirrored doors at the end of the long runway.

The only interruptions in the design were at the back corners where two screened-off doors entered the room. The one on the right opened into the bar, kitchen, and dressing rooms. The one on the left led to the bathrooms, telephones, the elevator to China's office, and a circular staircase to the private party rooms on the second floor. Halfway down each wall runway, a short extension protruded into the room, and on the front wall double-decked platforms offered twice the stimulation for your buck. Mirrors were everywhere, reflecting the revolving ceiling fans, Tiffany lampshades, and softly lit undulating female bodies in varying degrees of nudity.

The walls above the mirrors and the ceiling were painted black, with constellations of stars to represent the summer night sky over the South China Sea. Bamboo and chrome cocktail tables and an occasional leather sofa were strategically positioned about the inlaid floor. The room was about a third full, and here and there a table dance was in progress.

China glanced at his watch. The Rolex was one of the few luxuries he had allowed himself since his dirt-poor childhood in Copperhill, Tennessee. It was 5:30. Happy hour was about half over—not bad; things would start moving into high gear in a couple of hours.

He was approached by a beautiful, dark-haired Eurasian woman in a black leather miniskirt, black leather tux jacket, and thigh-high black patent leather boots. She wore a black leather bow tie and no blouse. The effect was stunning.

She raised a panatela cigar to her full lips and took a light drag. The smoke caressed her high cheek bones.

"Evening, China. Would you like a drink?" Her voice was intimate, but in control.

The only protocol in the club was that the male employees refer to him as Mr. Beach, and the women call him China. It went back to his days in Vietnam when he was setting up his first drug operation. It helped the men remember who was boss and permitted him a more casual, intimate rapport with the women.

"Thanks, Daphne. The usual. Is Passion on tonight?"

She smiled. "She should be out for the next number." Her eyes reached out to him. "Your special?"

He nodded. "I'll be at my table." He turned to Marco who was still standing behind him. "Thank you, Marco, that's all for now."

"Just let me know if you need anything, Mr. Beach." Marco took a step back then returned to his station by the door.

China maneuvered across the floor to a front corner table that kept him out of sight from the entrance and allowed him an unrestricted view of the room. By the time he arrived, his Singapore Sling and Daphne were waiting.

He took a sip of the drink. "Have there been any calls or messages?"

"Nothing I couldn't take care of," she said.

"That's good. What would I do without you?"

"I'm sure you'd think of something." She leaned over and kissed him on the cheek.

He took his cell phone out of his pocket and handed it to her. "Hold on to this for me."

She took the phone. "Passion will be out in a minute. Think about me on the way back." She slipped the phone into her jacket pocket, covered his hand with hers for a moment, then stood up and drifted off into the darkness.

Fred T. Beach had been in the arousal business for three years. He saw it as a natural extension of his drug enterprise, a legitimate front and a conduit for laundering the increasingly profitable returns from his growing empire. It had succeeded beyond his wildest imagination. He twirled his glass and watched as Daphne moved across the room, stopping to speak to customers here and there, then his gaze tilted up and panned along the mirrors and pulsing bodies. He was pleased. It was, by God, a long way from the hunger of Tennessee and the firefights and stinking jungles of Southeast Asia.

The whole world was turning pink. The sky, the water, the white stucco, and tile buildings lining the manicured Palm Beach golf course two hundred yards off to port, even *September Song's* white hull appeared to be dusted with pale rose talcum. Jamison checked the tension on the anchor line, then stood up, settled back against the forestay and let the sunset soak in through his pores. He took the perfume bottle from his pocket and removed the silver stopper. Her fragrance infused the air and she materialized next to him in the bow pulpit.

He smiled.

"I'm pleased you chose to show up."

She looked up at him, then out over the water.

"How could I resist on such a lovely evening?"

"So I do have a little power to influence you?"

She took his hand.

"The more you let go, the more power you have, Jamison."

Her lips found his fingers.

"How's the writing going?"

"In the Chronicle? As if you didn't know."

She smiled.

"It's coming along. What do you think?"

"I like the style. There's still some poetry left in you."

"I haven't thought like that in a long time."

"It's kind of nice to break away from the bottom line for a while, isn't it?"

He nodded.

"Yeah, but I'm not sure where it's headed."

Her hand brushed his face.

"I think you'll know when you get there."

She shifted her body.

"There's not much room right here. Isn't there some way we could get a little more comfortable?"

"Sure. I'll pull the sailbag over."

He grabbed the jib bag and pushed it around to form a giant pillow.

"How's that?"

She sat down and settled back against the dacron.

"Much better."

Jamison leaned back next to her.

"What you said about power a minute ago doesn't make any sense."

"Does it have to make sense?"

"There you go again."

"You're confusing power with control. They come from different places."

Her fingers toyed with his body through his shirt. She pressed against him, her lips found his and he tasted her tongue as it searched for him. His body came alive, and he let the warm, visceral energy flow up through him.

Her lips broke contact.

"How does that feel, Jamison?" she whispered.

"Wonderful."

"How about powerful?"

He hesitated, turning the word over in his mind.

"I'll buy that."

"Are you frightened?"

"No."

"Why not?"

An amused smile played across his face.

"I forgot to be."

"Who did you forget to be afraid of, Jamison?"

His smile became a look of acceptance.

"Me."

Her expression softened and she took his face between her hands.

"Look at me, Jamison. Tell me about my eyes."

He dove into their emerald depths.

"They're like two windows on the universe."

"Your universe or mine?"

"I'm still not sure."

"What do you see through them?"

"Passion, joy, wonder, peace, pain...and hope."

The five-foot-ten strawberry blonde walked slowly toward China. By most standards in the club she was fully clothed. The white satin camisole was suspended by thin spaghetti straps that allowed her breasts to sway with the movement of her hips. She stopped beside his table with legs slightly apart, weight on her left hip, back slightly arched and arms by her sides.

She looked directly into his dark eyes and smiled. "Hello, China."

He put his drink on the table and turned the wheelchair toward her. "Hi, Passion."

Her violet eyes sucked him in.

"You look beautiful," China said softly, then took off his ball cap and laid it on the table behind him. He leaned back, took a deep breath, and felt an emotional rattle in his chest. He let out an inaudible sigh and nodded.

A sensuous ballad began to transform the darkness. Passion began to sway to the music, her eyes never leaving his. They worked inside him, probing all the hot spots, caressing all the wounds. He felt each one respond as her hips brushed against his arm and her lightly tanned hands stroked his ebony face. He felt, rather than saw, the straps fall from her shoulders as she moved behind him, and caught the delicate fragrance of her perfume as she draped the camisole around his neck.

She moved around him, her breasts inches from his face, her right hand stroking her body as she slowly slipped out of her satin G-string. Her eyes searched deeper and deeper as China released lock after lock, until the music, perfume, and the intimacy of her naked flesh opened the circuits of his devastated neurons. His legs began to burn as the scars hemorrhaged poison; the jungle opened its steaming maw, and for the thousandth time, crushed him in a blinding explosion. Then he heard the demon wailing and saw himself in a surreal, slow-motion tableau, falling head over heels through eternity, with only stumps for legs.

Passion watched China carefully. She knew all the signs. She that knew her body would take him out and her body would bring him back. She was therapist, nurse, and sexual fantasy all rolled into one. The perspiration beaded on his forehead, then his eyes flickered. He was returning. She picked up the rhythm and her movements became more sensual. Her hands explored her breasts and traced the lines of her swaying hips. It was time to heal.

CHAPTER 23

Small silver missiles launched themselves on either side of *September Song.* They zipped along for fifty feet or so just above the deck then sailed back into the waves, only to be replaced with another sparkling flight holding formation just ahead of the bow. Charlie was astounded.

"I'll be damned, flying fish," he exclaimed.

One landed on the deck, but before he could catch it and toss it back into the water, the tiny aeronaut gave a flip and was gone.

"Must be the welcoming party to the land of enchantment. Whoops, there goes another one." Jamison laughed as another chrome bullet brushed the deck before peeling away.

They were running in three hundred feet of deep blue water two miles off the shimmering white condos of Palm Beach. The tall, candy-striped smoke stacks that identified the Lake Worth Inlet were dropping below the horizon as Jamison checked their course. *Right on the money,* he thought; it looked like a perfect day. During the night the wind had shifted to the east, which, when combined with the shoreline's westerly slant, made it possible for them go offshore for the final stretch to Miami. It would make for a long day, but the opportunity to sail and avoid the confusion and congestion of the Waterway south of Ft. Lauderdale made it an easy decision. The happy-go-lucky clowning of their flying hosts seemed to confirm they had made the right choice.

Susan rolled her chair closer to the window and opened the envelope with the Melbourne postmark dated three days earlier.

> *Dearest Susan,*
>
> *We are in a lovely marina within walking distance of downtown Melbourne. Came in with some rough weather, but the front moved through and today is beautiful. Went for a run early this morning and blew a little dust out of my system. Boy, did it feel good!*
>
> *I'm a little concerned about Dad. When I got back from my run he was cleaning the waterline in the dinghy. He told me about an unusual experience he had while he was working. It seems that a manatee came up from under the dinghy and almost turned him over, then allowed him to rub her body while she just lay back in the sun. Which is cool, I wish I had been there, but he seemed very distracted, almost spaced out.*
>
> *When we started the trip he was really uptight, even irritable at times, which, according to Mom, he's been lately. Now he's more laid-back, but every now and then, he seems to drift off—almost as if he's in another world. I don't know, its probably nothing to worry about, maybe he's just unwinding. He might say the same about me since we left St. Simons. You are always on my mind, and I do float off into a little fantasy every now and then. 'Course everybody knows how screwed-up men are these days—guess that's why you love us so much. Damn, I do love you! Seems like months since St. Simons.*

Probably won't be in touch for a few days. Looks like we'll be anchoring out the next couple of nights before we hit Ft. Lauderdale or, if we can go outside, Miami. Got to run. We need to do some shopping and I want to put this in the mail while we're out.

Love you,
Charlie

There was a small drawing of a leaping dolphin with a smile on its face just below and to the right of his signature.

Susan folded the letter and slipped it back into its envelope. *I think Jamison is going through withdrawal, switching to island time,* she thought. *I'm sure that's all it is.* She checked her watch. Her parents were due in at the airport at 3:45. Their flight from Rome had touched down in Atlanta at noon and the connecting flight to St. Simons took off just minutes ago, according to the airline's website. She couldn't wait to tell them about Charlie and the change that had occurred in her life since they left. *I'll do it after dinner over a glass of wine, when they've had a chance to get settled down.* She smiled, picked up her keys, and headed for the door.

China sat in his office studying the computer's glowing screen. The month was looking good. *Sex, drugs, and cash are a hard combination to beat,* he thought, as he scrolled the computer spread sheet. Since Passion had exorcised him, he felt damn near whole.

The darkness had been recurring ever since he had awakened in a Medevac Unit and realized he would never tie his shoelaces again. He never knew when it would come. Sometimes months would pass between attacks, then for no apparent reason the demons would switch to a weekly schedule. He had been to the VA and done all the therapy and support groups, but nobody had been able to offer him solace until Passion stepped out of the mirrors and gave him the gift of her body. Now the assaults were less intense and further apart. He was beginning to think he had the beast on the run.

The phone on his desk rang. He punched Ctrl-S on the keyboard and hit the speaker button. Daphne's voice filled the room.

"China, director of player personnel on line two."

"Thanks, Daphne." He picked up the handset. "I'm here."

"The Nassau farm club just okayed the bonus for our holdout." It was the familiar island voice.

China was silent for a moment. "I understand. Any information on where he'll report?"

"Miami. Close to home plate."

"Interesting. Send me the final program via the dugout."

"It's on the way, mon." The line clicked and went dead.

So Prescott's headed for Miami. He thought for a second, then punched line six.

"Daphne, would you ask Marco to come to my office? Also, player personnel is sending a fax. Would you bring it to me as soon as it comes in?"

Jamison was in the nav station checking the approach and entrance channel to Miami. It had been dark for an hour and the GPS indicated they would be at the sea buoy in about thirty minutes. Government Cut and the channel looked pretty straight forward: straight in, then bear to the right to pick up the lights of South Beach Marina. His biggest concern was shipping, since Miami was a very busy twenty-four-hour port. Their radar reflector was up, which made them a bigger target, but they still had to keep a sharp watch. He dimmed the chart light and climbed back up to the cockpit.

"How you doing?" he asked Charlie.

"Okay. Good thing we took the jib down when we did; the wind is picking up and the seas have started to break. How much farther to the channel?"

"Two and a half miles. Any shipping?"

"Haven't seen anything. What're the characteristics of the lead light?"

"White, Morse Code A. The second light is a red flasher—four seconds."

"Thought I saw the white a minute ago, but I lost it."

A wave broke against the hull and Charlie had to steer up into it. "I think we could use a little power." He reached down, flipped on the ignition and punched the starter. The diesel kicked in and he put it in gear.

"Is your harness hooked on?" Jamison asked. They both were wearing safety harnesses with strobe lights attached to the webbing.

"Yep. Wouldn't leave home without it. There it is! Just off the starboard bow—about 12:30."

Jamison squinted into the inky darkness. With the boat surging up and down the waves it was hard to find the pinprick of light. He scanned back and forth, then caught the dot-dash flash out of the corner of his eye.

"I see it, and I see the red ten degrees to the right." He felt a silent sigh of relief. Their guardian angels were in sight.

Charlie swung toward the light. "What's the channel like?"

"Plenty deep right through the cut. When you round the sea-buoy turn to two-five-two degrees; that should put us in the channel. About halfway up the—" He never finished the sentence.

Suddenly Charlie straightened up. "What's that noise?" He jerked around toward the stern.

Over the crashing waves and wind, Jamison heard it: the roar of high speed engines at full throttle, going like hell and coming at them from out of the darkness. Jamison leaped to his feet, but before he could gather his senses, the stiletto shape of a Cigarette boat exploded off a wave at their stern and crashed down twenty feet off their port beam, then accelerated, howling airborne off the next wave and was gone into the night.

"Holy shit! What was that?" cried Charlie, as he struggled with the wheel, trying to regain control of *September Song*. He was so startled by the screaming turbos and the near miss that he momentarily lost the helm.

"No lights! Did you see that? He's running without lights! Son-of-a-bitch, I can't believe it!" He was back in control and trying to find the buoy.

Jamison was stunned by what he had just seen. "It was a Coast Guard boat."

Charlie looked at him in disbelief. "A Coast Guard boat?" He found the buoy and was steering back toward it.

"There was a Coast Guard emblem on the bow. They were so close I could read it."

"What a bunch of hot dogs. They could have killed us— heads up, heads up, we're almost at the buoy."

There wasn't time for further discussion of the incident. They had their hands full as they swept around the flashing white marker and tried to line up on the channel. The wind was almost behind them as they surfed toward Miami. With the waves slamming past them, Charlie had all he could do to keep the bow pointed in the right direction, and Jamison was hard pressed to separate the channel lights from the neon glow of the Miami skyline. It was like being slam-dunked into a pinball machine.

"You want me to take the wheel?" Jamison asked.

"I'm okay. How much further to the jetties?"

"We bear right at the next red flasher; then it's about three quarters of a mile."

As they made the turn, Jamison confirmed what he had suspected for the past few minutes. "Charlie, do you see running lights on the right side of the channel just ahead?"

Charlie searched the darkness, then he spotted them. "Yeah, just out from the jetties."

"I've been watching them. They're not moving."

"You think somebody's anchored in the channel?"

"Looks that way. Better give them plenty of room."

As they approached the stationary vessel Jamison could see the prominent red, white, and blue marking of a Coast Guard patrol boat. When they arrived abeam the patrol boat it got under way, swung around off their stern and followed them into Government Cut.

Damn, thought Jamison. "Are you ready for more excitement?" he asked.

"What do you mean?" Charlie replied.

Jamison nodded toward the patrol boat, which was closing the gap between them.

When they were almost alongside, an amplified voice addressed them. "*September Song*, this is the U.S. Coast Guard. We intend to board you for a safety inspection. Are you going into South Beach Marina?"

Jamison waved and nodded his head.

"We'll board you at the fuel dock, Captain."

Charlie was incredulous. "A safety inspection? At this time of night?"

Jamison smiled wearily. "This doesn't have much to do with safety."

Charlie looked at him. "Drugs?"

Jamison nodded. "I'll get the fenders out."

When they arrived at the fuel dock the Coast Guard boarding party was waiting. They were dressed in navy blue, with orange life vests and carried side arms. Once Charlie left the boat, the commanding officer and Jamison went below, where Jamison presented the ship's papers and their passports for inspection. Once that was completed, a total safety inspection followed. Everything from the dates on flares to the Oil Discharge Placard in the engine compartment was scrutinized and checked off a long inspection form. Once the officer was satisfied that all was in order, he requested that Jamison leave the boat and wait on the dock while another team went aboard. Nothing was ever mentioned about drugs or contraband, but from what Jamison could see through the ports, this was no scavenger hunt.

Thirty minutes later the searchers reappeared and, after conferring with their commander, returned to the patrol boat.

Jamison and Charlie were beginning to feel the stress of the long day, the rough seas, and the evening's events. They were disheveled, windblown, and were still strapped into their safety harnesses and strobes.

Charlie turned to his father. "How are you feeling, Dad?"

Jamison tried to stretch. "I'm bushed. How about you, son?"

"Yeah. All of a sudden I've started to crash."

The Coast Guard officer appeared out of the dark. "Captain, you and your son may go back aboard and clean up. I'll be back after we complete a computer check on you."

Thirty minutes later Jamison heard a knock on the cabin top and climbed into the cockpit. The officer was waiting for him.

"Captain, we have completed the inspection. The computer indicates that this is not a stolen vessel. Here is the inspection report. You passed." He handed Jamison an official looking yellow copy. "Keep this document; it may be of help if you are boarded again. Thank you for your cooperation."

The inspection had been very polite and professional, but there had been no mention of the Cigarette boat, drugs, or the second inspection team.

"Thank you." Jamison gave him a tired, frustrated salute. A moment later the patrol boat's engine rumbled to life, and the boarding party pulled away from the dock.

When Jamison returned to the cabin, Charlie had crawled into bed. Jamison stuck his head in the aft cabin and held up the inspection form. "Welcome to Paradise, Charlie."

Charlie managed to crack open one eye. "Right. Paradise gained or Paradise lost?" he mumbled, and fell fast asleep.

CHAPTER 24

The Dolphin Chronicle #7

By every Post-Eden standard, love is subversive. It is the secret agent that breaks the analytical seal and opens the window on a reality that is totally creative, regenerative and transformational—a presence that defies quantification, computation and the status quo.

In a calculated world predicated on bottom lines and managed control, love is the barbarian at the gate; a crack in the ramparts of legal and statistical piety. It is the impulse that resists the linear tide, the genie of unpredictability, and the ultimate leap of faith. Love is the guide through the thickets of fear, and the angel of life waiting in the valley of death. It is the coincidental flower that transforms the linear garden.

"Tommy, Jamison's on line three," the receptionist called out as Tommy hurried past the front desk.

"Oh, thanks, Marlene." She stopped and looked at her watch. "Would you buzz Elliott and tell him I'll be a couple of minutes late for the Shaffer meeting?"

Marlene smiled. "Sure, they can talk about their golf game."

"You're a dear." She turned and hurried back to her office, went in and closed the door.

"Hi, honey. Hope I'm not interrupting anything." Jamison's voice bloomed in her ear.

"I was on my way to a meeting with Elliott and some of the staff, but they've got plenty to talk about before I get there. Where are you? I haven't heard from you for a couple of days." She tried not to let the apprehension show in her voice. For some reason she had felt anxious the past day or so. Call it feminine intuition or overwork, whatever; she had been a little on edge and they had been on her mind. She was successful. He didn't pick up on it.

"We anchored for two nights, but we made it to Miami last night. This is the first chance I've had to call."

Tommy smiled. Miami sounded safe. "Miami? You've really covered a lot of ground since Melbourne."

"We went outside yesterday and got in here a little late. Had some excitement, but I'll tell you about that tonight. Just wanted to let you know we're here safe and sound."

"Excitement?"

"Nothing really. The Coast Guard stopped us for a safety inspection, which was interesting. I'll call after dinner when you have more time."

A Coast Guard inspection? That seemed harmless. Her spirits brightened. "I'm glad you're safe. How's Charlie?"

"He's doing great. He sends his love. By the way, we're in the South Beach Marina."

"Let me get a pencil." She found a pencil and wrote the name and phone number of the marina in her appointment book.

"Looks like we'll be here for a few days. I want to have the compass adjusted before we leave for the Bahamas, and the earliest appointment I could get was two days from now."

"Think of me while you're lying on the beach."

"It's tough duty, but I'll give it my best."

"I love you, Jamey."

"Love you too. Talk tonight."

Tommy hung up, picked up the pencil and drew a smiley face next to the marina name, then reached for the phone. "Marlene, ring Elliott and tell him I'm on my way up."

Hink stood in the shade of the apartment's entrance and inspected the bank across the street. There was nothing unusual about its appearance. It was pretty much a blend with the other buildings on the block: two-story, stucco with a little tile, glass block, and the MIB logo on a Decco appendage that thrust up from the round-cornered roof which sheltered the glass and chrome front doors. A parking lot was to the left and a beauty salon to the right. Parking meters lined both sides of the street, and the sidewalks were shaded by occasional palm trees and accented with hibiscus. He noted that the bank served a variety of customers of differing age and circumstance. Some business suits, a couple of young-and-beautiful, and a few retirees had come and gone while he watched.

The black man in the wheelchair was still sitting by the front door relaxing in the sun. Occasionally he adjusted his baseball cap to shield his eyes from the morning glare. He and his hefty companion had arrived a few minutes earlier in a van and parked in a handicapped spot in the parking lot. The big man had gone around to the back of the van and unloaded the wheelchair, then opened the passenger side door, carefully lifted the amputee out of the seat, and gently placed him in the chair. Then they rolled around to the front door, where they talked for a moment, and the larger man went into the bank and left his friend to enjoy the warm rays and pleasant breeze.

Nothing out of the ordinary, Hink thought, as he looked up and down the street. There were no parked cars filled with banditos, and he had yet to see anybody smoking a skinny little cigar.

Hink had called the bank after breakfast and confirmed that the transfer had taken place. All he had to do was walk through the door and haul it off in a gunny sack. It gave him a rush to think that freedom was only fifty yards away. *But it isn't going anywhere,* he told himself. He was this close, and he could afford to be patient, at least for another day or two. He watched as the big man came out of the bank and loaded his cargo back into the van. Then they pulled out of the parking lot, turned into traffic, and drove quickly away. Hink took one more look up and down the street. *Just your average, quiet day in the neighborhood,* he thought.

"I'll do it! I'll work it out with Mom and Dad. They owe me a couple of days, and besides, they're thrilled about you. I can be there by dinnertime." Susan's excited voice danced in Charlie's ear.

"I'll get you a room at one of the little hotels by the beach. We'll have a day, maybe even two."

"How do I get to the marina?"

Charlie propped the phone on his shoulder, opened a road map, and gave her the directions. "Once you're in the marina you can't miss us. We're on H-Dock next to the pink high-rise."

"H-Dock, I've got it. If you don't hear from me, I'll be there for a late dinner."

"I can't wait to see you. Drive safely."

"I will. Charlie, this is a great idea."

"And there's still Nassau."

"I can't stand it...love."

"Lust."

She laughed. "See you tomorrow night."

Charlie leaned back against the phone booth and looked out over the marina. The sky was Miami blue; the sun, Bahama warm; and a big, beach-white cruise ship laid on its whistle as it sliced out Government Cut, headed for the islands. For a moment he thought he could hear the rhythmic bonging of steel drums gathering the faithful. It was party time on the Tropic of Pleasure.

Billy set down his can of Mountain Dew and salted his French fries. "Your boys are in Miami."

Johnny looked surprised. "How do you know they're in Miami?"

"Coast Guard picked them up and searched their boat last night. They were coming into Government Cut."

"I'll bet that was a pain in the ass. What's the word?"

"Clean as a shark's tooth. No drugs, no violations, very cooperative. An excellent report."

Johnny felt a sigh of relief. "Then they're out of danger?"

"I'd say so." Billy sipped the Dew. "Thought I'd run down and have a talk with them. Like to pull some R & R?"

"If they're out of danger why do you want to talk to them?"

"Other than Jake Dupree, they were the last people to have any contact with Prescott. I'd like to know if they talked to him and if so, did they pick up anything we might have overlooked. It's a long shot, but at this point it's about all we've got."

"Sounds reasonable." Johnny dipped a French fry in catsup. "Any more word on Prescott?"

"Yeah. They found his dinghy at Melbourne."

"The inflatable?"

"The very one. He had slit the tubes and scuttled it. A fisherman accidentally hooked it with his anchor and pulled it up."

"Do you think he's in the Melbourne area?"

"I don't know. A man fitting his description checked into a hotel on the river and then checked out a couple of nights later. The Melbourne police are checking car rental agencies, airlines, and busses. My guess is he's vamoosed."

Johnny nodded. "Sounds that way." He squeezed some more mustard on his hamburger and smiled. "A little R & R sounds great. I could use a break. When do you want to go?"

"You got anything tomorrow? I thought I'd take an extra day if you can get away."

Johnny thought for a minute. "I can do that; what time?"

"You name it. If we're not too late getting in, we can have a drink, get some dinner and hit the town."

"We'll take the cab."

"Why not. Go first class."

"Does the department care if you ride in a cab?"

"Oh, hell no, as long as I'm not spending any of their money; besides this is part vacation."

"It'll make great cover; nobody'll ever think you're a cop." Johnny laughed. They were both warming to the idea.

"What's going on over here? You boys are having entirely too much fun." Marge smiled as she refilled Johnny's tea.

"We're taking a couple of days off. You wanna come with us?" Billy asked.

She leaned over the menu rack. "You're sweet, but this sounds more like two for the road. But that offer will get your partner another glass of tea."

Billy grinned and shook his head. "What a woman!"

"Give me a rain check, cowboy." She winked and moved away.

Johnny had finished his hamburger and was mopping up his French fries. "So I'll pick you up about ten in the morning."

"Ten in the morning would be perfect. My turn." Billy picked up the check and they headed for the cash register.

CHAPTER 25

"No hablo ingles," the tall storekeeper apologized. His companion smiled and shrugged.

Jamison tried again. "Ah, mosquito net."

The two only looked more bewildered.

"What we have here is a failure to communicate." Jamison scratched his chin.

"Let me try, Dad." Charlie started to wave his fingers around in the air, attempting a flying motion. "Mosquito…bzzzzzzzzzz!" He dove a finger into his arm like a mosquito attacking and grimaced. He was greeted by good-natured laughter.

The four stood pondering each other.

"Don't anyone leave. I'm going out on the street and find somebody to translate." Jamison motioned with his hands, trying to indicate that he would be right back as he backed out the hardware store's door.

"He'll be right back." Charlie smiled. The two owners nodded at each other then smiled at Charlie. A moment later Jamison was back leading a middle-aged Latin man dressed in a suit and tie.

The owners immediately recognized him. "Juan, amigo!" They broke into even bigger smiles.

"Raul, Jesus!" He clapped them on the shoulders, then turned to Jamison and Charlie. "And now, you say we have a little language problem?"

"That's right. We need to get some mosquito net and heavy elastic bands."

Their benefactor smiled. "That should be easy enough." He turned to his two friends and explained Jamison's request.

They listened intently then broke into laughter once again. "Ah. Buzzzzzzzzz!" They waved their arms.

"Right. Buzzzzzzzzzz." Charlie and Jamison laughed and waved their arms.

Juan looked bemused. "Did I miss something?"

Jamison explained their attempts to communicate "mosquito." Juan nodded and joined in the laughter.

A few minutes later they waved good-bye to Raul and Jesus and left the store with the needed supplies.

Jamison turned to their newfound friend. "Thank you for you help, Juan. It's been a pleasure meeting you."

"No, amigos. The pleasure is all mine. I wish you a safe voyage and don't let the buzzzzzzzz get you in the islands." He smiled and wiggled his fingers.

They all laughed and shook hands.

"What's next?" Charlie asked, as Juan headed down the street.

"What time are you expecting Susan?" Jamison replied.

"I'm going to start watching for her around five-thirty."

"Why don't we see if we can find the grocery store the harbormaster recommended. If we can get stocked up for the crossing, then I'll tend to the rest of the chores and you can be free to spend your time with her."

"Thanks, Dad. I appreciate it." He smiled at his father. "Where's the store?"

"A couple of blocks from here. They're supposed to deliver to the boat."

"Really? Maybe things are looking up in paradise."

Johnny climbed back up on I-95 and hit the afterburners. The cab responded with a whoosh and they were at altitude and cruising speed in seconds. He scanned the sky. *Lot of action today, and it's going to get worse once we pass Ft. Lauderdale and get into Miami air space,* he thought. *Have to stay on my toes, but damn, it's great to be doing a cross-country again.*

"This is a rocket sled you have here, my man. I think the damn thing could fly to Miami." Billy leaned back and took a sip of Mountain Dew.

Johnny grinned and adjusted his sunglasses. "That's closer than you think, big man."

"Shit, gives me a sense of power. I feel like we're Thelma and Louise in drag."

"Hell, I can fly across the Grand Canyon."

"Don't doubt it for a minute, not for a minute."

Even factoring in the pit stop, it appeared to Johnny that they were right on schedule. Not only that, they had picked up a tail wind. It looked like an early arrival at MIA.

"I checked with the office while you were in the head back at the Exxon station." Billy popped open a tube of peanuts.

"How are the constables doing?"

"Not bad, considering St. Augustine ain't exactly the Bronx." He chewed a couple of nuts. "Your boys are still in Miami."

Johnny glanced at him. "That's convenient. Do they know we're coming?"

"Nope, I'd rather just drop in."

"You inspectors are all alike—no social graces. How long are they going to be there?"

Billy grinned and studied the design on the soda can. "That's us. Antisocial peas in a pod. According to the harbor master, they're registered for a couple of more days. Getting a compass checked or something like that."

"Which marina are they in?"

"South Beach, right down by Government Cut."

"I'm looking forward to seeing them again; they're great guys."

"Thought you probably would be, but get a grip on your knickers; it gets even better." He leaned back, took another drink, chewed some more nuts and smiled.

Johnny squinted at him. "I'm waiting, Thelma."

"Prescott's headed for Miami, too. He took a bus out of Melbourne."

"Damn, the party's getting crowded."

"Don't fill up your dance card, honey, we could be the hottest dates in town."

"I tell you, I don't know about Lorraine."

"Whaddaya mean?"

"Veg-ass for God's sake. Why Veg-ass?" The over-styled woman took a drag on her cigarette. The smoke enveloped her companion.

"Because she wants to be a dancer. Vegas is where she thinks she has to be." Her escort glared at her and tried to wave the cloud of nicotine away from his face. "I wish you'd give those damn things up."

"But Veg-ass. I just don't understand…." The couple drifted away.

Charlie smiled across the table at Susan. "I don't think they're from around here."

"I don't think anyone is." She sipped her wine.

The moon was breaking over the palms that separated Loomis Park from the beach. Cars cruised slowly by on Ocean Drive while an eclectic mix of beauty and gloss, wanna-be-seen, wanna-be-famous, and just-wanna-have-fun cruised the sidewalks and lounged under the colorful umbrellas and awnings of the hotel restaurants and open-air bars.

"How are you feeling?" He played with her fingers, gently stroking one, then another.

She watched him and thought how nice it was to be touched. "I'm a little tired, but it's nice."

She traced the back of his hand with her finger nails and noticed how they made a brief impression on his deeply tanned flesh.

"Does that feel good?" Her leg pressed against his.

His eyes met hers and he nodded. "I love you."

"I know."

The waiter brought their salads.

"Could we have another glass of wine?" Charlie asked.

"Of course, sir."

His hand dropped to her knee. "Do you like your room?"

Her fingers followed his hand. "I love my room."

"Do you think the moon is shining in it?"

She looked past him at the moon, now completely above the trees. "I think in about thirty minutes it will be the only light in the room." Her fingers made a circle around his index finger.

His hand moved deftly. "I think we should make it an early night."

Her fingers tightened around his and tugged gently. She felt herself opening to him and turned as his nose brushed her cheek. Her eyes caught the flame of the table lamp, and she tasted the smoke of wine on his lips. The silver orb in the sky silhouetted his face. *Oh, God,* she sighed to herself, *I'm in love with the man in the moon.*

China had been watching the two men at table three. He motioned to Daphne. "Would you ask Marco to come to the table?" She nodded and headed toward the front door.

A moment later Marco appeared. "Did you ask for me, Mr. Beach?"

China nodded and indicated a chair. "Sit down, Marco."

Marco pulled out a chair and settled his huge body next to China. "What can I do for you, Mr. Beach?"

"Marco, do you know those two guys at three?" He gestured toward the men.

Marco studied them. One was tall, well built, had good features and a mustache. The other was a little shorter with a receding hairline and was slightly overweight. The tall one had on jeans and a navy polo shirt. The shorter was dressed in tan Dockers and a black tee shirt. They both wore sport jackets. "I've never seen them before, Mr. Beach."

"I think they're cops, but I don't recognize them either. How did they arrive?"

"I'll check, Mr. Beach."

He moves like a shadow, China thought, as Marco disappeared in the dark.

"They think we're cops," Billy muttered to Johnny, as Marco got up from the table.

"What do you mean? Who thinks we're cops?" Johnny looked surprised.

"Don't look around. There's a guy in a wheelchair at a table in the corner that's been watching us ever since we came in. A moment ago he called the bouncer over and now he's left— gone to check on us."

"How do you know?" Johnny resisted the temptation to look behind him.

"It's my job." He shrugged. "You develop a sixth sense. Sort of like hunting, you sense things before they happen. They'll really be confused when they discover we came in a St. Augustine cab." He laughed.

"What do we do?" Johnny was beginning to feel uneasy.

"Nothin', just relax and enjoy the evening. Tonight I'm not a cop."

Marco slipped back into the chair next to China. "They came in a St. Augustine cab, Mr. Beach."

"They came in a what?" China looked at Marco in disbelief.

"Honest-to-God, Mr. Beach. Tony says they came in an All American Cab from St. Augustine with St. Johns County tags. The tall one was driving."

Goddamn, I must be losing it, China thought. "That doesn't sound like heat, Marco."

"No, Mr. Beach, it doesn't."

"Well, have Daphne send one of the girls over to them. We'll see if we can start taking their money, but keep an eye on them anyway."

Billy set his glass back on the table and leaned toward Johnny. "I think the cab threw them. The Big Man just reported back and confusion reigns. Shit, this makes the whole trip worthwhile. I can't tell you how much I'm enjoying this. The cab was a stroke of genius." He raised his empty glass to the waitress.

Johnny grinned. "I'm glad my modest contribution to this excursion has given you so much pleasure, old buddy."

A stunning redhead clad in black leather straps and stars materialized at the table.

"I think the pleasure has just begun, my man."

Jamison stepped into the shower and adjusted the temperature.

"Taking a shower is a great idea, Jamison."

"I thought you'd like it."

"You know I'm a water person."

She squeezed past him into the flow of water.

"So am I. We have a lot in common."

He opened a plastic container and took out a bar of soap.

"We have everything in common."

She threw her head back into the spray and let her hair wash down her back.

"Is the temperature about right?"

"If it feels good to you, then it feels good to me."

He took the soap and lathered her breasts and shoulders.

Her face came back out of the water.

"Oh, I'm glad I didn't have to ask."

"God, I love your body."

He buried his face between her breasts and she pulled him back into the spray. The water surged over his head and down his body.

"How does that feel?" she gurgled.

Her fingers found his nipples. He felt a tingling, nipping sensation. He pulled back and looked at her.

"It feels good."

"Try it on me."

She pulled him back into the shower and her fingers slid around his back.

He caught her in his teeth, and again he felt the erotic sensation on *his* body. He jerked back out of water and stared at her.

"What's going on?"

She laughed and kissed him, her mischievous tongue dancing.

"Well, at least that's better than 'I don't understand.'"

Her finger traced his nose.

He was bemused.

"I felt what you felt."

She smiled.

"Yes you did, Jamison."

He flashed back to cleaning the waterline in Melbourne and remembered that when she responded to his touch and gasped, he felt her electric release surge through his body. Suddenly he heard a moan from the next shower stall.

"Shhh. There's somebody in the next shower."

For the first time, he was aware that the other shower was running. He looked down. He could see four feet, and two of them had red toe nail polish.

"Oh, my God, there're two people in there, and one of them is a woman."

He heard a giggle and a little gasp. He looked at her.

"What are we going to do?"

Her eyes twinkled.

"Remember they can't see me, or hear us talking. This could be fun."

"Surely they know we're here."

"They obviously know we're here. Why else would they be in there?"

She pulled him back into the water and her hands slipped down his thighs. He kissed her and felt the full length of her body against him for the first time. She was soft and firm, cool and warm, and hot and urgent. He broke out of the flow for air and glanced down at the feet. Three were still on the floor, but one with red toe nails was no longer in sight.

"Oh, shit, I think they're doing it!"

"Doing what?"

He stared at the feet.

"Having sex."

She laughed.

"Of course they're having sex."

"I've got to get out of here."

He turned off the water and reached for his towel.

"Jamison, I believe you're embarrassed."

With the shower off he could hear the level of intensity rising three feet away.

"Jamison!"

Her body glistened in the low light and her eyes pleaded.

He pulled on his shorts, slipped into his sneakers, and pushed open the stall door.

"Come on, I don't want to be here when they come out."

"Come on?"

He turned around and looked at her.

"I can't leave you here."

She stared at him.

"I don't think you realize what you just said."

He smiled quizzically and hurried to the shower room door, his towel and shirt in one hand and his bath kit in the other. The last thing he heard as he stepped into the moonlit night was, "Oh, yes, yes, yes!" coming from the steaming shower.

CHAPTER 26

Hink was up early. He showered, shaved, and put on his only pair of slacks and a clean polo shirt. He carefully combed his hair and checked his appearance in the mirror. He looked good. In fact, he looked damn good. *Ought to try this more often,* he thought. He packed his duffel, set it by the door along with the cheap briefcase he had bought just for the occasion and scanned the room. Everything looked in order.

This was it, the big day at last. He checked his watch. By the time he walked down to the Burger King and got some breakfast, the bank would be open. He had discovered that the restaurant afforded a good view of the street in several directions and gave him an opportunity to see if he was being followed. He would enter through the corner door, and when he was through eating, leave through the opposite side, then loop around and head for the bank.

He took a deep breath, picked up the briefcase and looked around the room. It was showtime.

"You know that Coast Guard boat that blew us off the other night when we were coming in?" Charlie stuffed his bathing suit, an extra-large tee shirt, suntan lotion, and a beach towel into a sports bag.

Jamison stirred his coffee. "You mean the Cigarette boat?"

Charlie nodded. "One of the guys here at the marina told me it used to be a drug boat. The Coast Guard impounded it following a shoot-out off Ft. Lauderdale about a week ago. It was red, so they zipped it in, painted it gray, decked it out with radar and now they're using it as an interdiction boat. They call it *The Ghost*. We were their first interdictees, and it sounded to him like they were a little too aggressive."

"So we made a bit of history." Jamison leaned against the galley counter and peeled a banana.

"Yep, we were at the right place at the right time." Charlie tossed his bag into the cockpit.

"Quite a coincidence," Jamison mused.

"Call us lucky." Charlie grinned.

"Well, they need to work on their technique before they give somebody a heart attack."

Charlie started up the companionway steps. "If you need me for any reason, leave a message at the hotel desk. We'll check in there around lunchtime."

"I think I've got everything under control. "You and Susan have a nice day."

"See you later." The boat rocked gently as Charlie stepped off onto the dock.

Jamison finished his cereal, settled back, and sipped his coffee. His thoughts drifted back to the night before in the shower, and he smiled at the mix of emotions he felt: passion, amusement, embarrassment, but most of all, the astonishing feeling of having her emotions and sensations alive in his body. He remembered his reaction when she came to him in Melbourne, and he was amazed that this time he wasn't threatened by the experience. On an impulse he called to her.

"Are you there?"

"I'm right here, Jamison."

He felt her hands over his eyes, and for a second he couldn't see, then his vision returned, and he realized he was seeing through her eyes. She uncovered his face and walked around facing him. He could see himself.

"This is phenomenal."

"I can tell you're not frightened."

He saw himself nod.

"I can't believe it. Actually, I feel very comfortable."

"How do you look?"

He almost didn't recognize the person smiling back at him. He was tanned, appeared rested, and the two-martini roll around his middle had firmed up. But what surprised him most was the aura of relaxed confidence he generated. This was not the stressed, burned-out agency executive who had crawled out of a demolished Lexus seven months ago.

"Damn, I look pretty good."

"You're right. I like what I see."

He nodded.

"So do I."

"There may be hope for you, Jamison."

"I think you may be right."

Her hands closed back over his eyes.

"Take a deep breath."

She removed her hands and he could see through his own eyes again.

She leaned over and whispered in his ear.

"Your universe or mine, Jamison?"

He turned to her.

"I'd like to have both."

"You already do."

Her lips caressed his eyes and cheek, then she vanished.

Jamison sat for a moment holding on to her fragrance and the touch of her lips, and as he pondered the meaning of her words an image began to form in his mind's eye. He saw himself standing on a beach looking out at a stormy sea. Across the water he saw the dim outline of another shore. He knew in an instant the answer to her question lay in getting to the other side, but as far as he could see, there was no way across. There was no bridge and he had no boat.

He bent over and dipped a finger into the water. It was cold and threatening. He quickly backed away and stared across the foreboding barrier at the tantalizing vision. He felt a tingle of anticipation as the scene faded away. *At least I know it's there*, he thought.

He looked at the clock on the bulkhead. "The bank opens in twenty-five minutes. I'd better get the dishes cleaned up and get out of here," he said to himself. He turned to the nav station and picked up a piece of notepaper. He ran down the list of things to do he had written on the paper. Number one was traveler's checks and cash.

China sat at his table at the First Edition studying the National League standings. He took a bite of cheesecake as the morning light embroidered fans of palm shadows on the table cloth. He was pleased to note that the Braves were back in first place. He put the paper down and looked toward the beach. He was on top of the world. In only a few hours his customers would be picking nickel bags right out of the trees—just like the orchards at home where he used to steal apples, only this time the harvest was Meth and Ecstasy. He was interrupted by the beeping of his cell phone.

"I'm here."

"Mr. Prescott is closing out his account at this moment," a nervous male voice said.

"Slow him down. Don't let him leave before we get there!" China ordered.

"Yes, sir, I'll do my best."

China didn't wait for the man to hang up. He punched the phone button and the number for the Club. "Daphne, have Marco pick me up immediately! Prescott's at home plate. Tell him to come prepared. Chop, chop!"

"So there's a new lady in your life?" Billy asked, as he climbed into the cab.

Johnny slid into the cockpit and slipped the key into the ignition. "Yeah, Tracy, it looks that way."

He turned on the ignition and checked the instruments as the engine turned over: *Oil pressure, manifold pressure— everything lookin' good,* he thought.

"Are you going to tell me her name?"

Johnny looked over at him and grinned. "How do we get to breakfast?"

"You're stalling. Go over to Alton and turn south. There's a Burger King down near the marina. When we're through eating we'll walk down and see your friends, and remember, I'm trained in interrogation."

"Oh, shit, I'm in trouble." Johnny pulled on his cap and rolled out of the parking lot. "It's Cindy."

Billy considered the name. "Cindy sounds nice. Is this the end of Linda?"

Johnny looked at his buddy. "You know there's no hope for me there; she's married."

Billy paused. "It's a damn shame, too. Where did you meet Cindy?"

"She's the harbor master at North Point Marina." Traffic was light, so Johnny accelerated and entered the pattern.

"Been out yet?"

"Once."

"And it feels good?"

Johnny smiled. "Yeah, Billy, it feels real good."

"I'm happy for you, John. Turn left at the next corner."

Hink sat in the branch manager's office. It was glass on two sides, and from where he was sitting he could see the front door and the entire lobby. *Damn, this is taking a long time,* he thought. He looked at his watch. The manager had been gone for fifteen minutes. *How long did it take to issue a cashier's check and get five thousand dollars in cash?* He was about to go look for him when the little man returned and took his seat behind his desk. He appeared nervous. Hink could see a light film of perspiration on his upper lip, and he noticed that his little finger quivered when he passed the check across the desk. Hink's early warning system went on red alert.

"Mr. Prescott, here is the check, made out to you for the sum of one hundred and sixty thousand dollars, and in this envelope is cash in the amount of five thousand dollars all in fifties, as you requested." He paused. "However, there is one other—"

The front door opened and Marco stepped in, hesitated momentarily as he glanced towards the manager's office, then walked casually toward a teller's cage. The move was practically seamless, but Hink recognized him immediately from the previous day, and his heightened awareness read the unspoken signal between the two men. The alarms were going off, but Hink felt no sense of panic. In fact, he was almost at peace.

"Yes, Mr. Hunnicutt, you were saying?"

Hunnicutt regrouped. "Actually, it's unimportant, Mr. Prescott. Just details. We can deal with it internally. Now, I believe everything is in order." He handed Hink the envelope of cash.

Hink slipped the check into a number ten envelope, folded it and put it in his pocket. Then he placed the cash envelope in the briefcase and stood up.

"Thank you for your assistance, Mr. Hunnicutt." He shook Hunnicutt's hand and noticed it was limp and damp.

Hunnicutt came around from behind his desk and opened his office door. "Thank you, Mr. Prescott. If I can be of further assistance...."

They shook hands again, then Hunnicutt looked nervously at Marco, stepped back and closed the door.

Hink turned and walked casually toward the front door. He didn't look directly at Marco, but moved so he kept him in sight out of the corner of his eyes. When he was three quarters of the way across the lobby, Marco turned away from the tellers and started after him.

Hink picked up the move and broke for the door just as Marco shifted into high gear. In one smooth motion the big man lunged forward and drew a nine millimeter semi-automatic pistol from under his jacket. At the sight of the gun all hell broke loose. Women screamed and everybody dived for the floor or crouched behind desks.

When Hink saw the gun come out he swung the attaché case with all his strength. It hit Marco's extended arm, knocking him off balance, and as he struggled to regain his footing, he fired.

Jamison turned into the bank's entrance just as Marco fired. A split second later he was bowled over as Hink dived through the door with Marco in hot pursuit.

At the same instant, Johnny and Billy approached the bank headed south. Billy heard the gunshot and saw a man erupt through the Bank's front door with a black case. The detective knew a bank robbery when he saw one.

"John, stop the car!" he shouted.

Johnny slammed on the brakes, and Billy threw open the door and hit the ground running. Within two strides his weapon was out.

China was in his wheelchair at the corner of the parking lot on the south side of the bank. A man passed him and turned into the bank's entrance, then he heard the gunshot.

"Goddamn, Marco, not in the bank," he cried out. The next few seconds exploded with a flash. He saw the figure of a man knocking the other one down as he burst out the entrance. Then a third man leaped from a cab and dashed toward him with gun drawn. China recognized him immediately. From then on his world switched to slow motion.

Before Jamison could gather his senses, the man was off him and starting to run, then a huge figure with a gun leaped through the door and vaulted over him. While the big man was in the air above him, Jamison heard two more shots, followed by a shouted command: "Police officer, drop your weapon." There was a brief hesitation, then a single shot. In the midst of the chaos, he heard the urgent honking of a car horn. He rolled over toward the street and to his amazement there, with door open and Johnny Dash waving frantically, sat the red white and blue All American Cab.

Johnny had recognized Jamison before Billy hit the street. When he saw him collide with the "bank robber," he never thought twice. It was his assignment to get Jamison safely out of harm's way. He got his flaps up and was moving as soon as Billy was away. He took in all the action at a glance—the robber getting up to run followed by a huge man exploding through the door with fire blasting from his gun. Then he saw the man in a wheelchair sitting at the edge of the parking lot raising an automatic weapon. *My God, it's the two men from the club,* he thought. He was on the horn as he screeched to a stop.

"Jamison, Jamison, over here, over here!" he shouted. Seconds later Jamison dived into the car. "Close the door and hang on!" he commanded.

Hink had rolled off Jamison and stumbled to his feet running. He hadn't moved three feet when he saw the man in the wheelchair blocking his way. He sensed rather than saw the muzzle of the Mac10 swing toward him, and in desperation, threw himself between two parked cars as bullets whined over his head and the windshield of the second car exploded above him.

When the big man leaped over the fallen figure with gun blazing, Billy dropped to a three-point stance and shouted his command. The man landed like a cat and turned toward him. He barely hesitated, then swung his weapon toward Billy. The detective didn't have to think; this was it. He squeezed off one round and the man went down like a rock. Then, for the first time, he saw the man in the wheelchair and the Mac10. "Oh, shit!" he exclaimed.

It was all over in a roar, and a flash of red, white, and blue. Before China could zero in, Billy heard the screeching of tires and a blaring horn. And there it was: the All American Cab, with engine roaring, sliding broadside in the street. It leaped the curb and came to a halt with its bumper against the wheelchair. Then it nudged forward and slowly, almost gently, turned the chair and its occupant over.

As China tumbled to the ground, his gun clattered to the pavement. Through the windshield of the cab Jamison saw the weapon falling, and in his mind, the red pickup truck rushed at him out of the mist. A wave of anger swept over him. He'd had it with assaults on his life. The one-eyed pickup had almost gotten him, and now it looked as if a man with no legs was trying to finish him off. Rage kicked loose the adrenaline, and he did an insane thing. In a flash he threw open the door and leaped out of the cab. As he dashed around the car all he could see was the Mac10 lying on the sidewalk pointed toward him. A dark hand groped for it, but Jamison beat him to it, scooped it up, fumbled for the trigger, and leveled it at the outstretched figure.

"Don't even think about it," he ordered.

By the time Billy rushed up and Johnny jumped out of the car, China had managed to scrunch himself into a sitting position against the bank wall. He sat back, sighed, and looked at the three men surrounding him.

"I'll hand it to you, boys, you really had me fooled." He adjusted his baseball cap and smiled ruefully. "What do you think, will the Braves make the playoffs this year?"

"Looks like it's the bottom of the ninth, and you just struck out, pal," Billy said, then turned to Jamison. "I'll take it from here." He held out his hand. "Why don't you let me have the gun?"

Jamison hesitated and looked questioningly at Johnny.

Johnny smiled. "It's alright, Jamison, he's a cop."

Jamison nodded, handed the gun to Billy and collapsed on the bumper of the cab. His knees were shaking and he realized for the first time that his heart was pounding in his throat. He couldn't believe what he had just done. He had put his life on the line without so much as a thought of the consequences. He hadn't added up the numbers, rerun the calculations or checked the bottom line. He had risked everything on an emotional impulse, and it had turned out to be right. It was an exhilarating feeling.

Jamison took a deep breath, leaned back against the cab's warm grill and felt her arms close around him as she kissed him.

"You were incredible, Jamison."

Police sirens wailed in the distance as a crowd began to gather. In the confusion Hink had disappeared.

CHAPTER 27

Marlene poked her head into Tommy's office. "Surprise! You've got a fax from Jamison."

Tommy looked up from her computer screen. "A fax from Jamison?" That was a surprise.

Marlene walked across the room looking at three sheets of paper. "One's a map; one's a newspaper article; and oh, this one's a letter." She held it up and started to read. "Hi, Tom—"

Tommy jumped up from her desk. "Give me that." She playfully jerked the sheets out of Marlene's hand. "I'll bet you read everybody's faxes."

"Only the interesting ones. See ya." She stepped out of the office and waved as she closed the door.

The man is full of surprises, Tommy thought, as she returned to her desk and sat down. She looked at the top of the first page. The *time, date, South Beach Marina* and *page 1* were printed in the top margin. Then she studied the hand-drawn map. On the left side of the page was the east coast of Florida with a balloon drawn over Miami. *Here we are!* was lettered in the balloon. Then a big arrow was drawn to a group of islands to the right and up from Miami. In the midst of the islands was lettered *The Abacos*, and at the end of the arrow was a palm tree and *West End* lettered on the closest of the islets. On the arrow were the words *Here's where we're going!* To the right and below were other islands. A small island in the middle of the page was designated *Nassau*. She turned to page two. It was hand written in Jamison's familiar script.

> *Hi Tom,*
>
> *I'm faxing this from the marina office. Thought it would give you a better picture of what we're planning to do. I'll be careful what I say, because I know Marlene will read this. After talking with some cruisers here, we've decided our best bet for crossing the Gulf Stream is to head north to West End in the Abaco Islands group. It's a longer trip, but given the size and power of September Song, and the prevailing direction of the wind, it looks like it's to our advantage to ride the Stream north instead of trying to power directly across to Bimini. This means we may change our plans and have you meet us somewhere in the Abacos instead of at Nassau. Will let you know when we get to West End.*
>
> *We'll be leaving here about 1:00 tomorrow morning, hoping to arrive in West End after lunch tomorrow — that is if the weather holds. Will call tonight with a final update. Susan (the Susan from St. Simons) came down to be with Charlie for a couple of days, and they've been having a great time. Got a feeling this is serious. Cross your fingers; she's a neat lady — you'll love her. The compass adjuster got us zeroed in, which makes me feel much better.*
>
> *Also including a clipping from the morning paper. There're more thrills in paradise than I think I can stand. I have a few bruises, but I'm feeling fine. Tell you more later.*
>
> *Love you. Love you, too, Marlene.*
> *Jamison*

What's this about bruises? Tommy thought. She flipped to the next page. The headline of the newspaper article read: *OWNER OF MISS SAIGON CLUB IMPLICATED IN BANK SHOOTOUT. What is this?* She scanned the article.

> *Fred T. "China" Beach, the owner of the Miss Saigon Club of South Beach, has been implicated in a multi-city drug ring following a shootout at The Miami International Bank Branch Office in South Beach yesterday. St. Augustine Detective Billy Sparks credited cab driver Johnny Dash and Peter Jamison of Atlanta, in the capture. Mr. Jamison, who held Mr. Beach at gunpoint, corroborated the stories of witnesses in the bank and Detective Sparks. A second gunman, an employee of the club, was killed in the exchange. The object of the assault, who Beach has refused to identify, escaped in the melee. Mr. Jamison was treated for minor scratches and bruises and released from the emergency room at...*

"Oh, my God. I knew something was going to happen, I just knew it." The feelings of apprehension returned. She read the article again. *There's no mention of Charlie,* she thought. *He must have been out with Susan, but Jamison held a drug dealer at gunpoint!* Her heart almost stopped. She picked up the phone to call the marina, then caught herself. *He said he's okay, and he's going to call, and he doesn't seem to be taking this thing too seriously, so just relax,* she counseled herself. She put the phone back in its cradle. *In fact*—she read his note again—*he's pretty laid-back, almost like nothing happened, like the unflappable Jamey I fell in love with. Is he back?* She pondered the possibility and smiled.

Billy looked over at Johnny. "You're hell on wheels, Captain Midnight. You realize you probably saved my life, don't you?"

Johnny had just cleared out of Miami control on I-95 and punched in the GPS waypoint for St. Augustine. He adjusted his cap.

239

"Anything for a friend, Tracy. You were pretty impressive yourself."

"My only regret is losing Prescott." Billy tossed down a slug of Dew.

"You're sure he was the guy with the black case?"

"No doubt about it. Beach opened up after we'd spent a little time with him."

"Maybe it wasn't meant to be, but who knows? He might show up."

Billy stared out the window. "This time I think he's gone for good, but you're right, who knows?"

He was silent for a minute as he traced the rim of the Mountain Dew can with his finger. "I was serious about what I said a minute ago. You saved my life yesterday."

He turned to the boyhood friend whose misfiring heart had crushed his dream of flying Navy blue and gold. "You're Top Gun. You can fly on my wing any time."

Johnny couldn't speak. His vocal chords choked and his eyes threatened to betray him. He frantically checked the instruments: *altimeter, air speed, oil pressure.*

Billy took another sip and smiled. "Are we still on course, Lieutenant Dash?"

Johnny studied the gyro compass and nodded. "Still on course, Detective Sparks."

Charlie passed the salt and pepper across the table to Jamison. "How did Mom take the change of plans?" The lights of a large container ship slid silently out Government Cut past the restaurant windows.

"She didn't have any problem with it. In fact, she thought the Abacos sounded more interesting." Jamison sprinkled the pepper on his salad.

"Did you fax her the article about the shootout?" Susan asked.

Jamison grinned. "She was more interested in that little escapade."

Susan nodded. "I can understand why. That whole thing was pretty frightening. You're lucky you weren't killed, Jamison."

Charlie nodded. "Susan's right, Dad. You were great, but you really pushed the envelope."

Jamison pictured China's hand groping for the Mac10. He had replayed the scene over and over until the liberating rush of adrenaline had become a permanent entry in his memory bank.

"You're right, there wasn't much wiggle room, but when all your chips are on the table...." He smiled. "I must have a guardian angel."

"You've got something. Counting the automobile accident, that's two narrow escapes this year." Charlie laid his hand over his father's. "I don't think I can live through another."

"That's one reason I won't worry about you two on the crossing. I think Jamison is a good luck charm. As long as he's on board you're safe," Susan said, and sipped her wine.

"How does the weather look for tonight?" Charlie asked. The conversation shifted to the business at hand.

"Pretty typical. Ten knots of breeze, a few scattered thunderstorms along the coast, clear over the Bahamas. If the wind holds out of the south to southeast, and we don't run into a storm, we should have smooth sailing." Jamison buttered a roll. "What are your plans, Susan?"

"I'm going to see you off and go back to the hotel, and then drive to St. Simons in the morning."

"And you're planning to join us in the Abacos?"

"As soon as Charlie lets me know when and where." She reached over and took his hand.

Jamison was pleased with her show of affection. "Then it looks like we're ready."

Susan lifted her wine glass. "To the adventure."

Jamison remembered their first night in Bull Creek and caught Charlie's eye across the table. Charlie smiled and raised his glass. Then Jamison raised his. "To the adventure."

The night absorbed all light. It was absolutely impenetrable. Beyond the glow of their running lights even the water disappeared.

"Seen any more shipping?" Jamison shouted from the nav station.

"Nothing since the freighter," Charlie called back.

That's good news, Jamison thought.

As they were coming out of Government Cut a large inbound container ship had picked them up on its radar; at least that's what they had figured, since it began signaling with its whistle while it was still out on the horizon. The ship's location was never in doubt since it was lit up like a floating city, but it kept them informed of its progress with periodic blasts until it passed and they were once again alone with the night.

He hunched over in the dim glow at the chart table trying to keep his balance as *September Song* chopped up and down through the two and a half foot waves. In the dark of night under sail, all the bumps and sounds that reminded him of their fragile vulnerability were magnified: the gurgling and hissing of the sea exploring the integrity of the fiberglass hull a couple of feet in front of him and a few short inches below his feet, the creaking of the rig testing its strength and flexibility, and the whisper of the wind searching the character of the deck.

He opened the log book and recorded the 0200 entry: *Course-070 degrees, Wind-12 knots, Seas-2.5 feet, Barometer-30.10 and falling.* Next he checked his numbers and the GPS, then plotted their position on the chart and added it to his log entries. Several days ago he had carefully calculated their course and speed to compensate for the northward flow of the Gulf Stream. If he was right, they would ride the Stream north as they worked their way east, exiting the current south and west of West End, Grand Bahama, sometime in late morning.

He studied the chart for another minute. *Looking good,* he thought; then he put the pencil in its rack, dimmed the light, climbed the steps into the cockpit, and clipped his safety harness to the port jack line that ran along the deck.

"What's our course and speed?" Jamison asked, as he leaned against the cabin bulkhead.

Charlie's face glowed red from the compass light. "Still holding zero-seven-zero degrees at five knots."

That's good, he thought. *Right on course at the right speed.* "Seems like the wind's up."

Charlie nodded. "Yeah, we're heeling a bit more than we were before you went below."

"Any indication of storms?"

"Nothing so far."

Jamison stepped onto the first companionway step and shined a flashlight on the sails. The breeze was salty and warm. *Still some room for trim*, he thought.

"If the wind'll stay where it is and the seas don't build, we'll be all right." But he noticed that there had been a slight shift to the northeast and it concerned him. Ten more degrees and they wouldn't be able to sail.

He turned to Charlie. "The GPS indicates we should be entering the Stream anytime now."

Charlie nodded and glanced down at the compass. "It's hard to believe that we're finally there."

He adjusted his harness. He gave the tether a tug and checked the snap shackle attached to the D-ring by the helmsman's seat. It was securely fastened.

Suddenly a bright flash of light split open the sky. It was so sudden and intense that Jamison was momentarily blinded. All he could see was an after image of Charlie at the wheel etched into his optical nerves.

"My God, what—"

But before he could get the words out, he was bashed by the shock wave of a deafening explosion of thunder, followed instantly by a cold, crushing blast of wind. *September Song* heeled violently, and Jamison had to catch the companionway grab rail to keep from being thrown back into the cabin. He had just regained his balance and lurched into the wildly careening cockpit when another blast struck, smashing him into the cockpit seat.

He was on his back only inches from the rail. A wave broke in his face, showering him with spray as he rolled on his side and struggled to release the jib sheet. *Goddamn, so much for dodging storms. I've got to get the sails loose or we're going over,* he thought. He had to get in front of the winch to free the line, but the centrifugal force of the bucking hull kept pushing him down.

Charlie had been knocked out of his seat but had managed to keep his grip on the wheel.

"Dad, are you okay?" he shouted, as he fought to maintain control as the boat labored to right itself. The wind howled like a banshee.

"I'm okay!" Jamison shouted, as he grabbed the sheet, heaved himself forward and jerked it off the winch. It broke loose with a bang. "Get the engine on!"

Must be blowing fifty knots at least, he thought as he frantically tried to separate the mainsheet from the chaos of lines in the steeply slanted cockpit.

Charlie pulled himself back up into the helmsman's seat, braced against the pedestal and hull, turned on the ignition and punched the starter. Nothing happened. A bolt of lightning and a crack of thunder hit so close that Jamison could smell it. The concussion was so intense that he was sure they had been blown out of the water. His eardrums rang like a bell choir as a cold chill of terror swept over him. Charlie pushed and held the button again. There was a hesitation; then the engine roared to life.

"Thank God!" The wind sucked the words out of his mouth as he backed off the throttle and pushed it into gear.

Jamison finally worked the mainsheet free and broke it loose. The line raced through his hands as the mainsail jumped out and dumped the wind. *September Song,* responding to the added thrust from the engine and freed from the pressure against her sails, staggered slowly upright into the teeth of the storm. The combined noise of thunder, wind, waves, and thrashing sails and rigging was deafening. Jamison cupped his hands against Charlie's ear.

"Can you hold it?" he shouted.

"I'm not sure!" came the barely audible reply.

Then the rain began with a vengeance, driving in horizontally and ripping them with icy bullets. There had been no time to put on foul weather gear, so they were immediately soaked to the skin.

"Jamison, move, get the sails down now! I'll help you."

She appeared beside him.

He reached into his pocket. "Damn, I've lost my flashlight."

"Forget the flashlight! Use my eyes."

He leaned close to Charlie and shouted, "I'll get the sails down! Release the halyards when I'm in position!"

"For God's sake, Dad, be careful!"

"I will!" came the barely audible reply.

Jamison was glad he couldn't see Charlie's eyes. The sound of his voice said it all. He felt his way across the cockpit. She was just ahead of him guiding him onto the deck.

The phosphorus lightning and explosions of thunder burst one on top of the other, as broadside after broadside of screaming wind and rain swept out of the darkness.

He stumbled along the pitching deck going from one handhold to another, his safety harness tether snaking along the jack line behind him. The rain was blinding, but he was astounded at how well he could see through her eyes. Just as he got to the bow pulpit *September Song* burst off the top of a wave, the deck dropped out from under him and he momentarily lost his balance.

She caught him as he lurched toward the rail.

"Don't worry about falling. I've got you. Just get the sails down!"

Her arms tightened around him.

He grabbed the flailing jib with both hands. "Now, Charlie!" Shouting was a reflex. He knew Charlie couldn't hear him, but he prayed he could see him.

The bow tightened on the wind as he felt the sail go slack and he started clawing the thrashing fabric down. A huge gust shook the boat as a foaming wave crashed over the pulpit, soaking him to the waist. Then the sail was down, and he threw himself on top of it as he attempted to lash it to the rail. She held him firmly, then her mouth found his ear and a hand slipped under his shirt. He felt her heart pounding in his chest as she stroked his body.

"Please, not now," he begged.

Another bolt of lightning struck, silhouetting the bow against the angry clouds as it rose high in the air.

"Yes, now!"

Her breath was hot as her tongue probed.

"I've got to get the other sail down!" he gasped.

"We can do both, Jamison. You'll never get the sail down by yourself!"

As the bow came down, another wave swept across the deck almost tearing him loose. They were awash in a constellation of stars as plankton glowed and sparkled while the sea tugged at his body.

"Let go, Peter. There is no safe way to get to the other shore. If you're going to make it across you're going to have to risk everything. Your life depends on it!"

The noise, the overpowering fear, the physical assault of the wind and water, and the erotic urgency of her body drained the last of his sanity, and he gave up. His mouth found hers and her visceral passion poured into him in a searing transfusion. He let the adrenaline lift him, and he saw himself leap to his feet and dash to the mast, as she pulled him down and offered him her breast.

Charlie wiped the rain from his eyes. He could barely see as he fought to keep the boat into the wind, but what he could see terrified and amazed him. He had seen his father fall to the deck with the jib and for a terrible moment, he thought he had been washed overboard. Then in the next white flash he saw him lashing the sail to the rail. By some miracle he was still on the deck; then he was lost in a cloud of spray, only to reappear in the next blaze of light, leaping for the mast.

Charlie was stunned. Jamison seemed oblivious to the storm and the gyrations of the boat. His movements were fearless, perfectly balanced, powerful and graceful as he flew across the deck. The storm burst around him, but he moved to his own rhythm, leaping, diving, pulling lines, wrapping the sail, and all the while his feet and arms tracing intricate and graceful patterns in the phosphorescent light.

It was as if he were dancing.

The rain, buffeted by the wind, came in torrents. Her nipple was wet and rigid and he felt the electric response in his body as he caught her with his teeth and tongue. There was another burst of lightning, and he saw the sail was down and he was lashing it to the boom. Then he felt her legs open beneath him, and she reached down, slipped her hand into his shorts and drew him into her.

"*Oh, God,*" she cried out, as he entered her.

The lightning flashed, and he was drawn into a vortex of sensation as he felt himself entering and being entered, sucked and suckled. His neurofilaments exploded with the fire of their longing, until, in an implosion of ecstasy, he reached an epiphany of fusion. Eden bloomed in the garden of his cerebral cortex. Her mask dropped away, and he recognized her for the first time.

She reached up and took his face in her hand.

"*Look into your eyes, Jamison. What do you see?*"

"*Fire, passion, wonder, joy…and peace.*"

"*Your universe or mine?*"

"*Mine.*"

"*What's my name?*" her eyes pleaded.

He stared at her for what seemed an eternity. Then, in a voice that came from the dawn of his time—

"*Jamison. Your name is Jamison!*"

Tears of joy, mixed with rain, ran down her face.

The storm was relaxing its grip as Charlie dried his face and Jamison collapsed onto the cockpit seat. "I don't know how you managed to get the sails down, Dad. It was all I could do just to keep us into the wind with full power, but you were all over the deck like nothing was happening. I was scared to death you'd go overboard."

Jamison stumbled slowly back into reality. He tried to rub the salt out of his eyes and shook his head. "It's amazing what you can do when your life depends on it."

Charlie bent over, checked the engine temperature and eased back on the throttle. "Where did it come from?"

"I don't know. The first gust felt like a microburst." He shifted his harness. He was beginning to itch under the weight of the shoulder straps.

Charlie leaned wearily on the wheel. The wind had continued to drop and the waves were moderating. "We're lucky to be alive."

They were silent for a moment; then Jamison nodded. "I think you're right." He took a deep breath and sat up. "Guess I'd better check our position, and then we need to get into some dry clothes." He unsnapped his tether and started below. Halfway down the steps he stopped and turned back to Charlie. "I love you, son."

The tension flowed out of Charlie's face. "I love you, too, Dad."

In a few minutes Jamison was back. "We really got knocked off course."

Charlie nodded. "The wind has swung too far to the east to sail, and we'll never be able to power through these seas."

Jamison hesitated. "We're not going to make it across, Charlie."

"I know."

Jamison looked out into the darkness. The storm clouds were blowing away and the stars broke through in a dazzling array. The Milky Way blossomed and bathed the sky and sea in silver light. From somewhere, deep inside, he felt the arms of a giant tulip poplar reach up, and as he watched, they unfolded like a celestial fan and released the figure of a small boy into the universe. He felt an overwhelming sense of peace.

A long filament of lightning traced the horizon, followed by a faint rumble of thunder. He turned back to Charlie. "I'm ready to go home, son. How about you?"

Charlie watched the distant flicker. "Yeah, Dad. I think I've come far enough."

The next morning, after Charlie left to have breakfast with Susan, Jamison took out the blue perfume bottle. He carefully removed the stopper. Her fragrance was gone. If it had ever been there, no hint of it remained. He held it for a moment then gently replaced the seal, set it on the shelf and picked up the Dolphin Chronicle. The gold dolphin medallion glowed just as it had the morning it caught his eye in the book store on St. Simons. He opened it and slowly turned the pages as he read the entries he had so carefully inscribed.

Everything was just as he remembered until the seventh entry. When he turned the page he was taken by surprise. Directly beneath the final line of text was a small wildflower pressed into the paper. It had not been there when he wrote the entry three days ago, and since then the volume had been stowed securely in his locker for the crossing. Where had it come from?

He gently lifted the fragile blossom off the page and held it to the light. It sparkled and glowed with energy. It was as if he were seeing a flower for the first time. He examined its flowing lines, and the infinite variety of shapes and forms that defined its space. He noted with satisfaction that there wasn't a straight line in its entire structure. Then it dawned on him that he was seeing with her eyes, just as he had as a child, just as he had the first time he discovered art, and just as he had the first time he fell in love. His vision was clear, the shadows were gone, and he was free.

He lifted the fragile form to his nose and smiled. There was still a hint of her fragrance on its drying petals. He let her scent bloom in his mind one last time, and then carefully laid the flower back in the impression it had made in the paper. He knew the next time he opened these pages there would be only memories.

Once it was in place, he read the final line he had written and pondered his transformation. By every linear standard it was unlikely, outrageous and totally unacceptable. *But then,* he thought, *so is a flower.*

He read the entry one more time, then picked up his pen and added a final word: *Amen.*

Printed in the United States
71117LV00002B/454-498